CW00801473

Hunter Hunted

Hunter Hunted

The Eternals - Book II

Richard M. Ankers

Chapter 1

Ruby

"Life is a collection of colours when all you've known is night."

Sir Walter Merryweather

* * *

The trembling fingers were my own, they rattled on the cockpit like bones in a bucket. I stood before a sun I thought never to see and marvelled. Like a giant tomato cresting the horizon, our dying star illuminated the world with colour, the Arctic ice suffused blood-red by its near death. No longer was my world awash in moonlight, but actual daylight.

If not for Linka's steadying grip, my tether to the world I'd left behind, I might have drifted away swamped by such overpowering brilliance, but as her fingers tightened about mine, my confidence grew. If I'd had a soul to anchor, I'd have said she did, but I didn't, a salient fact I'd forever regret.

The Zeppelin we travelled in sped on in silence through a vampire sky, hues of vermillion, crimson, and ruby parting like red wine at our passage. A hushed still settled, and if I'd been alone with my darling, I should have said it a pleasure. The Nordic royalty, beacons of pearlescent light that competed with the weakening sun, a people of myth and majesty, were an ever-present reminder that alone was one thing we weren't. The Nordics stood almost invisible to eyes which sought the delights of the day, almost, but not quite.

The airship's inner tranquillity enhanced the Arctic landscape's barren calm, and for the first time in centuries, as I stood there enveloped in shades of blood, I experienced contentment.

"Look, Jean, the ocean," Linka gushed, her voice of unconcealed glee shattering my meditative peace.

I resisted her tugged enthusiasms, instead, preferring to stare out upon the ruby plain. Undeterred, she resorted to more direct methods and gave so hard a wrench, she almost yanked my arm from its socket.

"Good grief, an ocean of blood!" I exclaimed. And it was. "I wonder if it goes on forever?"

"Of course not," Grella's stern voice corrected.

He cut through my rouge world like an out of tune violin at a party making me feel quite stupid. "No, I don't suppose it does. I don't know why I said it."

"You're just excited," Linka beamed.

"Am not," I huffed.

"Are so," she retorted.

A trail of lavender preceded Narina's berthing at my side, as she whispered iced words in my ear.

"Ignore him, Jean. I was just like you all those centuries ago when first I saw the sun. So much more than one could ever imagine, is it not?"

"It has a certain novelty," I replied, unwilling to be made a fool of twice.

"Must you tell that old tale, sister? Don't forget, some of us were born to it."

"Ah, the voice of an impetuous twin," Narina cooed. "Let me introduce the pair of you to my brothers," she said, laying a pure, white hand upon my arm.

Narina turned me to the other ruby-goggled Nordics. Linka spun around too, but not without casting momentary scrutiny to my being touched by another woman; there was just a flash of anger in those blazing emerald eyes, but it soon passed.

"These two uncouth fools are my twin brothers Verstra and Serstra."

The two nodded and grinned as one. The action was a tad unnerving as it was the first time I'd seen the Nordic royalty show any sign of emotion. Even during the slaughter of Vladivar's men, they had remained impassive, predators at work. I returned their nods regardless.

"This is Ragnar their elder brother," she continued. Ragnar made a point of making up for his brothers' joviality by what could at best be described as a twitched response. "Grella, the eldest of us and future king of our people, you already know."

"Enough of the pleasantries, sister, we must prepare," Grella snapped. He spared neither Linka nor myself a single look. The future king, although lacking the bulk of Ragnar, or eloquence of his sisters, was indisputably the man in charge.

"If you would excuse us." Narina indicated to seats at the Zeppelin's rear; a polite dismissal.

I cared not, I was already quite bored with the Nordics' austere demeanours and glad to be rid of them.

I led Linka to the furthest end of the airship and sat down to peer out of the wrap-around windows.

"Are you well, my love?"

"Hmm."

"You seem flustered," Linka stated.

"Not really. You know how it is, five centuries or so in the dark, at last, you get to see the sun, and you can't be left in a bit of peace and quiet to enjoy it."

"I suspect there'll be plenty of time for that soon."

"There better be, I've dreamed of this all my life." I swept my arm across the ruby vista to emphasise the fact. Or to be more exact, the view that was solid ice to my left and churning red waters to my right. "Do you think they're following the conjunction of solid and liquid to achieve our destination?"

"We are," Ragnar interjected in a voice like rolling thunder.

"I wasn't asking you," I hissed.

"He was saving you the effort," laughed one twin.

"I don't care. It is impolite to eavesdrop on private conversations."

"We can't help it, good ears," replied the second twin.

"What if I discussed matters of an intimate nature?"

"But you weren't," the twins said in synchronicity.

"Wasn't I?"

Whether Narina sensed my bristled hostility, who knew, but she was quick to intervene. "Ignore them, Jean, they can't help their natures. And in polite answer to your unasked question, yes, we are. At a certain time and angle of entry, we are able to pinpoint our home. It cannot be located by any other means."

"You shouldn't have said that, sister," Grella growled.

"Oh, hush. Our guests will not be leaving anytime soon, and as you well know, Hvit's position will have changed long before then."

"Yes, but…"

"But, nothing."

Ekatarina span from the craft's controls in support of her sister and gave her kin a barely concealed glare. I felt the chill of her gaze even from behind her goggled exterior.

"Princess Linka, we shall be – landing, forthwith. Please be ready to move when we say so," Ekatarina said, returning to earlier formalities. I was not even spared a look.

I didn't care for my companions, nor the pause in our landing arrangements. Their eccentricities had already worn thin. I observed them with general disinterest as they went about their business in spectral personae. They glided from control to control without giving Linka or myself any further attention.

Speaking in hushed whispers the six did their best impersonations of porcelain dolls at the Zeppelin's controls. Only the pomade of lavender, which still circulated, marked the Nordics' earlier graceful passage. It was far too sweet for my tastes.

I soon got to ignoring their luminous closeness and stared out over the bloodied waters. They had somewhat calmed since I last looked, a swilled glass settled. If I hadn't known better, I should have said us surrounded by a world of ruby glass.

Linka snuggled against me in silent pleasure seeming less concerned of our hosts than I. Her nearness calmed me, and for a while, I lost myself in the horizon and relaxing, ruby expanse.

The bleeding sun soon sank back into its reflective home and I found myself saddened by its passing. In less than an hour, there was only a slit of boiling blood peeping above the waves. One side of the Zeppelin had returned to total darkness, whilst the other simmered in crimson. I still loved it, though. There was enough light left to keep the uninformed Eternal at bay, whilst still giving the enlightened the pleasure of a dawn, or sunset, I was lost as to which was which having never seen either. I could have sat in pleasant happiness for the rest of my years, my love at one side, shrouded in night, the sun I had thought to never see, glowing at the other. However, as per usual, my pleasure was not to last.

"Princess, if you will."

Grella had approached to less than a yard with a stealth I would not have thought possible. I prided myself on not being caught unawares least of all by those I had once thought legend. It was most disconcerting, and I chastised myself at my laxness.

"Have we reached Hvit?" Linka bubbled, jumping to her feet.

"We have, Your Highness."

"Oh, goody," she enthused.

"If you would stand by the doorway and prepare to jump when instructed."

"Of course."

"You too, Jean," he added, almost as an afterthought.

"Did you say jump?"

"Yes. We shall not be landing."

I did not pursue the point, but was reluctant to be dragged to my feet when Ragnar opened the Zeppelin's door. His action caused a blast of freezing air to invade the craft's stagnant innards, which swirled about in direct competition with the Nordics' own scents. I hadn't realised just how stale the lavender-infused interior had become until the freshness sought to banish it.

I was about to say as much to Linka when the whole craft lurched to port submerging us in darkness before making a slow and steady arc back toward the sun.

First out were the two princesses, who adjusted their goggles to an assured fit and leapt from the craft in tandem.

"Now you," Ragnar ordered.

Linka gave me one of her extra special smiles, an immense lightening of the load on my heart, then jumped into the night after the other ladies, myself in hot pursuit.

The distance to the ground was about thirty feet, nothing to an Eternal, and we landed as inaudible snowflakes. To my annoyance, so did the twins, one to either side of us. Ragnar landed next with less grace. His greater bulk displaced enough snow to leave a crater of sorts, although I suspected most of it for show.

The Zeppelin continued to nosedive towards liquidity. Down it plunged, and for a moment, I feared for Grella, until he launched himself clear of the hurtling machine landing with a crack at the point where ice met water. The Zeppelin followed him down in serene departure. There was something phantasmal about its demise. The airship drifted another half mile, dipped its head to the horizon, then disappeared beneath the becalmed ocean with more of a kiss than a splash. I would miss it in my own way.

Grella did not bother to watch it leave. He had already spun around and was striding towards us, his brilliant, white cloak billowing out behind him. I, in turn, walked the opposite way, as close to the edge of an ocean as a hydrophobe dared. The transition from dark to light was magical. It was hard to imagine how one could transcend the boundaries of such metaphysics in a matter of steps.

"Why do you watch it disappear, it is only a possession, a toy?" Grella asked as we crossed.

"I wasn't, I was watching the sun," my terse reply.

"Then, why do you watch the sun?"

"Because, I wish to."

"Why do you wish to?"

"Why do you not?"

"It is unnatural. Eternals desire the dark, deepest night. The sun offers security, nothing more."

"Is that not cowardice?"

"It is sense," growled Grella.

"Then, I am glad to possess none."

"Hmm, yes."

"What?" I spat, but Grella had already reached the others.

"It is time for us to descend," Narina called.

"Where is the entrance?" I returned, as I skidded my way over to them.

"Why, here, of course." And with a tap of a white booted foot on the ground, a sliver of glasslike ice popped up catching the last red rays of the sun. "Right here," she added, as the Nordics removed their glasses.

The sweet smell of lavender ushered forth from the slit-like hole almost overwhelming my senses.

"Hvit is down there?" I queried, a tad nonplussed, whilst wafting my hands before my nose.

"Yes, silly," Linka giggled. "They told us their city lay under the ice."

"I thought they were speaking metaphorically."

"Metaphorically?" the twins said in unison shielding their eyes from the distant wedge of sun.

"Yes, metaphorically. I thought it would tower over us in some kind of clear dome, hence, under the ice."

"You read too much into things people say, Jean," said Narina gliding to my side.

I noticed Ekatarina was quick to do the same to Linka. Narina laid her hand upon my arm and escorted me to the others.

Grella stooped to lift the ice door up, which was set on a pivot. He opened it with a creak just far enough to allow us entry. The obsidian interior came as somewhat of a shock after the advent of real light in my life. Ragnar rumbled through the doorway and descended straight down into the depths. Grella spared a moment to cast serious eyes about the landscape before following him. Ekatarina went next leading Linka below, my love giving me a reassuring smile before passing into the darkness.

"May I have a moment please?" I asked my shepherdess.

"Of course, but do not tarry."

"I won't."

"The doorway will close behind you of its own accord."

"I understand," I acknowledged, as Narina bowed her head and descended after the others in sparkling flecks of luminescence.

I needed to look at that wedge of sun one more time, it moved me in a way nothing else ever had, not even Linka, nor my once beloved Alba. I watched ruby borders pulse with cosmic life and felt something trickle down my cheek, most probably stray sea spray.

Turning my back on that segment of light was as hard a task as I had ever accomplished. I stepped back into the darkness bearing a frown and a heavy heart.

Fortunately, my senses were as acute as ever: someone, or something, observed me. A quick glance left revealed nothing, but I did not turn away. That's when I saw them. It was but a fleeting glimpse, a moment in time, but two blue eyes peered out from the demarcation of night and day. I stared back, unblinking. The whole confrontation lasted a fraction of a second, but those eyes seemed to stare for a lifetime. Twin, sapphire orbs gazed from an incorporeal shell, calculating, making a judgement. Then, with a blink, they vanished.

I stood there a minute more, sniffing at the air, narrowed eyes questing, but the flash of blue had absconded. Whoever, or whatever controlled them, had fled. I did not like it one bit. And much as I tried to convince myself of imagining things, I knew the encounter real.

My descent into Hvit was slow, not because of the darkness, I could see perfectly well in the blackest of holes, nor for fear of slipping on those treacherous steps of ice, but because of the trapdoor that closed, then reopened in my wake. I watched the faintest sliver of ruby illuminate the tunnel before me until it evaporated into the darkness, eclipsed.

The abyss swallowed me then as I hurried after my love.

Chapter 2

White

"I wondered where you'd gone, my love."

"One last sniff of fresh air before the descent into Hell," I replied.

"This is Hvit, not Hell."

"Thank you...Verstra?"

"Serstra," he corrected.

"Any chance of the pair of you wearing name tags?"

"I don't think our mother would be too happy about that," the other twin replied.

"Parents can be such a chore."

"Indeed," Grella mused. "Please be careful, these ice steps can be perilous at times." He cast back a withering look from below to make certain of my attention.

"Might I ask how far we descend?" I threw it out as a general question and then gave the tunnel the once-over in preparation for an answer: steps about as wide as an average man lying down; tunnel about the same in height, which accounted for my stooped posture; the whole thing of a polished, black finish.

"Can't you save your questions for later, darling," Linka teased, taking a playful grip of my proffered hand.

"I'm inquisitive by nature. You never know when such facts could come in useful. Plus, I would rather like for my feet to reach terra firma."

"Pfft!" huffed Ragnar.

"Pardon, have you something to say?" I snapped.

But Ragnar did not reply, and I was too weary to press the point. Once again, it was Narina who came to the rescue.

"Your feet will touch nought but ice whilst in Hvit, Jean. The staircase would have to go an awful lot further than it does to reach the sea floor."

"Sea floor! You mean the whole city is built of ice, not a rock in sight?"

"Not a rock, brick or wood beam in sight. From the doorway downwards, the whole structure is of solid ice."

"I can't say I find that reassuring. And is it me, or can I hear music playing?"

"You can."

"Oh no, it's Rimsky-Korsakov, isn't it!" I groaned.

"Sounds that way," replied one of the twins.

"Does that mean you shan't be dancing with me, Jean?" Linka pouted.

"For you, my little cauliflower, I should dance even to Rachmaninov."

"Thank you, I think!"

"You're welcome. Is it necessary for it to be played at such a volume, I have delicate hearing and prefer the quiet?"

"Jean, stop asking so many questions." Linka punched me on the arm to emphasise her objection.

"What have I said?"

"The answer lies in the sea," Narina responded with yet another Grella glare for an accompaniment.

"How very cryptic."

"Not really," she said, taking my hand and easing me over to the wall. "Put your ear to the ice and listen."

I gave her one of my best scowls, but did as asked. At first, I heard nothing and thought it some kind of practical joke from those who I expected it least of. But the more I listened, the more I realised there was another set of sounds running parallel to the music.

"Ah, I see by your look you hear them."

"Hear whom?"

"Orcas."

And right at that moment, as I looked out into the pitch darkness, I perceived something looking back. For a moment, I thought it whomever had regarded us above, but I was wrong. The eye was massive and set in front of a flash of white. The giant orb studied me, appraised, then vanished into the darkness. Instinct jerked me away.

"Don't be scared," Ragnar rumbled from his position ahead. "The ice walls of Hvit are impenetrable. You're quite safe, little man."

"Surprised is not the same as scared," I growled back.

"Now you know why we play the music, Jean," Narina gave a kind smile. "We do it to drown out the whale song. They watch us, you see."

"Watch you!"

"Do not worry, little man, it is only to this level. Orcas cannot swim much deeper."

"My name is Jean, not little man. I'll accept it once, forgive it twice, but I'll not be so lenient a third time."

"Princess, I suggest you teach your pup some manners," Ragnar boomed.

"That is enough!" Grella bellowed taking a step between the pair of us. "Jean is our honoured guest. You *will* treat him as such."

Ragnar, far bigger, and at first glance more powerful than his older brother, backed away down the stairs without another word. The act left Grella's seniority undisputed.

"I apologise, Jean, it is so rare that we entertain guests."

"I thought you said you never have guests," I snapped back glaring after he who had slandered me.

"Did I?"

"Yes."

"Well, either way, I apologise."

"Apology accepted," I replied, but it wasn't.

"Are you well, Linka?" Ekatarina retook Linka's hand and led her away down the staircase. "You look a little pale." I heard her add.

I would have objected, but couldn't help noticing the glance Grella cast over my shoulder. It seemed I wasn't the only one who knew us stalked from above.

Seeing my eyes upon him, Grella gave a slight nod, one last quick glance, then followed his companions into the abyssal depths. The twins had long since vanished, I suspected to warn of our impending arrival. A cursory look behind of my own to nothing but enforced night, and I set off in pursuit of the departing prince.

* * *

The staircase finished at an abrupt, right-angled end. There, I trailed Linka and the others through a passage draped in pure, white silks. The whole length of the thing seemed curtained for decoration, but I suspected the Nordics despised the whale's eyes upon them as much as I, and had decorated accordingly.

Along the passage we travelled, I in quiet observance of Linka's and Ekatarina's incessant chatting, Narina never far from my side. She was quite the distraction. I blamed her proximity for being caught unawares when Grella led us out of the enclosed space and into a hall that would have swallowed Vladivar's courtroom whole, possibly even that of the late King Rudolph's palace. The ceiling stretched away into the heavens behind a chandelier of such magnitude I almost thought it a miniature sun, so many candles did it hold. They lighted the area in eerie, flickering shadows that matched and accentuated the water which flowed all around the chamber's exterior walls. Music washed through the room, although there was no apparent source for it, and there tapping her fingers to it, sat upon a throne of brilliant, blue ice, reclined the chamber's sole occupant.

"Mother," hailed Grella, closing the distance between he and the distant figure. He bowed low to her, then rose and kissed the hand that never once stopped tapping upon the great throne's arm.

Ekatarina and Narina followed their brother's lead. A kiss to the royal fingers, then each took up a position at either side of their mother.

"Your Majesty," Linka curtsied. "I would like to thank you for saving us. I'm not sure we can ever repay you."

"You can't," came a clipped response. "I trust my children have looked after you well." She spoke with an air of the untouchable. I dare say she had good reason to. The woman was magnificent. She was everything that her albino daughters were and more. Cheekbones chiselled from marble stood against skin of milk. Eyes like burning pyres blazed from beneath alabaster, silken hair that flowed almost to her waist. Dressed all in white, she made for an exact replica of her children. Only an abundance of ermine trimmings and a tear shaped ruby the size of a fist that hung from a silver chain around her neck separated she from they. The jewel drew my eye, as it did Grella's, who stood to one side admiring it.

"Impeccably," Linka replied to a question I'd long forgotten.

"Good. One should always remember one's heritage and act with due accord. You are of royal blood child and are also one of the few enlightened."

The queen addressed Linka, but fixed her eyes upon me. It was unnerving, I'd never seen anybody stare so long without blinking.

For some unknown reason, I took it upon myself to stamp upon the clear floor in response. I put it down to nerves.

"Might I ask what you are doing?" said the queen addressing me.

Linka gave a look of such frustration that I had no option but to stamp harder still.

"I am testing the strength of your floor, Your Majesty."

"Serena," she instructed.

"I dislike the water and am reassuring myself that this place is as strong as your son claims it to be," I babbled.

"What if the floor breaks because of it?" she sneered.

"I hadn't thought that far ahead."

"If I told you it would not, would you believe me?"

"I would be obligated to."

"Then, allow me," she said, standing with the aid of her daughters' hands. She stepped, or rather eased herself from the throne, glared all the more, then stamped.

The action caused such an impact it almost knocked me off my feet, and I had to catch Linka before she, too, fell. Shock waves echoed around the room eclipsing the music that still played on.

"Reassuring enough?" she smirked.

It was, but I was not about to cow-tow to an obvious demonstration of her power. "Somewhat…Serena, but I doubt it will ever truly ease my mind."

"You are a troubled man?"

"I am a man with troubles."

"So I have heard," she said, returning to her seat.

"Whom have you heard that from, might I ask?" But the queen was already in some kind of discussion with Ekatarina who glided from the room via a large, ice, double door, and ignored my question.

"I am sorry to hear of your father's…death, Linka."

"Thank you, Queen Serena."

"I had known him a long time. I even danced with him once many aeons before my family left for these more peaceful climes."

"My father danced?"

"Oh yes, perhaps your mother's stifling influence prevented him from showing you."

"My mother!"

I saw the steam rise from Linka's head, but luck was on our side. Ekatarina reappeared at that moment followed by a throng of her albino brethren. The queen's underlings, attired in simple, white trousers and shirts, blouses for the women, all trimmed with azure strips across the cuffs, hurried to serve. The entourage bore large silver trays, which held glasses and carafes of slopping, red liquid.

"Time for a toast," Serena called out as I slipped my hand into my love's own. I felt her trembling ire, so kissed her cheek to calm her. It didn't work. "I think we'll have the lights dimmed," Serena added.

I don't know what I expected to happen; a flick of a switch; the lowering of the chandelier to have its candles snuffed, or something more mundane. What happened was more dramatic.

Serena leant from the throne, eyed the chandelier with chilling intensity, and then slapped her palms together with a force that dragged her pure-white cloak over her head from the vacuum. The chandelier swung so far up in the air I thought it sure to fall; the candlelight obliterated, but not light per se. Each wall morphed from a touch of gold to a neon blue that sparkled across the Nordics' clothing like cerulean raindrops on snow. Serena gave a crooked smile before she sat back down and resumed her finger tapping.

The lesser Eternals hurried to provide her with a glass of blood, as the tinkling chandelier realigned itself. Once attended to, they furnished the rest of the Nordic royalty including the twins and Ragnar who had inveigled his way back into the throne room, Linka, and myself, with drinks of our own.

"To old bonds, and Hierarchical loyalties."

"Hear, hear!" shouted all.

I couldn't even be bothered to raise my glass. The blue walls were far more interesting, as they lighted sections of the ocean beyond. I thought I should see mythical creatures swimming about the place, but much to my disappointment, I didn't.

A sip from my glass brought me back to the real world. It was awful. I'd half expected the crimson liqueur to imbue me with blistering speed, or superhuman strength, or to at least reinvigorate. No such luck. The stuff coated my tongue in a thick gloop, then slid down my throat like…well, thick blood.

"Good stuff," Linka commented, then punched my arm when I appeared to give my drink more attention than her.

"Do you mind," I exaggerated, "I almost spilled it."

"I'll spill you in a minute."

"Ah, back to your rambunctious best, my little sea-turtle."

"I'll sea-turtle you."

"You have such delightful dimples when pretending to be angry."

"I'm not pretending," she pouted.

"How do you like the blood of our mammalian cousins?" came the cool voice behind the hand that had materialised upon my arm.

"It is superb, Narina," I lied, turning to her. I thought it rude even by my standards to tell her the precious liquid I consumed was at best an average beverage.

"That is good because tomorrow you'll be helping us replenish our supply."

"What about me?" Linka interjected.

"Oh, of course, I meant the both of you."

"Hmm," Linka scowled.

"Do you think there's any chance of me getting a change of clothing? I'm not fit to be seen with attired like this." I gave my tattered garments a shake to prove the fact.

"That has all been taken care of."

"It has?"

"It has."

"Thank you in advance, then."

"You are most welcome. You will find new apparel laid out in your room. For you both," she added, giving Linka the once over.

"Thank you," a grudging Linka replied.

I took another swill from my glass and looked around the room that had become quite the hive of verbal activity. Only Serena, who sat aloof on her throne, remained in non-discussion. She eyed me through the crowd, or so I imagined. I could no longer see her but still felt those burning, ruby eyes boring deep into my skull.

"You seem distracted, Jean," Narina stated.

"Just a tad tired, that's all. It takes a lot out of one being almost drained to death by a lunatic royal. No offence meant, ladies," I added, as a courtesy.

"None taken." Linka punched me even harder than normal, in fact, very much harder than normal. Her drink had done her the world of good.

Narina looked at the pair of us as though we were children, or worse, then gave a glacial stare into the depths beyond the ice walls.

"They watch us from afar," she said.

"Who?" I asked, unable to see anything in the neon gloom.

"The orcas."

"Are you sure, I can't see a thing?"

"Very."

"But they are just fish."

"Never that, my friend. They are closer to us than you think."

"If you say so."

"You will see tomorrow. For now, though…" Narina broke off to clap to someone from within the crowd. A young-looking Nordic girl hurried over and bowed to her princess. "Please escort Princess Linka and Jean to their room."

"Yes, Your Highness, as you will it," the girl replied, bowing again.

"Good day to you, Narina, or is it night? I'm quite lost."

"Always night within the city, always day at the door."

"Glad you cleared that little mystery up."

"Good night, Narina, and thank you again for everything," Linka said with the required decorum.

There was no response as Narina returned to her mother's side, whilst we were led through a small doorway opposite the one we'd entered from. I slipped a glance to Her Majesty, as I passed her, but for once, her eyes seemed elsewhere.

No sooner had we left the chamber than the sound of voices dispersed and the tones of Tchaikovsky took over. The blue ice soaked up all the residual noise of the throne room with an immediacy I would not have thought possible. In an instant, all was still, and the three of us very much alone.

The girl led us along an arrow-straight corridor passing doorway after monotonous doorway. Many minutes elapsed before we came to one last room facing straight back whence we'd come.

"We have prepared this room for you," said the girl.

"Thank you," Linka replied and walked in through the open doorway. I followed, giving the girl a smile before closing the door on her.

"Thank god for that."

Linka chuckled.

"I was about ready to bang my head against the walls," I joked, as I looked upon the bland magnificence of the room. Four large walls draped in white silk with a large double bed and a single, gigantic wardrobe met my gaze. Laid out upon the bed were a set of white silks for my darling and a matching set in black for myself. "That's a surprise," I said nodding to the clothing.

"They must have known you were coming."

"Yes, they must," I agreed. "At least the curtains will keep out that infernal blue light."

"I quite liked it."

"You would, my awkward princess."

"I'll give you awkward…"

Before she could finish, I'd grabbed her in a hugged embrace, much to her squealed protests. "Got you alone at last."

"About time," she huffed.

"Certainly is." I kissed her forehead. "Have I ever told you what beautiful eyes you have?"

"Not enough."

"Well, you have. They're like ancient forests full of life."

"Ancient!"

"In a most beautiful way, my cherub. However," I said releasing her to slump onto the bed, "just one thing before I ravage you."

"Who says I'll let you?"

"A higher authority, my love. There is an inevitability about it to which you would be wise to acquiesce."

"Really."

"Yes," I laughed, as I lifted a curtain from the floor: water. I was less than happy about the fact, but before complete panic set in decided to check the other walls. Linka watched on amused. Two more abutted water, the third was frosted, and I presumed adjoined other rooms. It availed a degree of privacy but very little in the way of watertight reassurance. "We are three ways surrounded by sea and furthest from the exit."

"Five," corrected Linka.

"Five?"

"Above and below."

"Sleep may be an issue," I grimaced.

"Oh, sleep's one thing you will have to do without." Linka grinned like a she-wolf, and patted the bed.

"Ah, well, duty before oceanic obliteration, I suppose."

"You suppose right."

* * *

So started my first night in the submerged Nordic city of Hvit deep below the Arctic sea. It was better than death, but not much.

Chapter 3

Neon

"That better be angels disturbing my heavenly peace."

"Oh, Jean, how can you be grumpy after a night like that."

"I wasn't grumpy until now. I've been disturbed."

"You are disturbed."

"You'd think there was a war on or something. Who the hell's making such a racket this early in the morning? It is morning, isn't it?"

"Who knows?" Linka replied.

"I'd have said who cares, but it's obvious someone does."

"Do you want me to take a peep?"

"No, don't worry, I'll do it."

"My hero," Linka purred.

"I know, but I have an alternate reason for my heroic act."

"Really."

"If one of us is to give the Nordics a violent look of intent it's probably best it's me. I'd hate to ruin your angelic image."

"That can't be ruined, I am an angel."

"Not after last night you're not."

"Ah, but only you know."

"I may sing it to the world, my love."

"I didn't know crows could sing?"

"Raven, my dear, and of course they can. Not well, that's all."

I jumped out of bed to avoid Linka's swinging fist, slipped into my brand new jet-black trousers and opened the bedroom door. Princess Narina stood there in full white, silk splendour, her fist raised mid-strike.

"Oops, sorry, Your Highness."

"It is I who should apologise, Jean. I was about to knock." Narina made an undisguised once-over of my open-shirted frame and continued. "You are requested to hunt."

"Is that the same as commanded?"

"Jean," came Linka's chastising tones from the bedroom.

"My apologies, Princess."

"I much prefer Narina."

"You have my apologies, Narina," I said giving a low enough bow to expose Linka's uncovered form. Narina never even twitched. Instead, she watched me all the way to my lowest sweep and then back up again, as I did her. I suspected our reasons were different, though, as her ruby, unblinking eyes took me in. "How long have we got?"

"Now," she replied without hesitation.

From the exodus of pale shapes streaming down the corridor, and the clopping of booted feet on ice floor, we were already the last.

"Do you mind?" I asked, indicating for her to look the other way with my finger. She did not. Narina stayed exactly where she was. So, I did what any self-respecting Eternal should, I shut the door in her porcelain face.

"That was very rude, Jean," Linka chastened. She hopped out of bed with a shake of her head spilling out hair like ink on a desktop in the process and dressed post-haste.

"Aww," I sighed.

"What?"

"You look even more beautiful when you're mad."

"I'll give you mad," she laughed, jumping clean over the bed in one bound, fist poised to punch my arm.

Not only did I avoid her blow, but had donned both my boots before she landed.

"Are you ready, my little pumpkin?" I winked.

"I am," she replied. Her look of amazement said different.

I buttoned up my black shirt and swept the matching cape over my shoulders, as Linka did her snow-white one.

"You look almost Nordic, my dear."

"Is that a compliment?"

"I doubt it."

"Well, I'll take it as one. The princesses are stunning, after all."

"Not to me, my love. I'll take your raven locks and emerald innocence over their bland albinism any day of the week."

"Hush, Jean, they'll hear you."

"So what."

"So everything," she hushed. "Just be more discreet."

"I'll try, but I cannot promise."

"That's something, I suppose." She raised one perfect eyebrow, kissed me on the cheek, and then led us from the room.

Narina waited in the exact same spot I'd left her. She gave a nod to Linka, a wide-eyed stare to me, then whirled away down the now deserted corridor. She moved with effortless grace across the slick floor, her trailing skirts covering her feet so that one might have thought she hovered.

Down the corridor past the innumerable doors we went until exiting into the empty throne room. There was an eeriness to our echoing footsteps multiplied ad infinitum as they were. I did not like it one bit. And, for the first time, I noticed the music had stopped. The throne room sat in chilled austerity full of nothing but hollow echoes.

However, I had no chance to dwell on the matter. Narina ushered us out the other side of the blue-tinged hall at speed and headed towards the staircase in complete darkness.

We had caught up with the rear of the party by the time we exited the stairs into the half-light of the Arctic world. The low sun appeared as an ancient, red god brooding and ruddy-cheeked, as I took that last step out into the wan daylight. I was the last of Hvit's occupants to do so, or so it seemed.

Like a melee of snowflakes, the Nordic peoples gathered ahead in an arc about a central point that was their queen. Serena stood motionless looking to the ocean, for a reason I couldn't fathom, one fist raised to the claret sky. Her regal presence dominated the proceedings.

Linka followed Narina towards where her mother stood. I didn't, though. I couldn't. Unseen eyes were upon me. They froze my nape, so intense was their icy glower. So, whilst kicking out at the ice, I made a surreptitious circling of my position casting my eyes about as inconspicuously as possible. Like all such actions, I suspected it made me look more conspicuous than ever. Two complete revolutions later, I had revealed nothing. But those eyes were out there, I did not doubt it.

In an attempt to give myself something else to think about, I returned my attention to the motionless throng. All eyes were to Serena whose own were on the rolling, ruby waves.

"There!" she screamed, as a pair of black fins rose from the water like the dark sails of some bygone mariner's boat. "Follow me," she commanded.

Without another thought, Serena launched herself into the water in the orca's wake. As one, the Nordic peoples followed her into the ice-trimmed ocean. Plop after plop of departing Eternal marked the submergence of an entire race. With them, caught up in the excitement and general melee, went Linka.

I, on the other hand, seemed to have taken several inadvertent steps back from the hubbub, therefore widening the distance between myself and the water. It would be a cold day in Hell before I took that descent. My thoughts had already turned inward back to the city's dark embrace, and my feet were quick to follow, the halls of Hvit a safer place to summarise the pros and cons of immersing myself in such a lunatic endeavour. But before I made the doorway, I felt myself grabbed by both arms.

"Get your bloody hands off me!" I growled to my antagonists. Two quick glances confirmed it the grinning forms of Serstra and Verstra. The pair held me pinioned. "I would advise you to let go, my friends, or we may have an altercation, royalty or not."

"Gladly," said the two, as one.

And they did, but only at the point of swinging me backwards then forwards at so great a velocity that I flew through the air like a broken bird for fifty yards or more. The attack took place with such speed, I'd only concocted about ten separate murderous endings for them by the time I flapped into the water. Within moments, I'd sunk beneath the blood-tinged waves.

I saw the water erupt above my private nightmare as the forms of the twins shattered the ocean's ruby skin. More fish than Eternals, the twins looked at my floundering form, grinned the bare-teethed gape of sharks, before gesturing to each other and swimming off at pace into the ever darkening depths. I watched them go as the seawater entered my mouth; my throat; my lungs. It felt as though my innards were being quick frozen, not that it hurt, or even sent a particular chill, but my fear was no less for it. I hated the water. To have it enter me was worse than any torture, a true violation of self. I flailed about but found no purchase in that liquid environment. All I achieved was to swallow more sea and sink ever lower into what appeared a war.

Time lost all meaning as I slid down through the depths. The snow-white forms of the Nordics swam hither and thither, as a patchwork of fast-moving, gaping maws complete with full sets of wicked teeth struck for them. I wasn't even sure who was the hunter and who was the hunted? Not that at that particular moment I could have cared less.

Before I could give it any more consideration, two orcas hurtled past swimming for the surface as though their lives depended on it. Hot on their heels, speeding up from below like shooting stars in reverse, a shoal of Nordics pursued the black and white blurs. Caught up in the melee of their pale limbs, I tumbled over and over in the churning water, not knowing up from down nor left from right. Nobody gave me a second glance as I drowned; nobody cared, as the dark depths rose toward me.

Somehow amidst the chaos, I flipped myself back over, so my steady descent availed me a view of the sun through the water. I'd waited so long to see it. I could've slipped into the afterlife, or whatever awaited Eternal kind beyond our non-lives, with a degree of pleasure, basked in its glow, despite my circumstances, but it was not to be. The unmistakable forms of the elder Nordic princes surged into my immediate view both clinging to an orca's tail. I could not understand what they attempted until their mother sped towards them from within a cluster of her people. Only when talons like sharpened knives struck for the creature's eyes did I see the true ugliness of the hunt. They sought to blind the beasts and drown them.

* * *

Those were the last images I saw as I floated beyond my vision's limits. An Arctic oblivion reached out toward me like a comforting shroud of night. It wasn't such a bad way to go, or so I thought, even peaceful. If I could have seen Linka one more time, I should even have been happy, but I knew I would not. She wouldn't have seen my falling from the chaos of the battle above. A distinct faux pas in my choice of attire allowed for a seamless blending with the obsidian depths. If I hadn't known better, I'd have said it more than destiny how the Nordics had laid out black clothes the previous evening. Or I could have been overthinking things, a not unusual trait, as I prepared to meet my doom.

The last of what little oxygen remained in my lungs dispersed as tiny bubbles and an Eternal lord became one with a midnight sea.

* * *

I wondered how I'd know if I was dead? As an Eternal, I felt no murderous change in temperature, so doubted if even a descent into a fiery Hell would've told on me. If purgatory was my destination, then I may have already been a part of it, a weightless existence in absolute night was no worse than a weighted existence in the same. And, if Heaven, which I doubted, was my designated destination, then surely white light would've consumed me, wouldn't it?

At that moment, it appeared my questions answered. Most surprising of all, it was the latter destination. A brilliant white spark cut through the endless black. The distance between it and I was hard to gauge, I almost thought I might reach out and pluck it as a star from the sky, but it grew larger, stronger, more defined by the second. The speck of white became a snowflake, then a lantern, then a beautiful, luminous, blue-eyed form: blue eyes!

I flapped my arms like reeds before a hurricane. A dread set upon me, one might even have called it fear. Could it be? Had the one who'd spied upon me returned to guarantee my demise?

I watched a pale, slim-shouldered form descend into my nightmare. The demon bore goggle-less features, sharp, angular cheekbones and lips of ruby brilliance vivid against the luminance of an alabaster skin. A beautiful ghost, a murderous apparition, her features struck me hard, for I realised, as her hands reached out, it was no demon but a girl. She was an amalgamation of those females I knew most intimately. She had the ruby lips of my darling Linka, but not the same ethereal beauty; the skin tones of Narina or Ekatarina, but not the same aloof air; she wore Chantelle's innocence before her grotesque transformation, but not a false innocence, a real one. She was something else entirely.

She closed the distance between us like aquatic lightning, grabbed me by the lapels, and pulled me in a direction I presumed to be up before I could even react. All I managed was to waft my arms around in feeble circles as I tried to extricate myself from her trailing cloak. The girl gathered pace with each passing moment, faster and faster, she swam. The absolute dark soon gave way to tinges of rose petal, and I realised us to be nearing the surface. So enthralled was I by my saviour that the passage of several severed Eternal limbs, which hung in the sea like shattered marble sculptures, caused almost no distraction at all: almost.

We breached the surface as though powered by the machinery of the once almighty humanity. Clear out of the water, we hurtled, then back down again onto the ice, unfortunately for me and my head. The smack of skull on ground almost caused me to lose consciousness, but that was nothing compared to my embarrassment at retching up the liquid contents of a waterlogged system right in the middle of the assembled Nordic peoples. My saviour waited by my side until I'd finished.

"Jean! Oh, my god! What happened to you?" came the sweet voice of the angel that was my darling Linka. "Why'd you go in, you hate the water?"

"Help…me…up," I spluttered.

Supported by the arms of Linka and my mystery heroine, I stood tall and surveyed the massacre before my eyes. Blood shone everywhere, over everything, and everyone. There was so much red, I imagined the world sliced in twain, its lifeblood poured over those palest of peoples. A world that carried the subtle hints of a ruby sun had become painted in those of purest crimson, and at its centre stood Serena. For a moment, I didn't recognise her, or her siblings, with their faces thrust into the carcass of an orca pulled ashore to suffocate. They'd butchered the beast almost to the point of a bloody pulp. As if sensing my disdain, Serena swivelled from her gorging and eyed me. I tensed.

"Don't, Jean," I heard Linka's voice as if in a dream, and felt steadying hands grip that bit harder.

"If you value your life, stand down," came an Arctic blast of warning from my opposite side.

But, as ever, my actions were inextricably tied to my mood; my mood was not good. My two guardian angels tried to stop me, and to be fair, they caused me to slow to a stalking prowl. Nevertheless, I closed the distance between Serena's sneering face and myself, the others hauled in my wake.

"Can I do something for you, my dark, wet raven?" Serena asked when I was no more than a pace from her.

"I should very much like a word with your twin boys, Your Majesty," I grated.

"With Serstra and Verstra!" she exclaimed, sounding genuinely surprised. "And I told you to address me as Serena."

"Yes, you did, Your Majesty."

"Hmm, you seem like a man with a grievance." She wiped at the blood on her face, which caused it to smear all the more.

"It might be termed that."

"You do realise, they are two, have feasted on whale blood since childhood, and are without doubt each more powerful than you?"

"I do."

"What do you think, Aurora?" She addressed the girl to my left, who shrugged a response. "Well, I don't believe in people harbouring grudges whilst guests in my realm."

"How would you know, we were supposedly the first?" I spoke with barely concealed venom. A flash of anger in Serena's eyes showed I'd hit a nerve, but she soon recovered herself.

"Serstra! Verstra!" she barked.

In an instant, two unrecognisable, blood-soaked figures rose from within the bones of the orca carcass.

"Oh, Jean, my sweet, sweet love, please don't do this," Linka whimpered in my ear. "I beg of you, reconsider."

I looked at her, grinned, patted her arm with the hand Aurora had released, then placed a gentle kiss upon her beautiful lips. "I won't be many moments, my love."

By the time I set my attention back to the inanely grinning twins, they had taken up positions either side of their mother.

"I believe you owe me an apology, boys."

"Make us," they replied in unison.

* * *

"I bet a whale bone's never been used for that before?" Linka giggled, as I knelt by the water and washed the blood from my face.

"My mother will not look well upon you for making fools of my brothers."

"Aurora, lovely name," I replied.

"Thank you," she answered.

"And if they are your brothers, then I should say thank you for saving my life, Princess, and sorry about your brothers."

"No need to thank me."

"There is from my point of view."

"And mine," added Linka.

"I have no love for my family and if by saving your life I can annoy them even a little, then it was worth it."

"Ah, so not entirely for my benefit."

"I did not mean it to sound that way."

"He's joking," Linka giggled.

"Oh."

"You'll get used to him."

"Maybe?" she almost smiled.

"I gathered you didn't want to be seen the other day."

"You are, and were, very perceptive."

"I try, but the blue eyes gave you away."

"And, no, I did not."

"May I ask why?"

"You may ask."

"Ah, I see. I shan't ask again, at least, not for a while."

"Thank you," Aurora spoke, sweeping her long, milk-white hair from her pretty face. "I think it would be wise for us to return to the throne room. The merriment of the kill shall continue in the depths of Hvit for some time to come."

"Do we have to?" I implored. Both beauties nodded together, as the sound of a whale breaching close by drew my eyes back to the ocean. "Will they not disperse after what has happened?" I asked, looking to Aurora.

"They have as little to eat as we have to drink," she replied. "In their own way, I am certain they look forward to the hunts as much as my kind."

"I sense you are not of the same opinion."

"Your senses do you justice."

"Circle of life, then."

"Or, non-life."

"Yes, that too," I said, as I gave the descending fin of the hunted one last look. For a second, its flukes caught the sun's ruby rays before dripping, blood-like, back into the ocean after the rest of it.

"Come, my love," Linka said, "we should be getting below."

"Yes," I returned, "I could do with a drink."

"I bet," said Linka, as Aurora raised one perfect, white eyebrow.

Chapter 4

Red

"Scratch that drink," I hissed to Linka.

There was something manic about the whirling, twirling madness in the throne room. They seemed oblivious to the fact they looked like abominations. Gone was the snowflake elegance, the feeling of delicate myth, in its place, crimson hysteria.

Linka's fingers tightened their grip in my own. I realised I was not the only one appalled by our view.

The throne room doors closed behind us with a thud audible even through the badly played Strauss.

"Aurora!" hailed Serena. She beckoned to her daughter with one blood-dripping finger, and by association ourselves.

"They could have at least got changed," I whispered into Linka's ear. She did not reply. I couldn't say I blamed her.

We weaved our way through the turbulent throng until we stood before her crimson magnificence.

"Ah, I see you have gathered the flock unto you, my dear."

"I have, mother," Aurora acquiesced.

"Good, good," Serena mused, her gaze flitting from one person to the next before it settled upon me. "My sons will not be the same for quite some time."

"They will not, Your Majesty."

"Serena!" she barked.

"I do apologise, you're almost unrecognisable in your new attire."

Serena mopped at her eyes with the back of her saturated robe and flicked the blood over my face with something akin to a dare shining in her ruby eyes. "Is that better?" she asked.

"Oh, yes, now I see. It is you, Your Majesty."

Serena moved with a speed I'd never witnessed. Her right hand was about my throat whilst her left slapped me so hard that even Vladivar should have quailed before it: I laughed.

"Do I annoy you, Your…Serena?"

"No more so than a gnat. I would advise you to watch your rather smart mouth whilst in my company. Do not forget your place, young man. You are a guest here due to your acquaintance with Princess Linka, and that alone. You were within your rights to maim my children, unfortunately for them, but being disrespectful to one of the Hierarchy is an unforgivable sin."

"Oh, I don't know," I mused, licking the blood from the inside of my cheek, "Vladivar never complained."

"Vladivar was an oaf."

"Still is," I agreed.

"Yes, still," Serena somewhat reluctantly agreed, as she released me in a heap to the floor. It wouldn't have been so bad if the music hadn't have stopped and every leering face turned upon me.

"Verstra! Serstra!" Serena called, as she returned to her brooding position on the ice throne.

"Don't provoke her," Linka pleaded, as she helped me from the floor.

"Where's Aurora gone?" I asked ignoring her warning and peering about.

"I don't know? She was here a moment ago."

"Ah, there you are boys," said Serena as the twins entered the hall through the far doorway.

And just for an instant, I thought there the merest flash of opulence in yonder rooms. Colour adorned the world beyond my vision, a design far removed from that in which we stood. However, the closing ice doors soon extinguished it.

"He is still here!" exclaimed one of the two pointing in vulgar fashion mid-limp.

"He is, Serstra, my son," Serena's iced reply. "And here he *shall* remain for as long as the princess resides here."

"That is not fair," said the other who had wrapped a bandage over his missing eye.

"That is the law."

"You wrote the law, mother."

"And until I choose to un-write it, that is how it shall stay."

"But look what he did to us," the two chimed.

"That is due to your weakness, not due to the law."

"But we were only doing as…"

"That's enough," Serena interjected.

"But…"

"But, nothing." Serena barely raised the tone of her voice; she did not need to. A joint ripple of terror swept over the newly washed twins. They feared her, and no matter their posturing, they could not disguise it. The two flicked nervous gazes from their mother to me. I smiled back. Neither child said another word. Instead, they took up silent positions either side of their mother as before; neither twin raised their eyes to she, or I.

"Music!" commanded the queen clapping her hands together in a spray of red liquid. The music and waltzing renewed.

"Now, Linka," Serena began in cooing tones, "what with your sudden arrival and the hunt's excitement, I have hardly had chance to talk to you. Come sit by me and we shall discuss the state of this ever-changing world." Serena tapped the floor at the base of the throne to indicate exactly where she expected my darling to sit.

Obediently, Linka stepped forward without releasing my hand.

"On your own, my dear," Serena added. "If you don't mind, Jean," she said through a crooked smile.

"Are you all right without me?" I asked.

"I'll be fine." Linka stood on tip-toes to kiss me, fear reflected in her emerald eyes.

"I shall sit with you," came the cold tones of Ekatarina who materialised from nowhere resplendent in shining white robes.

"And I shall accompany you, Jean," ghosted the voice of her sister in my ear.

"I'll return topside for a while, if that is all right with you, my darling?" I said to Linka. "On my own," I added. I thought I heard the ice crack in Narina's heart such was the vehemence in the glance she cast. She swept back out of the hall rather less silently than she had entered. Ekatarina showed no sign of her sister's impetuousness as she gave a polite smile and extricated Linka's grip from my own.

"Don't be too long, Jean," Linka wavered.

"I'll be looking down on you all the time."

"Like an angel?"

"A dark one, I fear."

"They're the best."

"Always." I kissed Linka's free hand, stroked her hair, and then allowed Ekatarina to lead her to the throne.

I did not look back at the ruby eyes I knew upon me, their chill alone was enough to bore a hole in my skull.

* * *

Exiting the sweet-smelling claustrophobia of the stairwell, I stepped out into the half-light of that doorway between the real and the dreamed. I was not alone. For there, growling in defence of their requisitioned meal stood three enormous wolves. The creatures put those Vladivar had set upon me to shame. Their monochrome magnificence stood in sharp contrast to the ruby-hued light and crimson splattered ground.

"There, there, nice doggies," I spoke with all the niceties I could muster, whilst edging towards the lapping sea. I had no intention of harming any beast ever again after seeing the butchery committed by the Nordics. The wolves knew better than to hang about near my kind and were soon off. Yet one paused long enough to give me a quizzical stare. His or her piercing blue eyes examined me. I felt I could have patted the thing if I'd wished to, but that wet dog smell was prevalent and I did so like my new clothes. After sizing me up and finding me not worth the trouble it turned tail and scarpered after its fellows. I was sad to see them go, especially the latter, the Arctic landscape seemed too vast to be alone in. Good job I wasn't, really.

I strolled over to the water and stretched. Whether the sun had weakened since I'd been below the waves, I was unsure, but the waters had the faintest trace of a crystalline crust formed upon them. Like a spider's web catching moonbeams, the sea water refracted the ruby light at strange angles. The effect was both beautiful and moving.

"Do you like it too, Aurora?" I asked into the slightest stirring of a newborn wind. There was a hesitation, perhaps a hint of surprise in the voice that replied.

"I like nothing more."

"Shall you not reveal yourself?" I asked.

"I thought I already had."

"Ah, don't want to be seen, eh?"

"It is for the best," came a reluctant reply.

"For whom?" I pressed.

"Why, for me, of course. I enjoy the view too much to have it stripped from me."

"Your mother?"

"My mother," she confirmed.

"Say no more, I quite understand."

"I wish others did."

"Such is the way of things when unbalanced opinions collide."

"I suppose."

"It is beautiful," I said, attempting to change the topic and spare the girl any further unease.

"For now, but a storm brews. Soon, the sun will be smothered by a blanket of snow."

"That will be a shame."

"A great shame," she agreed, as something dripped onto the water, unable to puncture the semi-solid surface.

"Would you care to talk about what troubles you?" I asked in my kindest voice.

"No," came a blunt reply.

"Fair enough, child, I prefer the silence anyway." I stared out over the dimming, ruby eye that just crested the horizon. "Hmm, you appear to be correct about the storm."

"I am always correct."

"I shall remember that for reference."

"Ha!" Aurora laughed.

"Ah, so you do know joy."

"Is that what it's called?"

"I'm not really sure, I haven't known much myself."

"Are you orphaned too, Jean?" she asked, a touch overeagerly. I think she sensed a kindred spirit in that moment, or hoped for one.

"I am. Although, you are hardly an orphan whilst your mother remains so hale and hearty. God, I hope she isn't. Tell me it's true."

Aurora went silent.

"I'm sorry, I shouldn't have said that. She is still your mother, after all."

"I am an orphan to her, I can assure you." Aurora spoke as though having not heard me.

"I see," I said, although I didn't. "The rest of your brothers and sisters don't appear to feel the same way."

"Half-brothers and half-sisters."

"Ah, that would explain the eyes."

"I've been told I have my father's eyes, but cannot confirm it."

"Did you not know him?"

"No," came a blunt response.

"A sore subject?"

"I am reminded of it at every opportunity."

"I'm sorry. Being different has its pros and cons."

"How would you know?" Aurora's petulant response.

"Being different does not just come in shades of eyes, my dear."

"Now it's my turn to apologise, Jean. I did not mean that to sound as it did."

"Don't give it a second thought," I said, as the ruby light dimmed to a deep claret.

"It comes," she said. Then added, "The other direction."

"Well, if you would unveil your arm," I protested, but the sun's obliteration spun my head back to the sea and the oncoming snow. "Hmm, you were right."

"I told you, I am always right."

Before Aurora could say another word, I was swept off my feet and onto my rear end by a sudden Arctic blast of some magnitude. Strangely, my immediate thoughts went to the wolves and where they should have found sanctuary from the weather. I would have given them even greater thought if not for the distinct sound of something very un-stormy.

"Did you hear that?" I called into the wind.

"No!" she bellowed back

"Sounded like an engine."

"I heard nothing, Jean," Aurora restated, her voice closer. "We must get below before we cannot find the entrance. Take my hand," she commanded.

"I can't see your hand." But before I could complain further, I felt the soft flesh of another slip into my left palm. Aurora did not stop to talk, instead, she pulled me back to my feet and dragged me into what by then was a whiteout. I saw only snow, heard only wind, and within a few instants, smelled only lavender. My feet sought the top step's security, and it was with some relief I descended the windswept stairway. There was no thud of the hatched doorway closing only the silencing of the elements and a strange vacuum sensation for a second or two. A few stray snowflakes drifted idly by until deciding the ground their chosen destination, the staircase becalmed.

"Can you find your own way?" came a hushed voice.

"Yes, of course," I replied, "down."

"Then, go. I shall follow soon. It would not bode well for us to be seen entering together."

"I suppose not," I conceded. If Aurora heard me she did not acknowledge it and I perceived myself suddenly alone.

* * *

By the time I reached the doors to the throne room, the sound of revelry had somewhat diminished. In fact, upon entering the chamber, I realised the music had gone replaced by the sound of the Nordics chanting in sombre tones. The still blood-soaked citizens stood in one massive circle all holding hands. The massive chandelier had been relit although it appeared lower than before and the light fainter. It felt like I had disturbed something extremely personal, and I would have returned to the corridor if not for the fact an arm had slipped into my own.

I was about to say something devastatingly charming to Linka when I realised the limb entwined with my own was that purest of porcelain that only a newly washed Nordic could quite pull off.

"Shush," came a sound in my ear. I had no choice but to allow myself to be led around the edge of the assembly in silence. I said nothing to Narina for my eyes already quested for Linka. Much to my chagrin, the blood-spattered throne stood desolate. The pang beneath my ribs suggested a heart less vacant than I took it for.

We hugged the wall until eventually Narina opened the doors to the sleeping quarters and pulled me through them.

"That was all very cloak and dagger."

"It is a lament to those who died today," Narina replied.

"Oh, sorry, I spoke without thinking. Were there many?" I asked with genuine sincerity.

"Six."

"Is that usual?"

"It is not unusual, though still too many."

"Six of your people for one whale. I would definitely say that too many."

"We shall not need to hunt for a long time, though."

"What is time to an Eternal?"

"It is a great deal when your people only ever diminish."

"Good point," I agreed.

Narina half smiled at that and eased me away down that longest of corridors. The clip-clop of her stilettoed feet marked our passage along the ice. All else was silent. Only when we reached the doors to Linka and mine's room did she speak again.

"I am sorry for my brothers' actions."

The apology caught me somewhat off guard.

"You have no need to apologise, Narina. The actions were not yours."

"Still, they brought shame upon me and my family."

"Don't give it a second thought," I said. "I only hold a grudge against those who deserve it."

"A lot of grudges then," she said with a smile of dismissal. She bowed and made to leave, but I caught her by the arm.

"Why would you think that?"

Narina looked to me, then to the hand that grasped her. I had hold of her so tight that the skin around my fingers turned blue. Accordingly, I released her.

"I...I...do not know, Jean. I just..." Her words trailed off as I saw her struggling with something below that smoothest of facades. "Good night," she eventually said and was away down the corridor as though a spectre in a breeze.

I watched her fade into the distance, took a deep breath, for some unknown reason, and entered the room. How I wished I hadn't.

Linka sat on the edge of the bed, head slumped, her thighs moist from fallen tears. She held an opened envelope in her up-turned palms. I knew without a word passing between us that my blackmailers had found me.

Chapter 5

Blue

Something about the colour blue had always evoked a sense of emptiness. Blue always reflected my mood. Being surrounded by walls, curtains drawn back, ceiling and floor all flickering in subtlest shades of neon, whilst seeing Linka tinged by that same emptiness, saddened me beyond words. Blue took a deeper meaning then.

Linka never stirred, nor once acknowledged my presence. She sat there catatonic.

I slid the envelope from her hand, sat beside her and allowed the thing to disgorge its contents. A rather grubby looking sheet of paper fell into my palm like a dead weight.

Dear Jean;

We find ourselves in the surprising situation where those we wished terminated are. No thanks to you, though. This has left us in the odd situation where we could either thank you and allow you and your puppy princess to live happily ever after, or not. We have chosen the latter.

We have re-evaluated our affairs and have decided that as seen as you have not, so far as we can see, taken any of our previous messages seriously, we have one final task for you to complete: kill Queen Serena. If you do not, then your precious Linka shall die.

The fact you hold this letter in the one place on earth we should have found inaccessible proves we are capable of said task and shall not hesitate to do so. Do it now, we grow impatient.

Best regards

My eyes closed, breath caught. A life changed, again.

I crumpled the note and threw it as hard as I could. The thing bounced off the adjacent wall and unfurled like a flower revealing a stamen full of vitriol. The words refused dismissal, and my rage grew without an outlet on which to vent it.

"We must not let Serena see this," I eventually managed unable to contain my boiling blood.

"Turn the envelope over." Her words lacked conviction, spoken without hope.

I spared Linka a look, but her head still hung over her chest. She sat impassive, broken, a fire put out by the rain.

I picked the envelope up off my knees and flipped it over. There was one word on it: Serena.

"Quite the dilemma we have here," came the iced tones of she who I was to kill.

I raised my head to the majesty that was Queen Serena of the Nordics. She stood in the open doorway resplendent in the colours of her domain, impassive. The albino queen could have killed me then, and Linka, if she'd wished. She did not.

"I shall leave," I said without hesitation.

"And, if I was not to allow it?"

"I give you my word, Serena. I will not return if you promise to shelter Linka."

"Why should I?"

"She is a member of the Hierarchy, is it not your duty?"

"Perhaps, and I realise she is innocent in this game. However, I dislike surprises. This is the biggest in more time than I care to reflect upon. I am disturbed. Your letter disturbs me."

"Not as much as I."

"More so, Jean. Someone placed this letter on my throne, whilst we Nordics hunted. This should not have been possible. Hvit is closed to all but my own people; they were all with me."

"I… I don't know what to say," I stammered like a nervous child.

"I gather this is not your first contact with whoever sent *that*." She pointed to the letter with a look of utter contempt plastered across her sculpted face.

"It is not," I confessed.

"I also gather you have not done as they wished."

"I did not have to."

"That is not very reassuring."

"It is the truth."

"Who were you to kill?"

It was the question I'd dreaded. I felt like I was drowning in subterfuge and lies, the truth, my only life-raft. "Linka's father," I whispered.

"Speak up, Jean, I did not hear you."

"I was to kill Linka's father!" I growled. My love's leg flinched at that, but she remained otherwise deadened.

"Rudolph!" Serena sounded surprised.

"Yes, it is a long story."

"One I do not wish to hear, fortunately for you. Why do you think leaving would be preferable to doing as they wish?"

"I have had, and never will have, any intention of doing their bidding."

"Ah, a man of principles, I see. What if their wishes coincided with what was best for you?"

"Pardon!" I exclaimed, burying my face in my hands.

"With me dead, the most senior of all Eternals, then you as courtesan to the oldest house remaining in this fractured world would be in a powerful position."

"You have children, don't you?" I snapped.

"They are not me, though some would wish it."

"Well, either way, I have never intended to be anything other than left alone."

"I don't believe that was always the case, Jean. I do not believe that for one second. Doubly so, now." Serena nodded in Linka's direction.

"You know what I meant." An insipid response from between clasped fingers.

"Possibly? One thing I do know with an assuredness to level mountains is the girl you sit beside is your entire world. Ironic, really."

"Why's that?" My tone was savage but toothless.

"That the vagabond prince should, at last, find true love, as the planet nears its end."

"I would sooner spend a minute with Linka than a lifetime without her."

"Yet, you would leave her."

"If it spared her, then yes. I am the magnet they are drawn to, not she."

"Do you not think your blackmailers know this?"

"How do you mean?" I said, taken aback by her words.

"These people are resourceful, knowledgeable, even. They may have foreseen your reaction."

"I don't know."

"Do you not think the note's true purpose is to act as a provocation?"

"I don't know, Serena!" I snapped. "It is a nightmare I find myself unable to wake from."

"Ah, at last, a little of the real man." Serena stroked the ermine trims of her robe. A dismissive flick of her milk-white hair followed, and then she spoke again. "You must go."

"I know."

"Now, Jean. I believe time is of the essence. Hvit's door shall soon move and the entrance to our realm will again become invisible to all but our own."

"Then, I will leave."

"I do not want that," came Linka's tremulous voice.

"Even though you know the truth, my love."

"I know it was not of your doing, nor of your choice."

"It never is."

Linka looked up then with eyes like flooded grasslands. Without even trying, I'd broken the girl's heart, her spirit swamped and floundering. Shame on me. Shame on the world.

"I have to go. There is no other way to guarantee your safety. I trust Serena's word, she is honourable. What happened with the twins is proof of that."

Serena shuffled uneasily in the doorway, but all my attention was upon Linka.

"She is the only one who can protect you, my love. She already has."

"I would rather die than be without you," Linka implored.

"It will not come to that, dear, dear Linka. I will not let it. I will find who seeks to manipulate me and end this once and for all. There is no other way."

"Unpleasant actions garner unpleasant rewards," Serena cooed.

"That is the sort of thing a good friend of mine would've said."

"Would he?"

"How did you know it was a he?"

Serena paused before answering, "You do not strike me as a man with female friends, only dalliances."

"You see, a lot."

"I have seen, a lot," she corrected. "Now, you must go. I can already hear the ice creaking. It signals Hvit's repositioning. Our city moves."

She was right. A crack of such magnitude split our conversation I thought lightning had somehow penetrated the ocean and struck us.

"Jean, I'm begging you, don't go," Linka wept.

Cascades of tears washed over the contours of her perfect face; they froze as waterfalls before reaching the floor. I couldn't bear to look.

"I promise, my one and only love, I shall return when I can."

My words did nothing to assuage her dread. Linka threw herself upon me, a limpet to a rock, whilst I remained impassive. Only Serena's surprisingly gentle coaxing extricated her from me. Perhaps the queen still possessed some trace of humanity after all.

"Go, Jean, I shall watch over her," Serena said, as Linka clung instead to her, as though her very soul depended on it.

I stood, looked to the two, and then walked from the room. I could not say another word for I did not have the strength.

The long walk down that silent corridor was like a path to my doom. The echoes of my booted feet were my sole accompaniment, nothing more.

Through the doors to the throne room, I departed. The chamber, pristine again, stood deserted apart from a guard of Serena's children. They stood in two lines of three with Narina at point holding the doors to the outside world ajar. I said nothing as I strode between them, and neither did they. Only the flicker of a crystal tear in the corner of Narina's eye belied any emotion. Even the maimed twins remained statuesque at my passing, silent and still. I witnessed my own wake, or so it seemed. Perhaps, it was? Narina handed me a backpack containing the reassuring slosh of bottled blood, but it was lost in the thud of the closing doors.

I reached the top of the staircase before I realised I'd even set foot on it and stopped with my hands pressed against the exit. I don't know why I looked back over my shoulder, what I expected to see? But when I realised my love did not follow, I pushed upwards and emerged into an Arctic maelstrom.

An acerbic wind bit deep into my bones. The tempest, violent and wild, threatened to upend me such was its magnitude.

I pulled my cloak closer lest it wrapped me in my own dark shroud and stared into a solid wall of white. I could not see nor hear anything other than the Polar storm. I should have been cold then, scared, perhaps even nervous, if any other creature. Yet, I was Eternal, and felt nothing. Nothing at all.

Knowing the ocean lay before me, I struggled to turn my back to the wind, slung my pack over my shoulder, then set off in the opposite direction. I left behind not only the hated water, Hvit, and those contained within it, but the sun. When I would see it again, I did not know. What little soul I had grew a shade darker.

The compacted snow, closer in composition to ice than the fluffy white stuff I loved, had already covered to a depth of at least a foot. I did not care, for what had I to worry from it? There were only two things on my mind: Linka's tears, and my determination to quell them. Those thoughts fuelled me, consumed me. My mind swirled with violent intent. Angry hands gripped my cloak, their clutching talons piercing both fabric and palms. The suppressed rage that stemmed from embarrassment and shame surfaced. My deception of the one person I'd not have wished manifested in a roar of such anger as I'd never before expelled. The maelstrom winds swallowed my anguished howl the moment it left my mouth. Even in despair, I was unheard, unseen, unwanted.

I stood there a moment swaying to the planet's will. I hadn't taken twenty paces, but I felt a million miles from Linka, and perhaps a few closer to Alba, wherever she dwelt.

* * *

A few yards became a few miles, and a few miles, many more. In truth, I was clueless to how far I'd walked, or for how long, but the Arctic did not loosen its grip upon me for even an instant. There was no up, nor down, in that world of devastating obliteration. All I knew was that sometimes the going seemed hard and other times, harder. My plane of existence teetered be-tween limbo and Hell, I cared not which. I deserved everything the Arctic threw at me.

I tried logic: I considered my situation, evaluated it and sought answers. But I had none. No nearer to finding who manipulated me, nor to finding who had ruined what life I had, I trudged on through the relentless blizzard. My one certainty was that with every difficult step my fury grew greater. Whether it was with them, or myself, I wasn't sure.

* * *

An absence of sun, moon, and apparently season soon told upon my body. The passage of hours became a confusion of whipping winds and blanketed white landscapes. I even imag-ined my fangs freezing, then cracking off in a sudden gust like icicles plucked from a ledge. My body clock was off and my mood with it. If I couldn't be moody, my one dependable state, then what had I left other than tedium. I mired in it.

Then, as if in response to my confusions, the storm stopped. As abruptly as it had started it finished. A few half-hearted snowflakes that descended from the sky like shed angel's feath-ers were all that remained of my personal purgatory. In its place, a pristine sky freckled by stars. The beauty above was matched by its star-filled and gently undulating reflection?

I had stopped less than three feet from an almost exact replica of the shoreline I'd left long behind. They were so alike, I imag-ined a circuitous route had returned me whence I'd came. But the momentary panic of the lost cleared like the skies, the sun's absence proving I'd not. What else was there to do but sit and have a drink.

I removed my cloak, folded it into a square, then sat upon it, as though picnicking with Alba, as we had by the once blue Danube. I'd have preferred it being in the shade of the Alps with

Linka, but an expanse of bland white would have to do. The sea wasn't included in my observations; I held only contempt for that.

I uncorked the only bottle of what appeared a fine looking liquid, sniffed it to no effect, and took a long draught. Within seconds, everything felt much better. I took another swill of the crimson liqueur, gargled it around my mouth until all my senses became infused with it, then lay back in the snow. The stars always looked better when laid on one's back. But unlike the old me, who would have happily laid there forever, the ever twinkling lights were a constant reminder of she I'd deserted. Every pattern in the night sky was Linka. Every glimpse of the moon, her porcelain skin. There was no submerging her memory in my inner depths, no purging my core of her infection. The thought I might even have tried revolted me. I cursed my pathetic self, then the onyx sky, then the sea, and resolved to do something about it.

I got back up, brushed myself off, put the bottle back in the backpack and replaced my cloak. There wasn't time to dally. I had to press on, but where?

I looked about like some pathetic lost sheep. There were no landmarks to note, nothing to give a clue as to my whereabouts. I even contemplated continuing in the same direction. I couldn't swim, of course, but I considered sinking to the seafloor and walking in a generally straight line.

However, I was robbed of even that ridiculous solution, for as I stared over whatever ocean lay before me three dorsal fins rose from the dark waters splicing the waves like black blades. They were graceful in their way, although I did not thank them for spraying me with their expelled breaths. The orcas awaited my entrance with a patience I myself should once have envied. They circled five yards from my position not even bothering to hide. They knew my thinking even better than I.

The Nordics and orcas shared so simple a living arrangements as to be admirable. Not only did they provide food for each other, to greater or lesser degrees, but a certain joint security. I doubted any stray Eternal should've sought entry to Hvit past those most fearsome sentinels even if they had discovered where it lay. Likewise, I suspected no Nordic of being so foolhardy as to risk escape in the opposite direction. It was a marriage made in Heaven and consummated in Hell. If Serena had planned it, then she'd given more thought to her circumstances than I'd given her credit for. I would not make the mistake again.

The orcas swam in languid circles. On occasion, they'd rise clear of the water like half-submerged carriages to spy me through those gigantic eyes. Like kittens, the orcas toyed with their prey, their actual lion selves never far from pouncing.

I contemplated numerous miraculous escapes: springing atop their shiny backs, riding them to safety, etcetera, etcetera, but each was more flight of fantasy than the last. One whale, a huge specimen, as if sensing my lunacy, leapt from the sea and bellyflopped not two yards away, saturating me from head to toe. Unamused to start with, and even less so then, I was on the point of lavishing my antagonist with a verbal lambasting when I was deprived of even this. The three leviathans gave me one last wide-eyed glare and then each dived below the waves, lost to their liquid world. They did not resurface.

At first, I was surprised, then suspicious. I even suspected the creatures of hatching some master plan to dispatch me. I soon saw why, or rather, heard, why they'd departed with such permanence.

It started as a slight drone, a bee on the wing, then a wail like a trodden on cat, if I'd ever had a cat to tread on, then louder still. Out of the distant sky, a flying platform sped towards me over the rolling waters. I was so ecstatic to see it I almost waved my arms about in joy. Almost. I could not see the machine's pilot but did not approve of his trajectory, nor his erratic movements.

So much so, I dived full length to avoid being flattened by the strange device, as it ploughed unceremoniously into the snow. In a great crash of unyielding metal on even tougher ice, the contraption sent volcanic amounts of snow raining down in all directions.

I picked myself up, dusted off my shirt, then strolled nonchalantly over to my visitor. I would not give them the pleasure of seeing me ruffled. That cool demeanour dispersed when I recognised the pilot, hurt, bleeding and half covered by snow. It was the aged form of my one true friend, my blind friend. It was Sunyin, alive, but just.

Chapter 6

Grey

Collecting Sunyin's crumpled form was a bittersweet torment. The tang of blood, which seeped from both a cut forehead and gashed arm, was like a natural aphrodisiac. I had no choice but to resist.

"Sunyin," I said taking a handful of snow and mopping at his injuries. "Sunyin, it is I, Jean."

There was no response. I tried to compress some snow to water to provide a drink, but the cold hands of the dead refused so simple a task. Instead, I took a handful of that most bountiful provision and tried to feed him it. Most fell from Sunyin's mouth to his robe, but some melted into his mouth if judged by his gulping throat. Scant else revealed any sign of life. His milk-white eyes stared off into the night at I knew not what as he lay otherwise limp. I offered him a little more snow until a short cough signalled the precursor to words.

"I knew a Jean once. I dreamed him."

"Yes, yes, my old friend!" I exuded. "It is I, Jean, the one you mistook for a good man, but you did not dream me. Do you not remember?"

"Jean?" He rolled the name over his tongue as if tasting a memory. "I recall a raven called Jean. It was many lifetimes ago." A wracked cough made him wince in pain.

"Say no more, old friend, I shall care for you."

"Ah, that sounds like something a good friend would once have said."

If Sunyin was serious, delusional, or teasing, I was unsure, but I removed my cloak, wrapped it into a tight bundle, and laid his head upon it. That seemed to ease the monk's frowning features, but I noted from the shining crystals collected across his shuddering body, he was very, very cold. I removed my shirt, as it did nothing for me, slipped it over Sunyin's head and rested him back down again.

"Jean…Jean," he mused. "I cannot remember his last name."

"I have not got one," I said, wiping the last smears of blood from his blue-tinged skin.

"Everybody has one. You have merely forgotten it…" Sunyin's words trailed off into the Arctic night, as his eyes slid closed.

I shook my head in despair not knowing what else to do? Caring was not my forte, Alba and many others would've testified to that, but I was not about to let humanity pass from the world without trying to prevent it. So, I did the only thing I could, I righted the craft, laid Sunyin in its rear and in mimicry of Merryweather's handling of the last flying platform took the controls. Through clenched teeth, I depressed the red button.

The vehicle stung into action. The front end trembled, spluttered, then lifted from the snow. I wasn't sure what to expect next, but a sixth sense told me to hang on. I did. Good job, too.

Within an instant of placing my hand upon the flying platform's strange handlebars, it was up into the air. The thing paused, rotated one-hundred and eighty degrees, then shot off at a velocity that almost ripped my fingers from their sockets. Over the choppy sea, we flew, higher and higher. Up and up in a graceful, arcing ascent we rose, then sped off into the endless horizon.

I soon grew bored with staring off into an unknown, unchanging vista, so risked a tricky manoeuvre. The platform, level as it was, seemed sturdy enough for a shuffled passage to Sunyin. I saw no point remaining at the steering column for I contributed nothing to the ship's control. So, I dropped to my knees and with a degree of trepidation did just that.

Sunyin rested upon the low rail that ran around the back of the machine. There, I took my place in silence beside him. He looked peaceful in his own way; unwell, but peaceful. The blood had ceased running from his wounds and instead formed miniature pools of red ice. Blood: it had so much to answer for. I sat there, the wind streaming through my hair, freshest of fresh air assailing my senses, and thought back to she who I'd abandoned. I hoped Linka fared better than I. Serena had appeared sincere, but I'd felt compelled to hurry from Hvit. As a rule, I preferred time to think things through. My flight was most unlike me. I sat and stewed over my questionable decision making amidst visions of emeralds and long raven hair.

I stood by the Rhine in gleaming light. The sun shone brighter than any star, and I felt warm, or what I imagined warmth to be like. I liked it. I'd even have said it made me happy. Shading my eyes from the celestial orb above, I watched on as Linka picked pretty flowers from the riverbank. She seemed happy, too. Perhaps, it was real? Perhaps, not? For the crystal, clear waters that ushered passed in gurgling glory began to thicken and transform. The Rhine slowed almost to a stop as its waters darkened from clear, to pink, to crimson, then black. The sun strayed behind a cloud that dripped ruby rain, and I felt a dread upon me. I could not move as the waters churned, could not react, as two female forms rose from the depths. Twinned they were in evil, one turning eyes of ruby upon me, the other obsidian black. My voice deserted me as I tried to shout to my love, to warn her. But without words, she heard nothing. They tore her apart from the throat down. Her un-

blinking eyes were the last to go. I could do nothing; feel nothing; hear nothing, as the sky exploded and what was promised came to pass. The end laid heavy on my soulless shell as all faded to dust.

"Sir, are you well?"

My eyes flicked open to the misted globes of Sunyin. He looked at me, or through me, as though I was a ghost? His face reflected the panic of my dream, as the words from his blue lips sought to reassure.

"Jean, not, sir."

"Ah, yes, you said. My apologies, Jean."

"No need." I dismissed his words with a waved hand.

"You were screaming, Jean. I was worried about you."

"I am fine, old friend. Nothing more than a bad dream."

"You dream like that often?"

"I don't dream at all, as a rule. Too busy trying to escape my little slice of death."

"You seek to escape death?" he asked, sitting back down beside me.

"I seek to escape the feeling of death."

"But, you are alive?"

"Am I, old man?"

"Do you not wake, live, feel love?"

"I sometimes think I do," I said more to myself than my inquisitor.

"Then you are alive."

"Glad to hear it," I said. "But I'll feel more alive when we get to our destination. Which I must say," I added, "looks considerably closer, wherever it is?"

"Yes, it is good to see soil again, even if it is not as rich in life as it should be."

I was clueless as to how Sunyin knew we no longer flew over the Arctic waters but instead a vast expanse of tundra? However, experience had taught me not to doubt my companion's observational skills despite his infirmities.

"I think it's about time you and I had a chat, old monk." I climbed to my feet, arched my back in a raking stretch, then grabbed for the rail before the turbulence propelled me overboard.

"I would be glad to," he replied with a smile.

"Well, how did you escape the Marquis is the one that first springs to mind?"

"I do not know this Marquis of whom you speak."

"Hmm, then, how did you find me?"

"I do not remember."

"Not going great, is it?"

"Not really," he agreed.

"Is there anything you do remember?"

"I don't even remember you," he said. "Only that I should find you. Do you understand what I am trying to say?" he asked with a puzzled expression.

"I could lie if it made you feel better."

"Lying is not a good trait."

"At least you remember that," I said.

"I remember many things. Just not the answers to your questions."

"Then how *did* you find me?"

"I can only presume it fate."

"I do not believe in fate."

"But I do, Jean."

"How can you be sure?" I thought I had him there, but Sunyin, as always, had an answer.

"Faith, Jean. I found myself on this machine. Somebody had put me here for a reason. I now know that reason was you. I do not question, only follow my preordained path."

"I have no preordained path, though I feel the draw of the Rhineland."

"Is that where we are headed?"

"I don't know!" I laughed out loud. "I hope so. I think so."

"How can you be so sure?" the old man pressed.

"Hmm," I mused. "I suspect it's fate."

"Then our conversation has come full circle, my friend, and the Rhineland is undoubtedly our destination."

I huffed a response, but was already investigating the landscape we sped over. There was no way to describe it other than dead. It didn't even contain the memory of life. Barren dirt and rock, punctuated by a slight but ever increasing vista of twisted, stilted trees, swept before us. On and on the same view until we shot out over endless water and I realised we had crossed the ancient Scandinavian continent and out over the sluggish remains of the Baltic Sea.

The Baltics weren't high on my list of places to visit. In fact, I prayed we'd not stray too close to Duke Gorgon's domain. If I could've wrenched the controls from the floor and aimed us in another direction, I would have.

I had issues with all of the Hierarchy, but none more so than Gorgon. He was ever bad tempered. He and Chantelle's new husband made quite the pair. Gorgon and Vladivar were equal in their obnoxiousness and shared hatreds. Both held a grudge against the world and more so each other. However, Gorgon had some redeeming principles; Vladivar had none. Duke Gorgon's non-appearance at his enemy's wedding suggested knowledge of his counterpart's machinations. He knew things. However, I'd be the last person he'd share them with. It would've been ill-advised to venture there, so I crossed more than just my fingers that we weren't.

Sunyin had nodded back off to sleep. The exertions of his interrogation had been too much in his frail state. I rested his head back on the makeshift pillow and stared into the distance as the Rhineland's crumbling coast came into view. The distant, gaping hole that had once been the River Elbe's outpouring looked somewhat pitiful with nothing but brown sludge emanating from its maw. A lifetime ago, the boy I was once stood on those cliffs with his parents and marvelled at such an expanse of water. On reflection, it was probably those crumbling cliffs that had created my phobia. I'd almost slid over their edge and into those particularly turgid waters, my father catching my hand as my mother screamed. A memory best forgotten.

We were soon back over more familiar territory although hanging too close to the East for my liking. I put up with it for a while before determining to adjust our trajectory. So, I mounted the high stool that stood before the handlebar controls and tried to turn them. Merryweather had manipulated the ship to some extent, so I saw no reason why I couldn't manage it if that idiot had. But much to my chagrin the thing wouldn't budge an inch, and we hurtled on in an almost arrow-straight line. Only when the amalgamation that was the Alp/Himalay massif rose into view did the device alter its bearing. Veering towards France, unfortunately, the thing made a beeline for that vascular river that was the amended Danube. I remembered my parents' tales of how the Eternal engineers had carved out a second exit to the northern coasts so the river might flow in either direction to both the Baltic and Black seas as the occasion demanded. All very unnecessary in my opinion but unsurprising with there being so little else to do. Like a serpent of hellish proportions, the blood-red waters of the leviathan cut through my immediate grey horizon. The craft, as though sensing its snaking trail, then cut a sharp south-east line and made an approximate navigation of the thing. From such a height, one appreciated the sorry state of my homelands: I duly averted my eyes. I focused, instead, on the line of the mountains and their snow-crested summits. But the white caps only reminded me of what I'd left behind. Those tiny tips of Arctic dreams made me miss my darling all the more, and no matter how hard I tried to think of something else, I failed.

Lost in my moroseness, we shot in between a line of two separate sets of peaks and along a winding, steep-sided valley. The area looked vaguely familiar although I had never seen it from such an angle. In the past, I'd paid little attention to my whereabouts, after all, I'd spent most of my time wishing I wasn't amongst them.

We followed that crease in the planet whipping occasionally from one side of it to the other, adjustments made for no apparent reason other than to annoy me, before the flying platform decelerated to a gentle jog. I found it a tad surprising as I'd convinced myself we were to veer off toward the Comte de Burgundy's palace. Instead, we rounded a bend in the mountains to be confronted by the oncoming blemish I recognised at once as the Marquis de Rhineland's ivory palace. By choice, I'd have avoided that most inhospitable of places. If not for Sunyin's enthusiastic intervention, I still might have.

"Look, Jean, isn't it beautiful," he said pointing into the distance.

At first, I thought him senile. Nobody could think that appalling construction beautiful, but I followed the line of his arm and realised he meant the rising sun: I had forgotten the course of time still moved. The constant sameness of the Arctic darkness that lingered beyond Hvit's limits had thrown my usual astuteness out. I would have stern words with myself later.

"I'll admit to something, Sunyin, if it was not for the fact we were charging into yet another perilous situation, I would agree." And I meant it as the burning outline of that molten orb illuminated both mountaintop and palace in a darker shade of blood.

"I don't think I've ever seen the sun before?" the old monk chuckled.

"Quite the reverse, my forgetful friend, you have seen the sun many times, if not with your eyes, whilst for me, this is still rather unique."

"You'd have thought I'd have remembered such a beautiful occurrence."

"Could be the bang to your head, or that you've forgotten you're blind." I winked, then realised it wasted. "Right now, I think the palace should be our main concern. Do you recognise this as your starting point?"

"I do not. I am sorry, Jean, I know it is not what you wish to hear," Sunyin responded, his face downcast.

"Never fear, old friend, but if this confounded contraption should alight, you would do well to stay behind me."

"As you wish," he agreed with a sage nod of his bald head.

The Marquis' palace was undoubtedly our destination as the craft slowed almost to a standstill, took a leisurely once around the place, then came to a hovering stop between it and the valley we'd just navigated.

"At least we have the daytime on our side, Sunyin. No Eternal would stray into sunlight."

I said it more in hope than expectation.

"Why?" asked the monk, as I surveyed the palace's upper windows for any sign of life.

"They would think it their death, as once did I."

"Then, what is he doing?"

I must have looked very startled, as Sunyin laughed out loud at my jerked movements and slapped his thigh in a way most out of character.

A peep over the craft's prow, down into the depths, all the way to the gigantic, double glass doors at the palace's rear, confirmed what the monk had spoken of. The enormous, velvet drapes behind the doors-cum-windows were drawn back to reveal a beaming face.

"Do you know him?" asked the old monk looking not for a second to the madly gesticulating idiot behind the glass.

"Yes. Yes, I do. That, my blind friend, is Sir Walter Merryweather, and we may be in more trouble than I first suspected!"

Chapter 7

Ivory

The glass door drew back to reveal a grinning Merryweather.

"Have you put on weight, Jean? That craft's listing like my old girlfriend's knickers!" he bellowed, even though we'd descended to eye level and were less than ten feet away. "You look like you've seen a ghost, or toast, or a little of both?"

"I see you survived then."

"No thanks to you. But, hey-ho, I'm not one to hold a grudge. At least you came to find me."

"Well, to be honest, Merryweather, I'd forgotten all about you."

"Meeeee! But, I'm unforgettable!

"Apparently not."

"That's deeply regrettable."

"So you say."

"I find it quite incredible."

"Do you?"

"And so inedible."

"Stop talking nonsense. Have you lost your mind, man?"

Merryweather paused, scratched at his chin and shook his head, his floppy mess of blond hair looking like a bird's nest dislodged by the wind. He gazed down the valley, then back to the flying platform, and then up into the rose-tinged sky. "Do you know what, Jean, I think I just might."

"Your friend is very excitable," noted Sunyin.

"He is not my friend."

"That's harsh! After all I've done for you."

"You didn't even have the decency to die when I wanted you to."

"I'm un-killable, un-murderable, un-slaughterable, and un…I can't think of any others!"

"Maybe, you were just first time lucky," I suggested. "And stop shouting."

"I blame you."

"Thought you might."

"And I will stop, but only because my throat hurts."

"Hm."

"Well, if you'd done the job right, I wouldn't have had to mope across the landscape looking for somewhere to hold out, would I?"

"Rest assured, Walter, I shan't make the same mistake twice."

"That's not very reassuring. It's not very reassuring at all. How's Linka by the way?" he added, with an exaggerated wink.

Unable to contain myself any longer, I made a lunge for Merryweather, who ran off into the Marquis' palace screaming like a girl. If not for Sunyin grasping my trouser leg, I would probably have gone right over the flying platform's ledge in my efforts to scrag him.

"Thank you," I said, pulling myself back together.

"You're welcome, Jean," Sunyin beamed. "But please explain, why can you not settle your differences with that funny man? He seems happy enough to see you."

"It's a long story."

"I have time."

"NO!" I bellowed.

"Does he always generate such hostility?" Sunyin's calm reply.

"Yes," I said, this time at a more sociable level.

"Do you need a helping hand?" grinned Merryweather from his masterful hiding place behind the velvet curtain.

"You're back, are you?"

"Seem to be."

"You weren't gone long."

"I soon get bored these days, and hungry," he said licking his lips in Sunyin's direction.

"Trust me, Merryweather, touch the monk and I'll rectify any mistakes I made in finishing you off the first time." I gave Merryweather one of my dirtiest looks to emphasise the point.

"Ah, but that implies that you won't touch me if I don't, which by a process of elimination leads me to the conclusion you've already forgiven me."

"It may imply it."

"Still as grumpy as ever."

"Where you're concerned."

"Oh, well, might as well invite you in."

"Yours now, is it?" I said with a nod to his new home.

"Well, I can't see the Marquis hurrying back here, can you?"

"How would I know? Dear Vincent has mastered the art of avoiding my attentions. I don't suppose not being in his own home when I should most desire to throttle him will be any different."

"You do have some strange reasoning."

Merryweather leaned out over the abyss so far I thought he should fall at any moment. I watched him, alive in his own little world of eccentricities. He hung there by his fingertips releasing one at a time until a single digit dug into the doorframe.

"Merryweather!" I barked.

"Oh, sorry, old boy," he said snapping to attention and pulling himself indoors.

"Can you catch Sunyin if I toss him?"

"I really do worry about you."

"Grrr! Just do it," I growled.

Merryweather took an exaggerated step backwards and stood there with his arms poised as though cradling a baby.

I shook my head and helped Sunyin to stand. "I'm sorry, my friend, it's the only way to get you inside."

"I trust you, Jean."

"Right, here we go," I said, grabbing two fistfuls of his robe. "One…two…"

"Chuck him!" shouted Merryweather.

So I did. And much to my surprise, my antagonist not only caught him but gently placed him back on his feet. I followed, with the grace of an overstuffed duck.

"Jean?"

"What, Merryweather?"

"Why didn't you just park in the grounds and come through the front?"

"You could have made that brilliant suggestion before we went through all the throwing and jumping."

"And rob you of such dynamic decision making. I could never do that to you, my dark avenger."

"Hmm," I mulled. "Anyway, I couldn't."

"Why?"

"I don't know how to drive it."

"You mean it was a fluke you ended up here."

"Fate," interjected Sunyin.

"Whatever," I replied.

"Tut-tut, old boy. Didn't I teach you anything?"

"Only to push that damn red button, which did nothing, I might add."

"Ah, but that's the trick, I'm good at pushing people's buttons," he said to an accompanying raucous laugh.

"Where did you get the outfit?" I asked, changing the subject. "I seem to remember your last one being a bit the worse for wear."

"Ooh, you noticed," he beamed. "That's just made my day."

Merryweather stood there in a heroic pose, his pristine, red-velvet attire glinting in the sunlight. The fact he hadn't put a comb through his blond mop of hair and still had twigs sticking from it did nothing to compliment his ensemble or sanity.

"Well?" I repeated.

"Leave him be, Jean," Sunyin said.

"Yes, leave me be, you misery."

I allowed a flicker of anger to flit across my face, leapt back to the platform for my cloak and pack, then returned in less than a second. I then closed the palace's glass doors just in case Merryweather got any grand ideas on how to dispose of me. Merryweather, however, had a different expression playing over him to one of revenge.

"I don't suppose you have any blood, have you, Jean, old boy? I'm really rather famished."

"I suspect you know I do."

He beamed at that and gave a salacious slurp of his thin lips. His tongue lolled like a slug rolling off a cabbage, his mouth unable to contain it, as a glob of drool dropped to the carpet.

I shook my head, but, regardless, offered him the bottle.

Merryweather's eyes lighted up like all his Christmases had come at once. He snatched the thing from my hand and did a merry jig, much to Sunyin's pleasure, before downing the lot in one.

"He's a thirsty fellow, isn't he?"

"Looks to be," I agreed with the old monk.

Only when Merryweather had finished licking every last drop from the bottle's rim did he take a deep breath and look to his supposed guests.

"Oh, do forgive me, I haven't had a drink for days," he whined.

"Thanks for leaving me some," I grumbled.

Merryweather pretended not to notice and waved his hands about in front of Sunyin's face.

"Do you have to?" I said with a shake of my head.

"Is he really blind?" he asked, turning to me conspiratorially.

"Yes, but not deaf."

"Ah, I see, it's the old one and not the other routine."

"It is not a routine," Sunyin's polite reply.

"If you say so," Merryweather said with a dismissive wave. "I suppose you'd both like somewhere to rest for the day."

"Not really." I took Sunyin by the arm.

"Hey! Where do you think you're going?"

I ignored Merryweather's protestations and made to lead Sunyin from the room. I had no particular place in mind other than to be away from my nemesis. But before I could reach the doorway, Merryweather had rushed past and stood barring the way with an outstretched arm.

"He's a lively fellow, your friend," Sunyin commented.

"He is not my friend. And you!" I bellowed, pointing at Merryweather's grimacing face. "Get out of my way."

"I think it's best you don't, Jean. This room has a lovely view, infinitely preferable to any other. When sunset comes it's as though the whole place is filled with blood." He licked his lips at that. "Why don't you two stay here and I'll fetch us something to sleep on."

I drew my fist back, sick of him already, but Merryweather had already skipped to one side in screaming hysterics.

There before me, strewn throughout the main hallway, lay what I presumed to have once been the Marquise's staff. What little remained of the contorted cadavers, drained to husks as they were, no longer resembled human forms.

"Oh, no! What a terrible, terrible waste," Sunyin said. He daubed at his milky eyes with the back of my borrowed shirt sleeve.

"Merryweather!" I snarled, but my foe had high-tailed it outside and already mounted the flying platform.

"Oh, Jean, so easy to manipulate. I do so miss your company," he crooned. "But unfortunately, I must be off. Destiny beckons, and all that. I couldn't have got there without you. You've just saved me a very, very long walk and I'll ever be indebted to you."

"Your true colours show at last," I said, attempting to stall him.

"I have so many, I've forgotten which colour is truly my own."

"Yellow," I suggested.

"Oh, no, a deep maroon, or perhaps a nice forest green." He shuddered at that. "Maybe not the green, I've seen quite enough decaying forests of late."

I was about to make my move, as Merryweather's hand strayed toward the aforementioned red button, when the strangest thing happened. Merryweather stood statuesque, as his eyes glazed over, and a, "Bugger!" slipped from his throat. The next thing, he was flat on his back.

I tried to process the event, but no matter how hard I concentrated just couldn't come up with any explanation. When Merryweather's limp form raised itself to a four feet high horizontal position, hands and feet dangling, and propelled itself from the craft into the palace, I was left dumfounded. There it descended back to the floor until resting on the carpet like a corpse.

I scratched my head in bewilderment as Sunyin took the lead. The old monk shuffled his way to the comatose Merryweather and raised a hand in welcome to thin air.

"Very pleased to meet you," he said.

"And I, you," came the response as of a crisp winter's morning.

I was only mildly surprised when the owner of the invisibility disguise drew it back to reveal a snow-white attire and a pair of glistening, sapphire eyes.

"Hm, I wasn't that heavy, after all."

"No, you weren't, Jean. Not one bit," Aurora replied.

We ambled into the living room like friends at a dinner party. I chose a deep, luxurious, red-leather seat, Aurora diagonally to my right in the same, Sunyin to my left on a sofa he looked quite lost on. Merryweather sat cross-legged and bound between us. His face was redder than a beetroot, until then, something I'd have thought impossible for a pale-faced Eternal to pull off.

"Can I interest anyone in a drink?" I asked offering out one of the three blood bags I'd rescued from the fridge.

"I thought he'd drunk all the blood?"

"Ah, my dear Aurora, I think Master Merryweather here prefers his blood to be non-fabricated. Once sampled and all that, eh, Walter?" Merryweather remained in full pout mode, focused upon the state of his slightly be-smudged boots.

Aurora took the proffered bag, turned away and partook of a drink. The face she pulled on returning her blue eyes to my own told she, too, had the same Achilles heel.

"Not to your taste?"

"It shall suffice."

"She is very polite, Jean. You could learn a lot from this girl."

"Is that your professional opinion, Sunyin?"

"I believe it is, though I know not on what it's based."

"I can be polite just not necessarily when around the impolite," I said casting a glance to our prisoner.

"Ah, a victim of circumstance," the old monk said rubbing at the wound to his head.

"Are you well, Sunyin? I'm afraid there was nothing in that refrigeration unit for you."

"I shall...suffice. Thank you for your concern, Jean."

"Oh, god, you're all talking like bloody Nordics," huffed Merryweather.

"Ignore him," I said. "Perhaps, he'll go away."

"I tried, but you stopped me."

"And that leads nicely to my one and only question, dear Walter. Where were you going in such a rush?"

His shrugged shoulders were not the answer I wanted. So, not finding anything better to hand, I threw the ivory-coloured cushion I reclined against, at his stupid head. Merryweather did not react. The cushion bounced off his scruffy hair and away down the room.

"I am not enjoying these surroundings, Jean," Aurora said with a grimace.

"I will take that as an indicator of your own good taste, dear girl. The Marquise de Rhineland would have been better titled as the Queen de Gaudy."

"Been?"

"She was in Rudolph's palace when it was destroyed."

"I know nothing of that," Aurora frowned.

"It's a long story, but needless to say, Crown Prince Vladivar blew almost all of Europa's nobility into kingdom come. Or is it King Vladivar now, I'm unsure?"

"Pfft!"

"What was that, Walter, do you not approve of your new monarch?"

Merryweather tongued the inside of his mouth, but would not be drawn into an answer.

"So that's why my family aided you," said Aurora. She turned her big, blue eyes from Merryweather to me.

"I can't speak for Linka, but I'm pretty sure I was an unwelcome guest," I sniffed.

"Perhaps?" she said, giving the room's ivory interior the once over. "It is a shame my family does not discuss such matters with me."

"Because of your father?"

"And, our physical differences."

"Eyes and lips do not make for much of a difference, my dear."

"Yes, eyes and lips," she mused.

"It is the tiny differences that make us unique," said Sunyin.

"Pah! How the bloody hell would you know, you're all the sodding same!" screamed Merryweather, suddenly agitated. "Well, they are," he added, softer again.

"That is how I know," Sunyin replied with a smile.

"This is getting us nowhere," I commented. "Are you going to tell us where you were going, or not?"

Merryweather shrugged his shoulders once more, unfortunately for him.

I only slapped him, not even hard, but Merryweather burst into snivelled tears. I looked to Aurora, perplexed; she shook her head. Merryweather cried until the tears streamed down his pale face and dripped to the floor at his feet. I ignored him and continued to drink from my blood bag, as did Aurora in polite sips, hoping him soon to cease. He had other ideas and balled his eyes out to such an extent, he fell on his side kicking his bound legs about in a tantrum.

"Good grief!" I exclaimed after too long of his antics. "I wish it had been the Marquis I was interrogating, and not this pathetic fool."

"I could take you to him," said Merryweather stopping that instant.

"You what!"

"I could take you to him. I could, you know."

"That sounds like a good idea," expressed Sunyin, whom I'd thought fallen asleep.

"Is that not what you want?" Aurora asked.

"Well, yes," I said, a little nonplussed.

"Why didn't you just ask?" Merryweather bemoaned.

A scowl silenced him.

"How do I know I can trust you?" I enquired.

"Well, I've been trying to tell you from the start, you can."

"Yet, you won't answer any question you do not wish to."

"I'm a man of mystery," he laughed.

"You'll be a dead man of mystery if you try anything untoward."

"I wouldn't dream of it," he chirped and beamed a grin.

"You realise, this man wants me dead?" I said to Aurora.

"Everybody wants him dead," Merryweather laughed. "Except for me, of course," he added, with as best a mock bow as he could manage.

"Of course," I said and rolled my eyes.

"If you are implying danger, Jean, I would not worry. I'm perfectly capable of looking after myself." Aurora sat a touch stiffer in her seat.

"I'm sure you are, dear girl."

She looked defiant then, as though I taunted her.

"Did I not follow you without incident?" her iced response.

"Indeed. And whilst we're on the subject, why did you follow me?"

"I wondered when you'd ask."

"Well, now you have your answer."

"I believe it is my duty to look after you, as I already have, twice."

"But, why, Aurora?"

"Jean, I may be young by Eternal standards, but like you, I have already lived a long life. A long, tedious and troubling life, to be more exact. The advent of Princess Linka and yourself into both mine and my family's lives is the first excitement I've ever known. I wish it to continue."

"Did I just hear a Nordic express joy?" Merryweather sat bolt upright and raised a dishevelled eyebrow.

"Not joy, my dapper friend."

"Ooh! She called me dapper."

"Shut up, Merryweather!" I snapped.

"As I was saying, not joy, but life, something I've not had until the last few days."

Aurora's voice trailed off there, and for a second, I thought I saw a crystal tear form at the edge of one of those deep blue pools.

"And you, Sunyin?"

"Our fates are intertwined, Jean. I believe if I am to recover any memory, it will be whilst being at your side."

"Then it's settled," I said. "We shall set off after we have rested. You for one need to do so, Sunyin."

The old monk's response was instantaneous. Sunyin nodded and curled up in his chair. I watched as a calm settled over his amiable features, his eyelids closed over clouded orbs, and he fell asleep on the spot.

"There are quarters upstairs, Aurora."

"I do not need to sleep," she replied. "I shall keep an eye on our friend here."

"Are you sure?"

"Quite."

"Then, I shall adjourn, and leave Walter to your more than capable sentry."

Aurora inclined her head as I stood to leave.

"And what about me?" Merryweather moaned. "Jean, what about me?" he repeated.

"Night, Walter."

"Jean! Jean! What about me?" he yelled as I left the room.

The last words I heard as I made my ascent to the second level shepherded a wicked grin to my face.

"Do you think he's coming back?"

Chapter 8

Sand

"Did you sleep well?" Aurora asked, as I jumped onto the flying platform, Sunyin gripped in my arms. The thing hadn't moved since last I saw it hovering like a stagnant cloud awaiting the wind.

"I am well, thank you. Although, I found sleeping in a coffin most unpleasant after sleeping in a real bed."

"You should have tried sleeping on a bare floor," Merryweather grumbled.

Aurora untied the fop to which he made a great show of dissatisfaction until the task was finished. He then stood and clicked into position just about every bone in his body, much to my annoyance. After a thorough check of himself, including a variety of tongue clicks and patted limbs, he swept his hands before Sunyin's smiling face in a repetition of the previous day.

"Do I need to threaten you, Walter, or will you behave?"

"There's no need for violence, I'm looking forward to our little adventure."

"I'm not sure I like the sound of that."

"That's because you're a misery. This is all very exciting if you'd but acknowledge it. What could be better than two old friends, an albino, Nordic Princess with weird eyes, and a human thought once extinct, flying over a dead landscape without a clue where they're headed?"

"Human!" Aurora exclaimed.

"Didn't you know, my pale strumpet?" Merryweather crooned.

"Is this true, Jean? Is this man un-Eternal?" She made a point of ignoring Merryweather's beamed grin.

"If un-Eternal means human, then, yes."

"But…aren't they extinct?"

"I thought the self-same thing until the Marquis de Rhineland proved me wrong. The Sunyins are home-grown, so to speak, but as good men as you'll ever find."

"Oh, stop it, Jean, I think I might cry." Merryweather mopped his eyes in mock grief.

"I could give you something to cry about," I hissed.

"Ooh, we are touchy this evening."

I ignored the whining Britannian and straightened my cuffs glad to be adorned in new dark attire for the trip. I failed to see Portia minding my commandeering replacement clothes what with her being dead and all.

"Right, everyone ready?" Merryweather's trumpeted herald.

"No tricks, Walter," I warned.

Merryweather brandished his index finger for all but Sunyin to see, waved it about like a conductor's baton, then pressed the mysterious red button below the handlebar controls.

"The Marquis de Rhineland!" he bellowed, followed by something quieter I didn't quite catch.

I had no time to dwell on it as the flying platform lifted rapidly into the air. Higher and higher we rose until well above the Marquis' ivory palace. It was a phenomenal view but not one I'd ever have cared to see again.

Unsure what to expect next, the craft made a full three-hundred and sixty-degree slow pirouette. It was almost as if the thing sniffed out the Marquis' presence. Merryweather seemed particularly unconcerned by it all. He lounged against the handlebar controls with a superior smirk and a general nonchalant air. The craft made a few final adjustments, then shot off in a south-west direction. If not for Aurora's quick thinking, we may have lost Sunyin in the process. She grabbed him by the scruff of the neck just at the point of tumbling to the valley floor. There she eyed him inquisitively before assisting him into a seated position.

"We might as well all do that," Merryweather suggested. "Who knows how long the ride will be."

"Hmm, who knows?" I replied, but sat down anyway.

* * *

"What is it like to be human, Sunyin?"

Aurora's hair pooled out behind her in a slip-stream of spilled milk. Tendrils of softest white, the wind tickled them against Sunyin's face and made him sneeze.

"I do not understand?" he replied after itching his nose.

"Does it differ to being an Eternal?"

"I do not know; I have never been an Eternal."

"Do you crave blood?"

"I crave peace."

"Do your eyes hurt?"

Sunyin touched a wrinkled hand to his face before realising what Aurora meant. "No, it is all I have ever known."

"All?"

"My memories are unclear. I cannot remember the past, only that Jean is who I sought and that he has always been kind to me."

"Pfft!" Merryweather huffed but kept any further comments to himself.

"I think Jean is special, too," Aurora spoke bluntly.

"I am sat here," I interjected.

77

Aurora looked to me, or more through me, to be exact, before turning back to the monk.

"What does a monk do?"

"Monk-ey about. Get it? Monkey."

"Thank you, Walter." I cast him one of my most withering looks. He pretended not to notice, as usual, and picked at his nails with a twig he'd removed from his hair.

"A monk harmonises with himself and nature," Sunyin said after some consideration.

"I know nature!" Aurora enthused. "In the Arctic, we have whales, wolves, and I even saw a Polar bear once."

Merryweather twitched at that, pausing mid-prune. I observed as the cogs turned in his mind. Seeing my watching him, he returned to his former task.

"I know not the creatures you mention, but I believe this world possess so few that they must be precious to you."

"The whales are, although I do not believe there are many left."

"Do you watch them?"

"No, we drink their blood," Aurora's emotionless response.

"That is not good. Every creature has the right to life, the same as us. After all, there is not long left for them to do so."

"How long?" Merryweather blurted with wide-eyed intensity.

"Not long."

"How long?" he said rising to his feet.

"Sit down, Walter, there's a good boy." I patted the metal floor and clicked my teeth. But, for a second, a fraction of a moment, I thought Merryweather would rebel. He delivered such a look of malice, such utter contempt, I thought my insides should twist and knot. Of course, as is the nature of the game between men, I returned his glare tenfold. Even then, he tottered on the brink of madness before I made to stand and he quickly bowed and reseated himself.

"How do you know the world will end, yet you cannot remember your recent past, old monk?" Aurora asked her question as though nothing had transpired.

"I feel it."

"Is that all?"

"Yes."

"But you sound so certain."

"I am certain, Princess."

"I do not understand? You trust fate and feeling over fact and certainties?"

At that, Sunyin offered his hand to his pupil. She looked at him hesitant, then took it in her porcelain own. The old monk closed opaque eyes, then smiled the gentlest smile I'd ever seen.

"Do you feel the sun clipping the Arctic waves, Aurora? Do you see the darkness perforated by day? Do you know your father will one day find you, and love you, and shelter you?"

"Yes," Aurora replied as ice-blue tears slid across her glacial skin.

"Do you have any proof?" the blind monk asked, but with no hint of superiority, only love.

"I do not. I know only what I feel in my heart."

"Then, as I said at the start of our conversation, you and I are more alike than you realise, child." Sunyin released Aurora's hand, as the Princess curled up over her knees.

"What a load of crap!" Merryweather baulked. "Eternals don't have hearts. Not that work, anyway," he added with a dismissive wave.

The next thing I knew, Merryweather dangled by his throat over the platform's prow. Aurora said nothing, she didn't even twitch, as Merryweather screamed his apologies. She held him there at arms-length hundreds of feet above the barren floor, eyes narrowed, lips twitching. She was a goddess amongst men, an angered one at that, and even I feared her.

It was Sunyin who, as always, seemed to know just what to say in such a situation.

"Have we left the mountains yet?"

Aurora snapped free of her trance, unfurled two of the fingers that clutched Merryweather's throat, almost as if to prove she could, then lifted him back over the railings and dumped him to the platform floor.

"We appear to have, Sunyin," she said sitting down beside him and taking his trembling hand in her own.

"Are you well, my blind friend?" I asked as the tremors seemed to take hold of his entire upper body. Merryweather crawled further away as if the monk carried contagion.

"I… I do not know?"

"Would you like my cloak wrapped around you to better keep out the cold?" I offered.

"What is cold?" Aurora asked.

"I remember my father once calling it humanity's taste of the afterlife to come. That was a long time ago, of course, and may not apply now."

"I am not cold, Jean. And, as always, I thank you for your kindness."

"Think nothing of it, old friend, I only wear it for effect."

"What effect?" asked Aurora.

"You are inquisitive today."

"I do not normally get the opportunity to ask questions."

"Well, in answer, I should say I wear it to menace."

"How do you mean?" she asked putting her arm about Sunyin's quivering shoulders.

"In my experience, a scowl and a sweep of a dark cloak is worth a thousand words."

"I have only a white cloak. Do you think I should have scowled at Sir Walter and swept it before him instead of what I did?"

I laughed at that, her innocence was so refreshing. It felt like all my troubles lifted from my shoulders at her words. In fact, I burst into so intense a laughter it made Merryweather cower even further against the platform rails. I laughed with an infection that caused even the stoic Nordic to burst into her own. I should have likened it to the chiming of Linka's flowers back on the banks of the Rhine, but that just reminded me of her misery when we parted in Hvit. My laughing stopped.

* * *

We travelled on in silence over a dead and sandy landscape. The night wore on with its usual relentless pace, Polaris rising ever higher in the Northern sky. The moon shone down, unhindered by snow or cloud, and I watched its essence trickle over Aurora's luminescent skin. Sunyin's continued shaking made particles of pure light lift from her form and disperse into the passing night. She mesmerised me. It wasn't desire, fascination, or even inquisitiveness, just awe. How she and her people had remained a mystery for so long troubled me greatly. The fact I'd deserted my only reason for living, unless the murdering of one's blackmailers counted, with those I knew so little of, troubled me even further. But, even though the Nordic royals had proven so difficult to understand, there was something about them I trusted. I should have called it honour, perhaps, but as a man without any, I couldn't be sure.

"What is that?" Aurora asked. Her words shattered the silence as she pointed over the craft's edge.

"That's the beautiful turquoise of the Mediterranean Sea," Merryweather said without looking up.

"But there is no water."

"That's what was the beautiful turquoise of the Mediterranean Sea," he replied, still looking at his feet.

"How can it be a sea without water?"

"That is what was the beautiful turquoise of the Mediterranean Sea before it died."

"I think we get the picture, Merryweather," I interjected kicking his foot. "This is what remains of the Mediterranean Sea, my dear Aurora," I said. "The whole thing became defunct not too long ago. In fact, I should think it better called the Mediterranean Trickle, as that's all that's left. The Eternal engineers created a basin that holds seawater in the Aegean only. Any surplus trickles away into the Atlantic that is likewise barricaded and dammed."

"Who told you that crap?" said Merryweather.

"My parents, so choose your next snide remark with care."

Merryweather zipped his lips though his eyes remained furious.

"Then what are we doing over this sea without a sea?" Aurora continued.

"I can only surmise the Marquis had come to the brilliant conclusion I would not find him if it meant crossing water."

"The joke's on him, eh, Jean?"

I did my best to ignore Merryweather's attempt at humour and the return kick to my own foot. But it made me wonder just where we were headed. For one very frightening moment, I even thought he should have hidden in the all but deceased continent of Africania. Fortunately, I was wrong, as the flying platform took a sharp turn to the West. After all, who could've lived on a dead continent of nought but creeping deserts?

"Wheeee!"

"He's such a happy fellow," said Sunyin at Merryweather's aeronautical outburst.

"You're awake, my friend."

"I'm feeling a bit better, Jean, thank you."

"That is good," I replied. "Very good."

"I believe it is due to Princess Aurora's wonderful attentions." Sunyin attempted a teeth-chattering smile.

"I did nothing," Aurora said, surprised at his words.

"Kindness is never anything less than the best a person can give."

"Ah, Sunyin, always you see the best in people. You even see something in Merryweather, although only God knows what?"

"Thanks," said Merryweather.

"Welcome," I replied.

"Everybody contains some good, Jean, it just needs releasing."

"He really is a star," Merryweather chuckled. "Where did you say you found him, and can I have one?"

"There are plenty of me to go around," said Sunyin.

"Oh, I know there are," Merryweather sniffed.

"You what?" I leapt to my feet, then almost immediately regretted it such was the craft's velocity.

"I mean! I mean!"

"Spit it out, dear Walter," I hissed looming over his cowering form.

"I mean, there's the younger ones that escaped from Vladivar, plenty of them."

"How do you know, you weren't there?" I grabbed him by his velvet lapels and hoisted him to his feet.

"Instinct, Jean, that's how I get by. Same as knowing the Nordics would be at the wedding."

"How did you know they *were* at the wedding?" I felt the red-mist descending but did my best to control it, not that Merryweather would have known. The wind which blew through my unkempt mane and moon-maddened eyes must have scared his tongue into loosening.

"Someone was bound to have invited them."

"Not good enough, Walter. How could anyone invite them, when we thought them a myth, hidden, untouchable, gone?"

"Nobody's untouchable, these days."

I lifted him clear of the platform and pressed his limp frame over the handlebar controls. "The truth!" I roared.

"Chantelle told me," he blurted and started crying again.

"Do you mean the dead Chantelle?" I whispered in his ear.

"But she's not dead," he said perplexed.

"I know that. Sunyin knows that. But how did you know?"

"Oh…erm…bugger."

"Tut-tut, Walter. So unlike you to let your guard down."

"I couldn't help it, you're all so boring," he sobbed.

"In that case, I'm very glad that we are." I felt a sudden need to relieve Sir Walter Merryweather of the burdens of existence and lunged for his neck. But before I could make contact, fang to jugular, the craft lurched downward flipping me over the front end. I only saved myself from a life-threatening fall by retaining my grip on Merryweather's lapels.

"Help! Help! He's choking me," he shouted.

"You have no breath in your lungs to choke out, you idiot!" I yelled, as my cloak whipped over my head, blinding me to everything.

The rest was a blur. Walter struggled to free himself from my grip. I heard Aurora's iced voice, calm, yet indistinct of word. Sunyin shouted my name in panic. But most of all, I felt a shudder run through my entire frame as the ground rose up to strike me. It flipped me in the air and sent me tumbling head over heels in a tangle of clothing until I came to a jarred and very prickly stop.

I had no requirement for the deep breaths I took, but they helped settle me. I laid there some more to make sure I wasn't actually dead, or deader, then gripped my cloak and threw it off my face. The sight of the moon beaming down came as a blessed relief; the sound of manic laughter fading into the night did not. Sir Walter Merryweather had again eluded me.

A few more frustrated breaths, then I rolled onto my front and straight into a pair of high, brown-leather boots.

"Buenas noches, Jean. May I enquire as to why you are rolling around in my rose bushes?"

It was a voice I had forgotten still frequented the Earth.

"And, where is my hermana? I apologise. I believe you say in English, where is my sister? Where is Alba?"

Chapter 9

Orange

I raised my head to the annoyingly handsome visage of Raphael Santini. He stood, legs apart, hands on leather-trousered hips, long, brown hair swaying in the scirocco breeze before a mansion of orange-tinged gaudiness. The building stood at the end of a long and verdant lawn of lush green grass bordered by rows of exquisite coloured roses.

Ignoring Raphael's question, I raised myself to my feet, stretched to the accompanying clunk of my spine clicking back into place, then cast a glance over my shoulder. There, sticking out of a flowerbed of indigo-coloured roses was a very unhappy looking flying platform. Sunyin lay before it attended to by several women. There was no sign of Aurora, nor he who had come to be my bane.

"Did you not hear me, mi amigo?"

I gave each ear a bash before extending my hand to Alba's brother. "I'm sorry, my ears were ringing. That wasn't the best of landings."

"I can see that," he said taking my hand and heartily shaking it, much to my relief. "So, now you can hear, I repeat, where is my sister?"

Who knew why I lied, but Raphael had always been some-what protective, and I didn't think he would've taken too kindly to my admitting to his sister being dead.

"She's at home," I lied.

"That is…" Raphael paused there as if searching for the right words. The gears of his mind rattled in time to his grating teeth. He settled on, "A shame. I should have loved to have seen her."

"Well, you know how it is."

"No, I don't."

"She's a home bird, never leaves the place."

"This was her home until you stole her away."

"Oh, Raphael, don't you ever let that drop, it was hundreds of years ago?"

"A mere heartbeat."

"I forget how much older you are than your sister and I."

"Age is relative to those who span millennia."

"I haven't spanned one millennium yet, so I can't give an hon-est answer. By the way, how's the rest of the family?" I said, changing the subject.

"Dead. False plasma is no substitute for the real thing."

"I wouldn't know."

"Madre and Padre slipped into eternity about a century ago. They'd grown as bored with life as you always pretended to be. I would've let Alba know, but you know how it is."

"No, I don't," I replied giving him a taste of his own medicine.

"I'm not too keen on the Rhineland."

"It wasn't too keen on you, as I remember."

"True, true, I can't deny it. Have we buried our differences, you and I?"

I doubted very much that we had. I hated Alba's brother's guts, and I was certain he felt the exact same way about me. Regardless, I nodded and offered my hand again.

"Bueno," he said taking it and shaking the thing with a vigour I thought might dislocate something. It was whilst in the act of holding his hand, not a thing I was prone to with another man, that highlighted something I'd thought up to then a trick of the light.

"You're looking a decidedly darker shade of pale," I reflected.

"Healthy living," he replied, pulling his hand away. "Are you thirsty?"

"Dry as a bone."

"Then, you might as well come in. I can't have you loitering around my garden. It'll be light before long and I don't fancy cleaning smudges of Jean off my roses."

"And, my friend?"

"He, too, then you can tell me what you're really doing here."

Raphael slapped my back in an over-familiar manner, and painful one, then led the way to his front door. "Quite the spectrum of colours you've got going on," I noted.

"Gracias, I think!" he said with a slight inclination of his head. "I like colour. Living without it for as long as we all have, has left me feeling cheated; I dislike feeling cheated. This is my own small rebellion against our shadowed existence."

"I'm very impressed," I replied, as I stole another glance to Sunyin. Fortunately, he was not far behind, strung up between two impressive looking females. The little monk did not look in good shape. I dared not tarry to verify it though, Raphael had always been temperamental even at the best of times. I thought it wise to keep on his good side until such time as I wasn't.

He strode into the house with the swagger of a man that had total confidence in his own power. Of all the men I'd known, he more than any had earned that right. Raphael's temper almost surpassed my own. Almost.

The Santini clan's persuasion towards violence was the stuff of legend. Even though members of the Hierarchy, they had been cast out by their fellow cronies, banished with some relief to the shores of the Southern Americas. Raphael was the foremost reason for it. That he and his kind had returned showed

The New Europa Alliance, and with it, the Hierarchy, was as weak as I'd always suspected. I hoped to God he knew not just *how* weak.

* * *

Alba had believed she'd be safe within the auspices of the Rhineland. That was how she and I first met. She fled the evil that was her family to what she hoped would be a better life. Instead, she found me, and fell in love. A cruel circle of events that ultimately led to her death.

I hadn't really believed her tales of Hispanic life until Raphael happened upon our doorstep one day and demanded her return. He claimed it his parents' wishes, but Alba knew better. Raphael was, and always had been, infatuated with his sister, sickeningly so, and still was. My refusal to agree to his demands had not gone down well with either he, my neighbours, the ruination of several gardens, nor with several fellows who'd aided me in his departure. A most unhappy experience for all involved parties.

The fact he treated me so well the second time around was beyond suspicious. As my erstwhile brother-in-law had suggested, to an Eternal, it had all happened in less than the blinking of an eye.

* * *

"Take a seat." Raphael waved his hand in the general direction of an enormous, wooden table laden from head to toe with food, real food! A motley assortment of about thirty male and female Hispanics sat around the thing in absolute silence at my entrance.

"Evening," I offered in a way to break the ice. One particularly swarthy character, who if I wasn't very much mistaken had a tan, but that was surely an impossibility, looked me up and down and then burst into hysterics. A chain reaction of raucous laughter soon echoed around the grand dining room until silenced by another dismissive wave of their master's hand.

"This, mi amigos, is the one I have told you about."

For some unknown reason, I felt the need to nod to the host of Hispanics at Raphael's introduction. I soon wished I hadn't.

"He is, or was, the best blackmailer, most underhanded operator, and, of course, fighter, I have ever met. He is also my sister's keeper."

"Husband," I corrected.

"Whatever," he added, as Sunyin stumbled into the room and straight into my arms.

I pulled a spare chair from between two mean looking fellows and helped Sunyin into it. The two busty females left him to my care and took up a seat either side of where Raphael stood at the head of the table.

I ignored the looks the assemblage cast, for Sunyin shook again so violently that his chair's legs rattled against the tiled floor.

"He doesn't look too good, Jean. I'd suggest an apple, or perhaps a chicken leg, or even a glass of beer," Raphael beamed.

"Like all Eternals," I said, not wanting to give his true form away, "Sunyin does not need to eat."

"What a strange thing to say, are we not eating?"

"Well, no," I answered honestly.

"Show the man we Hispanics can feast as well as anybody ever has," he instructed. As one, the assembly tucked into the piles of food.

I watched as fang split meat, sucked juice from what I knew from history to be varied fruits, drank liquid of brown, not red. It should not have been, could not have been, but was. These societal cast-offs were eating because they could, not just for show. And throughout all the tearing, ripping, and chewing, not for an instant did Raphael take his brown eyes off of me. He observed, predatory.

I did not have the same luxury with poor Sunyin. The blind monk trembled so wildly that even with both hands applying pressure to his shoulders, I could not stop him. The mists that were his eyes seemed to roil like a sea fret, his head lolling back against my abdomen. I removed a hand to reach for a glass of liquid, but the moment I did Sunyin rattled himself off of his chair. I followed him onto my knees, but in truth knew not what to do. So, I did something which in the past I would never have done in front of those I mistrusted: I showed compassion.

"Sunyin," I whispered. "Sunyin, what is wrong? You must tell me. How can I help you if I do not understand what is happening?"

That drew jeers from the crowd, but I did not care. Sunyin was the kindest man I had ever met, and I should have taken his place in a heartbeat if I'd had one to do so. But I did not, and could not.

"Is there something the matter with your man?" Raphael called over.

"Nothing I can't handle."

"Are you sure? That doesn't look the case, amigo."

"Quite sure," I retorted, taking Sunyin's shuddering hand in my own. "Pray tell me, old friend, what can I do?"

"Je… "

"What, what is it, Sunyin?"

"Je… "

"Please, help me to help you?" I begged, as his legs thrashed against the floor.

"Jean," he managed.

I offered my ear to his laboured speech.

"It…is…fate… " Then the thrashing stopped. Sunyin was dead. Not dead, as an Eternal terms the word, but gone forever.

No sooner had I thought the words than the monk's body crumbled before my eyes. It was like centuries forced into seconds. The ravages of death stripped lairs from him at a pace accelerated beyond all reason. Sunyin's skin peeled away, then turned to dust like ash on the wind; his bones crumbled to chalk until all that remained was the robes he had worn and the shirt I had gifted him. It was not how things should have happened. It was all so wrong. Humans should not have decayed that way; I was sure of it. More important still, it was too inglorious a way for so great a man to pass from the world.

I couldn't help the tear that fell from my eye. The thing landed with a splat and merged as paste with all that remained of the one who'd been Sunyin.

"Do you weep, Jean? Does the fearless slayer cry? Does he who is supposed to offer strength to my sister, show only weakness? Tut-tut, amigo, you are not the man I thought you to be."

"I'm sorry to disappoint you," I said getting to my feet.

"No need to apologise on my account," he chuckled. A few of his cronies felt able to do the same.

"Oh, I am not apologising to you, Raphael, not at all. I am in fact apologising to the man who has just left us. I'm apologising to his soul as it leaves for grander pastures. You see, I know he had one, the best one, and I feel only pity that it passed on under the watchful glare of scum like you."

I didn't even bother to wipe the liquid from my eyes. I did not care who saw it. I did not care what they thought. For none of them could have lighted a candle to the man I'd known as my friend. My only friend.

"How wrong you are! How wrong you've always been! How misguided! How foolish! How played! You see, Jean," Raphael ranted, "we are as much men as your…whatever-he-was, was to you. In fact, now we are more so. We eat what we want. We drink what we want. And, when we can stand in the light of day, we shall be all that humanity ever was, yet still Eternal. Do you understand, amigo? Do you?"

Raphael bristled with spite. He all but shook with anger. However, that did not change the fact he remained there, a table's distance between us. In that moment, in that instance of clarity, he confirmed my suspicions: Raphael still feared me. For all his posturing, all his pretence of superiority; for all his attempts to portray himself and his followers as human, they were not and neither were they like me. The advantage was mine.

My calm unnerved Raphael. The Hispanic twitched, his eyes would not meet my own; they betrayed him. His own misgivings transferred to his followers. The whole thing was self-perpetuating, a circle of cowardice. I decided it time to strike, whilst still I could.

I would have too, if not for the jiggling, corpulent entrance of the Marquis de Rhineland followed in chains by the misty-eyed, wastrel figure of Sunyin?

The Marquis said nothing, he did not have to. A tug of steel, and a wail of pain from the man wrapped in chains had me beaten. What's more, he knew it.

"Ahhhh! Jean, Jean, Jean, will you ever learn? How long will you remain blinkered? How long before you begin to see the bigger picture? Raphael, myself and… others, have been so busy whilst you waltzed your way into eternity."

"Really, Marquis. Well, I hope it's soon, for your sake."

"Ever defiant, ever in the dark, but not for much longer, methinks."

"Oh, God, you're not going to regale me with your master plan, are you? Are you so stereotypical, my robust friend? Are these the lengths you must stoop to for pleasure? I can see from the eyes of our female companions that you do not get it from elsewhere." I cast a cursory look to those sat around the dining table. It had the desired effect. Two giggling tarts fell silent at my glowering.

"Look about you," said the Marquis, surprisingly undeterred by my refusal to submit. "You now look upon an apex predator, perfection in progress. These men, and women," he added with a smile to one of the busty beauties, "are more than you could ever dream to be, dear boy."

"If that is true, then why am I not dead, eh? Why go to all this trouble to get to me? Why?" I bellowed, smashing my fist against the wooden tabletop sending plates and food flying.

"I have no idea what you're talking about, Jean. As per usual, you have blundered into somewhere that you are not wanted. Actually, that is a bit of a lie, as poor Raphael here has wanted you in physical nearness for quite some time."

"Two of you that way inclined, in one room, at the same time, who would have thought it."

"Joke all you want, Jean, but now that we have you, although earlier than planned, you shall aid us in claiming the one thing we need."

"You need," Raphael corrected.

"And by default, all of us."

"If you say so."

"I do, Raphael Santini, soon to be Lord of all the world."

"I beg your pardon, boys, but exactly where in your schemes do I fit in if it's not for butchery?"

"Why, to draw out Linka, of course. Her solar resistance will be the last piece in the puzzle of Eternal evolution. That day will come sooner still, thanks to you."

My talons had scratched a set of three-inch grooves into the tabletop before I could control my anger. The Marquis believed himself so wise, yet knew so little. What disturbed even more was the fact Merryweather appeared to have done only as I'd asked of him. He had indeed brought me to the Marquis as requested, and not at the behest of either of my two antagonists. However, I had no intentions of sharing my thoughts with them.

"Now, now, now, what to do about Linka?" the Marquis continued his monologue.

"We have, Jean," Raphael snarled, turning on his compatriot. "Alba first, as you promised."

"I have not forgotten my promise to you, Lord Santini," the Marquis replied with a difficult bow. "I would not have gone to all the lengths I have, otherwise."

Raphael gave the Marquis a long hard stare but turned his attention to eating a slab of meat, instead.

"I presume the man who has passed away was another of your genetic duplicates?" I sought to stall for time, though I knew not what I had to gain from it. There was no way out of my situation. Even if the absent Aurora should have materialised like a ghost, I doubted the two of us able to subdue all of Raphael's horde.

"Congratulations!" the Marquis roared and started to laugh.

I looked away, not because of his condescending attitude, but due to the rolls of blubber that rippled below his many chins. The man disgusted me.

"For once in your life you are correct. That abomination was my only duplicate of this sorry specimen, the original Sunyin, unfortunately for me. But I'm glad he pried you away from the Nordics in time."

"In time for what?" I replied giving no indication that, in fact, he hadn't.

"Before he disseminated, of course. They all do sooner or later. I've told them many a time to eat, take on water, but they don't, so what do they expect."

"Not much of a father to them, are you? Not much of anything, really. I rather think the reason they don't eat is that you've already scoffed it all."

"Think you're very clever, don't you?"

"Not really, but cleverer than you," I taunted.

"Cleverer than me!" the Marquis boomed and tugged on Sunyin's chains to procure a whimper of pain. "Could you have mastered the sciences of humanity: no! Could you have developed a blood so fine that the Hierarchy would destroy kingdoms for it: no! Would you have had the foresight to see a future where all that was would be rendered pointless: no! All they have done is clear the table for Raphael," the Hispanic grinned on queue, "to take over the planet. Could you, Jean? You are a little man in a big man's world, that is all. You are a crow with clipped wings."

The Marquis frothed at the mouth such was the venom in his words. He was loving his moment in the spotlight.

"You are a one-time, petty, blackmailing thug who did only what his parents wished him to. You are a deserter of wives and murderer of women, which you couldn't even do right, as well as a general bore. That's what you are. Whereas I shall be Chamberlain to the Earth."

The Marquis tried to look triumphant, but only achieved in looking fatter than ever.

"Cat got your tongue, boy?"

"That was a lot to take in. Seems like you've got it all accounted for." I scratched my head and faked an abject expression. "Then again," I said.

"Then again, what?" the Marquis interjected.

"Well, the way I see it, is this: Raphael, and your good self, still cannot go out in the sun; there is now a power in Europa that is greater in anger than ever there was before; Linka is not in your possession, and I'm still very much alive and kicking. Call me old-fashioned, but isn't that abject failure?"

"B..."

"One more thing, Marquis, before you spit your dummy out. Don't ever talk of my parents again. Anything I did for them was for the greater good of us all. If they'd been listened to, we wouldn't be in half the mess we are. Only an idiot would say differently."

"Really."

"Really," I replied, and cast him such a vehement scowl it should have cut through stone.

Raphael was the one to break the impasse by throwing a bone from his food at Sunyin, then giving the Marquis a big, thumping pat on his broad back.

"Good for you, Vincent, you stood your ground. I'm really very proud of you, and all you've done. But, at the want of sounding pushy, amigo, I am getting impatient to see my hermana. So wrap up your little toy," he indicated to the bedraggled Sunyin, "I'll see to mine," he indicated to me, "and we'll be off. Entender?"

"You what?" I spat.

"Understand," he said. "Obviously, you don't, but the Marquis does, so I declare him the winner on points. Now," he said addressing his flock. "Tie that bastardo up. Oh, and make it hurt."

I didn't resist. What would have been the point? But never for a second through all the spitting, cursing, taunting and beating, did I take my eyes of the Marquis and his prize. He would not evade me again and I wanted him to know it.

Chapter 10

Tan

My reflection receded into the dark depths of the Marquis' frog-like eyes. The fact several Hispanics towed me across a hard, tiled floor had no bearing on anything. He'd got the message; the clinking chains around Sunyin's weak frame confirmed that much. However, I endeavoured to press the point.

"Sunyin. Sunyin, it is I, Jean. Do not worry, he dare not harm you. After all, his corpulent life depends on it." It was mostly bluster, and Sunyin heard not a word of it, but the Marquis did and that was its purpose.

One of Raphael's men kicked out, an impolite be quiet. I did not care; their pathetic chuckles drove home my words. It was not me they joked about.

The mob dragged me into the next room and deposited me in unceremonious fashion against the far wall. If Sunyin noticed, he did not show it. The old monk couldn't lift his head, he was so weak, a ghost of the man I remembered.

"Un momento." Raphael commanded his men to stop and came running after us. "I forgot to give Jean this."

He booted me full in the face, the bottled venom of several centuries compressed into one swift kick. The last laugh was mine though, I felt nothing. I was already dead.

I stirred to the musty smell of damp. Raphael had had me deposited in a chamber that possessed the home comforts of a badger: soil floor and excrement. Charming! It appeared I was in yet another cell, in yet another fool's residence. But wakefulness prompted memory and the image of a trembling Sunyin was foremost in my mind.

"Su…" I attempted to hail my friend but was silenced by excruciating pain. It took a moment to reset my dislocated jaw, not an easy task when bound, resolved by a swift explosion of face to wall. I then tried again. "Sunyin," I hissed into the darkness. "Are you there?" There was no reply. The cold silence of my personal tomb swallowed my voice. "Sunyin!" I said again, but louder. But the man I called for had disintegrated before my eyes and his real father would not be far from the Marquis. Poor Sunyin, even his copied self was a better man than any Eternal. I could not imagine the fear he must have felt on finding himself flying through the Arctic wilderness whilst searching for something formed from the shadow of his real self's faith. However, being bred to hunt down a specific quarry was something I related to.

I think I must have slipped the coils of lucidity then, for the next moment, my mind had travelled back in time to the once glorious New Washington.

* * *

I would never forget the day we stood before our new home, Alba looking radiant, as always, me in my usual black. Seeing her head slump to her chest in resignation, chestnut hair falling from the bun she'd placed it in to cover her eyes, hurt me.

"What is it, my love?" I'd said. "Does this not please you?"

"You know he will come for me now I'm revealed."

"You'd be noticed if covered by a sack and I at the other side of the world, your beauty shines so brightly."

"I'm being serious, Jean. Raphael will find me."

"Let him try."

I'd said the words with the assuredness of a man never bested in a fight, a talent that had served me well. I'd done as my father had wished unchallenged, a menace in black, a man without conscience. The odd ruffing up of those who sought to belittle he and my mother's work never seemed to do any harm. Only occasionally did I have to resort to worse. I became so used, so acquainted with violence that just turning up at another's door became enough of a threat. That was all well and good whilst the Eternals flourished, but as those who realised my parents' words to be true chose to take their lives, before destiny could take them from them, it became less and less the case. I grew bored. Alba changed all that. Where melancholy had consumed, happiness spread. Where I had courted violence, even enjoyed it, I grew to despise it. But that did not mean I would not have defended Alba with my life. As it happened, I'd had to.

Raphael arrived unannounced, unwanted, and very unhappy. His entrance to our beautiful home had paid testament to that. I had walked into our driveway to see him clambering over the front of the residence in an attempt to gain entry. Alba's screams had cut deep. I'd never heard such raw terror in a voice. She feared her own brother in ways I could never understand nor comprehend. The ensuing fight was more than the desire to harm. For the first time in my life, I fought to defend, not enforce. But it is said that one lost to madness can feel no pain; Raphael showed none. I might even have fallen to him in his blind rage if several neighbours had not intervened. They who owed me nothing – I kept to myself even then – yet they aided me. But they didn't really do it for me, they did it for Alba. She was so beautiful, so popular, who wouldn't have? We forced Raphael to swear he'd never enter the lands of The New Europa Alliance ever again. An Eternal's word is more than an oath, it is a life sentence. He knew he would be exterminated if he ever returned. But even as his mouth snarled the required words, his eyes betrayed him. I'd stood, talons poised around his throat, and still he'd quested for her. My father later said that desperate people did desperate things. That was never more true than in Raphael's sick obsession for his sister.

But, as the years crept by and Raphael and the rest of the banished Santini clan languished in the wastelands of the Southern Americas, Alba became all I could have ever dreamed of and more. I gave up my life of errant morals and misplaced dedication to my parents. As a result, they became derided without response. If I had realised they would take their own lives things might have been different, but I didn't, and they did. From that moment forth the seeds of my life were cast into a breeze that never allowed them to settle. I grew so despondent over their deaths, heartbroken, I left Alba to her own devices and vowed never to return to New Washington. The ladies of the Hierarchy's courts became my respite from self-induced insouciance and even that waned. I danced with a sneer and lived with less.

Linka changed all that. Raphael threatened to return it.

* * *

The sun sank beyond western borders, I felt it in my marrow and prepared myself for my captors: I did not have long to wait. A sneering triumvirate of Raphael's largest brutes burst into the cell and carried my trussed up form from the mansion in a jingle-jangle of unbreakable chains.

"Good Lord, is it raining?" I quipped, as the three threw me onto their master's well-groomed lawn. "I'd quite forgotten what it looked like."

"Let us hope it pools in your future grave," replied a leering Marquis. Vincent strolled past, or rather rolled, with the arrogant air of a man who believed himself victorious.

I struggled to my feet, eyes and ears searching for Sunyin. They held him some distance away under chained guard. Although I wouldn't have thought it possible, he looked in an even worse state than the previous evening.

Seeking not to draw undue attention, I gave the gardens a surreptitious once-over. The first thing I noticed was that the flying platform had gone. That was one means of escape ruled out. Raphael stood amongst a bed of roses not far from Sunyin that changed colour with every droplet of water that struck them.

"You like?" Raphael asked looking my way.

"In actual fact, I prefer the real thing."

"How would you know, they've been missing from this barren world for so long?"

"If only you had, too."

"I've thought the same thing about you for longer than I care to remember."

"I'm sorry to have proven so stubborn in my diminishing."

"True, amigo, but that shall soon be remedied," he chuckled.

"Do you have to speak like that? We all know you put it on. I think it contributed to Alba's hatred of you and your ill-bred colleagues."

Raphael laughed at that, but it was apparent for any fool to see that all he wanted was to rip out my heart.

"Marquis, take your dog and go fetch your ship."

"Too lazy to get it yourself?" I said as scathing as possible.

"Too much in charge," he corrected. "Now, Jean, you will get me into New Washington, won't you? I might have to take it upon myself to harm this Linka that the Marquis blathers on about if not."

"I don't think you could, Raphael, she is far stronger than you."

"Really? We may have to put that to the test once I've found out why you have cheated on my sister, something I would never have done."

"I should hope not too, you moron, she's your sister, not your wife."

"She will not be yours much longer," he said with such a disgusting look I almost baulked.

Fortunately, the glinting silver of the Marquis' craft settled like a fallen leaf upon the grass breaking the image. Raphael's sickness required new words to describe it. He'd be a hell of a lot more so when he found Alba unable to greet him. I still had no idea how I would handle that but tried not to dwell on it.

I replaced Raphael's ugliness with Linka's beauty in a surge of raw emotion. How I longed to see her emerald eyes and winsome smile. It focused me. It had to.

The Hispanics manhandled me into the Marquis' blood bank craft. They lashed me to one of the many light emitting contraptions that lined its interior as Raphael's full household trailed out after me. A long line of false tans and white, wicked smiles swaggered inside as though vacationing. Bringing up the rear in arrogant contentment came the Lord of the manor himself.

The Marquis had Sunyin tied to the only seat in his contraption, then hastily retired, as Raphael took it from him. The globular one busied himself with the controls, whilst Raphael stretched out like a cat, his feet rested on the control panel. He desired to look relaxed, carefree and in control, but where Alba was concerned, I knew it a falsehood.

We took off with the silence of a hunter stalking its prey and shot into a water filled sky.

"Confound this damn rain!" the Marquis cursed.

"I rather like it," I said more to annoy him than anything.

"You would, the only Eternal I know who could drown in a puddle loving the rain, what a joke."

"I can't say I find it funny."

"Oh, but it is. Big, bad Jean unable to stomach a little liquid. I found it hilarious watching you floundering in the Rhine, I could barely contain myself I laughed so hard."

"So, you were watching even then."

"Always. There are ways and means for such things. I watched it after the actual event, but it gave the same pleasure."

"Really," I said, a little annoyed, but unwilling to show it. "Then, I'm glad to have entertained you. Was it as funny to watch your wife being exploded, or whatever the hell that bomb did?"

"Portia was not at the ceremony. She entered, as did I, then left according to my instruction."

"No, no, no."

"What do you mean, no?" the Marquis said a little flustered.

"She did not leave. I had the pleasure of talking to her just before I left. Not for long, of course," I winked.

"You lie. Portia is at home. She took a horse, I told her to."

"Now who's the fool? Do you honestly think the Marquise would ride a horse, never mind all the way home? I doubt she'd even have mounted one. Then again, she mounted me several times, so I could be wrong."

"NO! She left, I know she did."

I said nothing. Sometimes a cool silence said more than words ever could. This was my gift to the Marquis. I watched the realisation of my revelation wash over him, then went in for the kill. "Your palace, castle, home, or whatever you call it is all well and good, though. I've recently been there, you know. All your staff are now dead, but I don't suppose you'd notice, what with spending most of your time in Shangri-La. Oops, sorry, I forgot, that's gone too."

The Marquis turned a deep shade of purple. For one frightening moment, I thought he might even pop. The implications of wiping Vincent fat off my clothes quite overwhelmed.

"You murderous bastard!" he screeched and lunged for me.

His blow never hit. Raphael grabbed the Marquis by the arm with the cool of a cat to a mouse. He held him on the spot with such languorous ease, I wondered just what the Marquis had been feeding he and his brethren.

"He is not to be touched until Alba is mine. Nothing must be done to him until then." He spoke with a steady calm, but left no doubt to those present, he meant what he said.

The Marquis looked from Raphael to me, then back again. The overtones of grape eased from his features until he was his usual slobbering self.

"That's better," said Raphael.

The Marquis said nothing but made to walk away.

"Marquis?" his Hispanic master said.

"What?"

"I am sorry about Portia."

"Thank you. I detested her mostly, but she was still my wife." He hung his head and shuffled off into the craft's nether regions.

"I'm sorry too, Vincent!" I called after him. "She would have made excellent ballast!" Raphael was up like a shot, his hand about my throat.

"I know why you mock him. I may even agree with it. But if you do anything to jeopardise his bringing me to Alba and your wooing her back to my side." He paused, searched to find the right warning before settling on, "I shall harm you."

"Your breath already has," I said with contempt.

Raphael breathed on me again, then returned to his seat where he cast his feet upon the console and leaned back once more in his chair. He regarded me with his brown eyes, watched me. His tanned skin showed even in the wan light of an inclement night, and I wondered if the Marquis truly knew what he'd unleashed upon the world?

I doubted it, or he wouldn't have done it.

Chapter 11

Ash

The Marquis did not return for some time. When, eventually, he deigned to honour us with his presence, he waddled straight to the controls, pressed a few haphazard buttons, then stood watching the incessant rain beat against the craft's window.

Raphael said nothing, preferring to keep his nervous fingers busy by tapping out an annoying Flamenco rhythm on his thighs.

I ignored both, my attention focused on the limp Sunyin. He hung from Raphael's seat head slumped against a console of flickering lights. There was no point wasting words on him, he wouldn't have heard them.

As always, I soon tired of it all. The craft was like a morgue inhabited by the ghosts of those I most detested and then some. There was nothing for it but to make the most of my one freedom: my mouth. I decided to antagonise my captors, whilst I still had breath to do so. One never knew, there was always a chance I might get lucky and annoy them enough to get thrown out the window.

"Got any jackets aboard this heap, Vincent?" I asked. "I don't imagine Alba would be best impressed if I turned up at the doorstep looking like a sewer rat."

"What?"

"A jacket, I'm sure you've seen them. A thing with two arm-holes and a back, maybe some polished buttons and a nice carnation, too."

"You've got a cloak, has it not a cowl to cover your bruises?"

"He's right!" exclaimed Raphael. His boots dropped from the console with a clatter as he sat bolt upright. "Alba might not recognise me."

"Me," I countered. "I was talking about me." However, a blind panic had swept across Raphael's handsome features, his tan visibly paled.

"Well, I haven't. And I'm quite sure your sister will remember you, Raphael. As for Jean, he's unforgettable."

"You can never be too certain," I offered, hoping to stir up more trouble.

The Marquis did not respond, instead, pretended to busy himself with a few of the blinking lights I presumed essential to the craft's propulsion.

Raphael's response hinted at manic. The Hispanic jumped to his feet and paced up and down the craft's metallic interior. His hands were a blur of motion: running through his hair; tugging at his shirt sleeves; fiddling with anything within range like they had minds of their own. Despite his earlier blithe manner, it was obvious to all he was wound tighter than a spring. Raphael was as nervous of reacquainting himself with Alba as I was of him not.

I had no time to dwell on the matter, as right then, my stomach entered my throat. The sudden change in altitude caused my feet to leave the floor and cloak to flap about like a raven's wings. The Marquis took us down.

In an almost see-saw change of view, we swept from the rain filled sky to one of rain battered ruins, instead.

"This can't be Vienna?" Raphael uttered in disbelief. He leaned forward for a second look, then slammed his fist against a flashing red light that shattered to the floor, fragmented glass exploding in all directions.

"New Washington," I corrected. "Perhaps, that is where you've gone wrong, dear brother-in-law? Have you consulted an old map? I shouldn't if I was you, they're always moving things these days, or at least they go through phases of it. I myself have entered the wrong house on several occasions."

"How long before you realised you were sleeping with the wrong woman?" the Marquis spat, a little of his old vigour returned.

"So many looked the same, Vincent, it was hard to be sure. Fortunately, Portia was easy to spot by the froth collected around her mouth."

The blow came from Raphael, not the Marquis, straight in the solar plexus. It doubled me over, but it was worth it.

With a clang of metal on broken concrete, the ship's door opened to a miserable and blustery evening. Spray from the torrent blew straight into the craft soaking all those ready to depart it, which looked to be pretty much everybody. In a release of nervous energy, I expected Raphael to stride out into the night like the prowling predator he was, but he didn't. It was the Marquis who seemed keenest to get on with things toddling his way down the ramp to stand in the middle of a deserted and muddied street.

"Which way, Jean? The whole bloody place has changed since I was last here."

"And when was that?" I asked, hoping to garner some clue as to his reasons for meddling in my affairs.

"City of music, city of dreams, a life amongst the finer things," he sang.

"If I said, eh!"

"When it was Vienna, you oaf."

"You could have just said."

"Now, which way?"

"I expect you'll find nothing but rather tall mountains to your right, so I would suggest left."

"Hmm, I see that now," the Marquis mumbled obviously feeling rather stupid. "Raphael!"

The object of the Marquis' barked request, finding renewed verve, grabbed me by the scruff and shoved me down the ramp. Three forward rolls later, I found myself laid flat on the ground, my face submerged in a rather deep and dirty puddle.

I struggled to my feet in a spray of spluttered liquid only to see Sunyin being manhandled out of the doorway by two of Raphael's testy colleagues.

"Be careful with him," I called, spitting another mouthful of wet mud onto the street. "I have warned you about your conduct towards my friend."

The two paid no heed taking it in turns to scrag the semi-lucid monk. I feared for him and decided stalling was not an option.

I turned my back on he who I most wished to aid, though it pained me to do so, and shuffled my way up the street. By the thudding of feet to my rear, the whole assemblage followed.

The Marquis had landed his ship at the city limits, luckily for me, within two streets of my old home. The craft was far too big to have squeezed into suburbia true, but it was close enough. Large gardens had spilled forth their once majestic contents into every place where soil had settled making the place a bitter parody of a jungle. Seeing the once scenic cityscape dishevelled and near death had troubled me on my earlier visit, but to see the grotesque forms of rotting trees weeping in the gloom of the rainstorm tore at my un-beating heart. Multiple mumbles of disapproval confirmed others thought the same, although I doubted with the same level of regret.

I made my way along the potholed street, took a sharp right into my own, and within ten minutes stood at the entrance to my old, gravel driveway.

"Ah, it's all coming back to me," I heard Raphael ooze, his smirk grazing my neck.

"Not much to look at," the Marquis remarked. "Kind of like its master." He chuckled to himself, then quickly shut up realising his partner's temper might take umbrage to the mocking of his sister's home. "What are you waiting for? Get a move on," he said, changing tact. He emphasised the point by kicking me behind the knee, which sent me sprawling across the gravel.

"She may be watching!" Raphael hissed.

"Sorry," said a supplicant Marquis.

The situation was dire. What was worse, as I lay there prostrate on what remained of my lawn – more weeds and ivy than grass – I hadn't a clue how to save myself. One step inside and Raphael would know Alba gone. I doubted I'd be far behind her.

My eyes darted from hedge to tree, verge to porch, but there was no place to hide, no place to run. My bonds were too strong to break, anyway. Rainwater trickled into my eyes, as I sensed the moon rising behind turbulent skies, my hopes retreating in the opposite direction. Even whilst laying so close to where I'd once been so happy, the only person I could think of sat imprisoned underwater in an icy cage too many miles away to count. I had to escape, for if I died, who knew what my blackmailers would do to Linka in retribution. As far as they were concerned, whilst alive, I was able to do their bidding, but dead! It was better not to consider such matters.

"Get to your feet, mi amigo."

Raphael's tremulous voice disgusted and disturbed in equal measures. A little of the darkness that had often overwhelmed my beloved Alba wormed its way into my own psyche. How she'd lived with such a beast both baffled and drew forth a pity I'd never before felt nor understood.

"You are my brother-in-law, Raphael, that is all," I retorted. "If you call me your friend again, I shall not look kindly upon it."

"Aww, poor Jean. What does it feel like to know you are about to lose your wife for good?"

"I believe I've faced that fear once and triumphed. I see no reason why I shall not do so again."

"Really."

"Really."

"We shall soon put that to the test." He kicked my derrière so hard I fell back to the gravel. "Now, move, MI AMIGO!"

I gritted my teeth, rolled back up onto my feet, tumbled again entangled in my cloak, then tried again. More successful second time around, I shuffled off down the drive. It was the sound of the most pitiful voice I'd ever heard that halted me.

"Jean," Sunyin moaned, but a slap to the back of my head prevented me from looking at him.

My mood aligned itself with the weather: miserable. The rain slipped down my arms rolling away to join the waterfall that cascaded from each fingertip. Only the sound of Raphael licking the inside of his cheeks rose above the pounding torrent. His lascivious slurping increased in magnitude all the way up the driveway until all of a sudden it stopped.

I risked a glance to my captor, who stared to the upper regions of my home. I followed Raphael's gaze to that of a pale, female hand waving from a grime-covered, bedroom window. It was a good job he didn't look back for I'm sure my countenance looked twice as perplexed as his own.

"Alba," he gasped.

My reaction would have been much the same if he'd not rushed past to bang upon the front door, knocking me flat on my face in the process. It appeared that Jean the bait was less and less required.

I watched from the dirt as Raphael stepped back and waited. It felt like the world held its breath. His Hispanic followers were marked by their absolute silence. Nobody dared disturb their master's moment. He had waited for centuries, dreamed of it in his own sick way, and his anxiety was palpable.

All was hushed except the beating rain. It rapped off the rotting porch, clinked off cracked windows and stirred the stink of the rotten ground so as it permeated my sinuses; I thought I'd never be rid of the stench.

It was the clopping footsteps of boots on wooden stairs that shattered the still. I counted their descent, step by creaking step, the tension causing me to bite my parched lips. After the thirteenth and final step there was silence from within. The occupier toyed with whether to answer the door or not. It did not last. One, two, three steps more, and the door handle turned.

Raphael ran greasy fingers through his long brown hair, much good that it did him plastered to his tanned face and neck as it was. He straightened his bedraggled clothing and waited like an expectant dog seeking to be fed.

The door groaned open like a rusted, coffin lid. A hiss of stagnant air escaped into the night. The interior was black as pitch and otherwise vacant. I held a non-existent breath.

Raphael turned nervously back, looked wide-eyed at me, then at his people, before striding inside. The door slammed shut behind him.

Those were the longest few moments of my undead life. I'd no idea who'd opened the door and even considered it the actual ghost of my once beloved wife. I had heard of such things but never believed in them. Not a sound emitted from the other side of the closed door, not a whisper.

"Crash!"

In the time it took to form a memory, everything changed. Raphael's body split the door asunder and hurtled past into the evening gloom, a trail of shattered raindrops the only evidence of his passing. I gawped to where he'd hailed from as something luminescent materialised from the obsidian darkness and spoke.

"What a disgusting little man, and such a strange colour."

"It is called a tan, Aurora. Apparently, humanity used to trifle in them." I grinned from ear to ear.

"I do not care for it," she returned in Arctic tones, as her sapphire eyes blazed a path through the night. She threw back the hood that covered those pristine, albino features and revealed herself to all, dropping the cloak that concealed her perfect, white self. She was magnificent. Spectral, she hung there and took them in. She regarded those who'd bound me, an avenging spirit that sparkled with crisp energy. The beat of hastily retreating footfalls informed that her dramatic entrance had served its purpose.

"Quickly, Aurora, you must untie me, they have my friend."

Aurora observed me with those oceanic orbs as though I'd said a foreign word. Then, with a shake of her head, as though clearing her thoughts, she swept to where I lay. A moment's grappling and the sound of snapped chains signalled my release. I got to my feet, wobbled, then fell over.

"Would you like my help?" she asked.

"Of course, I would!" I snapped unfairly, but desperation was already upon me. Aurora grasped me by the collar, lifted me to my feet, then held me there until I felt balanced. A second later, I was off.

I ran as fast as my aching legs would carry me. Out of the driveway, I sped, almost toppling in a pothole as I turned up the street. There was nobody there. Trying only to think about reaching the ship in time, I burst off down the decrepit road. The rain pricked at my skin like a million tiny needles. I cared not, it would not slow me. Neither would the wind that had picked up in protest at my good intentions; payback for prior misdeeds.

The instant I made it into the clearing, I knew it too late. The Marquis' ship was already fifty feet in the air and making rapid ascent into the dark and tempestuous sky. I remained where I stood until it had long passed from view.

* * *

Grief marked my short return home. Not only had the Marquis evaded me, yet again, but he still held Sunyin. I feared for the blind monk. I doubted his captors would take their failure well. There was nothing for it but to pray he was more use to them alive than dead.

It was a forlorn, bedraggled me that trudged despondently up my driveway. Aurora awaited my return just as I'd left her. Her Arctic presence ghosted a welcome I did not greet well.

"Why did you not come with me?" I growled into the wind.

"I could not."

"What the hell do you mean, you could not? You knew how much that man meant to me, yet you did nothing to save him."

"I saved you."

"I didn't want saving! I've never wanted it! That man was worth a hundred of me!" I raved. "Why, Aurora? Why did you not stop them?"

"I could not."

"Of course, you could! You're stronger than them, me, all of us put together."

"It would not have achieved our goal."

"What goal? We have no goal! I have no goal!"

"You wish to find those who've manipulated you. Letting Alba's brother and the Marquis escape was the best way to expedite this. You may never find out who does so, otherwise."

She spoke in that calm, disassociated way that all the Nordics used. It angered me. I felt so desperate that I almost struck her in my rage, or tried to. Fortunately, I did not. Perhaps it was the ever-present pattering of the rain across my skin, or the hypnotic effect of her billowing luminescence, either way, my passions subsided and I sat back down upon the sodden porch steps. Much to my shame, I wept.

"What are you doing?" Aurora enquired after standing watching me for a time.

"I do not know, Aurora, I really don't."

"You seem frustrated."

"I am. It is not a feeling I am used to, nor welcome, yet of late it has frequented my life."

"But we have achieved our goal."

"What bloody goal?" I snapped.

She stared impassive, unabashed at my outburst.

"I'm sorry, Aurora, I did not mean that. I am tired, hurt, and have just lost my only friend. I have achieved nothing."

"Sunyin is not your *only* friend, Jean. I thought you would have known this by now." She sat on the step beside me, milk-white hair streaming behind her in the wind. "I am your friend, as is Merryweather."

"Merryweather!"

"It was he who knew you would come here. It was he who insisted I did not intervene at Raphael's home though I wished to."

"What are you talking about?"

"Walter is on the ship, Jean. He will notify us when and where they land." She held out a small, metallic device I instantly recognised as that which Merryweather had spoken into once before.

For the first time in a long time, I smiled.

Chapter 12

Porcelain

"It is beyond my isolated comprehension how one man can know so much," Aurora continued. "Yet, make no mistake, Jean, he does. He is erratic in the way he releases said information, sporadic even, to the point of wanting to shake it from him, but he possesses it. Walter can be most frustrating," she added, doing her best squint-eyed impression of a look I knew only too well. "I do not understand why he should be so. Perhaps, in his own way, Walter is as troubled as you. But he was most insistent that I did not aid you when we crashed in Hispania. He said, at worst they would hurt you, and you enjoyed pain, or something very similar, so it didn't matter. The crash threw Sunyin too far from us to save him without giving Walter and myself away. Raphael's people were fast upon him. If I did not know better, I should almost have said they awaited our arrival. Their hasty attentions prevented my taking any course of action other than that which Walter demanded. For that, I apologise. I know Sunyin meant much to you."

"Means," I corrected.

Aurora hung her head at that and paused as she gave me time to digest her information. Ever impatient, I took the initiative.

"How did you remain undiscovered?" I pressed. "I heard Merryweather's laughter. One must surmise the Hispanics knew you there. Either that or the ringing in my ears played tricks upon me."

"He would not quieten, Jean. I asked him to cease, but he appeared unable. Concealed within my cloak, I was in no danger whatsoever, but Walter showed a disregard for his well-being that bordered on suicidal. By the time he eventually calmed, we had cleared the compound. Very unpleasant it was too. I had not realised a world without the cover of snow could be so colourless. I did not like it, Jean. I did not like it at all."

Aurora furrowed her elegant brows at that as though confounded, or perhaps just disappointed. A world on the cusp of death becomes an unhealthy obsession, and I hoped it did not become hers.

"We hid just outside the compound and returned for the flying platform when the sun came up," she continued. "There was a chance they'd have moved it, but fortune favoured us; they were preoccupied with you. Walter said Raphael wanted Alba above all else, and he suspected they did not know her deceased. He claimed they would come for her, as they did, and so formed his plan accordingly."

"Wait a minute." I stopped her mid-flow. "Are you saying you both came here on the flying platform?"

"Yes."

"Then we must follow them," I said leaping to my feet.

"Where?"

"Wherever."

"We cannot search if we do not know where to look."

"They'll return to Hispania and Raphael's bolthole."

"Walter did not think so," Aurora replied coolly.

"How can he know all this?"

Aurora just shrugged her shoulders. "You do not trust him?"

"I do not."

"Neither did I, but I was wrong. I told him so, and he laughed at me."

"That sounds like something he'd do."

"How long have you known him?" Aurora asked. She wiped a film of rain from her face and cocked her head to one side.

"Would you like to go indoors, it's a long story?"

"It matters not. I prefer being outside. Besides, I have never seen actual rain. It's beautiful in its liquidity, peaceful, all these little want-to-be snowflakes dripping from the clouds."

Aurora smiled then, a look of such angelic pleasure that under different circumstances I imagined my heart should have melted. The upturning of her luscious lips changed the whole complexion of her face revealing her true youth and innocence. It suited her being unburdened. However, time was as it was, and my heart belonged to another.

"Have you truly never seen the rain?"

"No, only wind, snow and on occasion falling ice. Nordvind and I remain in it whenever we can."

"Who?"

"My friend," she said the glow of life fading from her face. Aurora's thoughts turned inwards much as my own often did. "Hvit stifles me, Jean, more so than ever these days." She spoke softly, her eyes to the ground.

"I'm not surprised. Another few hours in Hvit and I think I'd have jumped in the ocean just for relief."

"Hvit is still my home, Jean." Aurora levelled her gaze back to my own.

"I'm sorry, Aurora, I was not thinking." I gave her one of my least reassuring smiles, but she seemed to bear no ill will.

"Hvit has much to answer for, but it is all I know."

"This must be quite the adventure then."

"I suppose so. I have my cloak, of course. Nobody would have found me should I have left, but I've never had anywhere to go."

"Quite a thing that cloak of yours. Where did you get it?" I asked.

"It is all I have of my father."

"He gave it to you?"

"Left me it."

"He had great foresight."

"Possibly?"

"Who was he?"

"I do not know."

"You do not know! Will your mother not tell you?"

"No."

"Hmm, sore subject?"

"It is."

"Then, in way of apology, I shall answer your enquiry as to when Walter and I first became acquainted."

The wind picked up then, a restless squall. The rain came down with such intensity as to send raindrops bouncing off my jet-black boots back towards the sky. My old home creaked its pathetic resistance to the gathering storm, the tiled roof taking a thunderous battering. Aurora appeared not to notice. She sat there serene at the first thunderclap, as I tried to find the words to start my tale.

"I was a very different man back then, Aurora, I cannot stress that enough. I was an idealist. Those that wield so powerful a weapon often wield it unscrupulously. I was no different to anyone else."

I stopped there and apologised, jagged forks of lightning that illuminated the clouds in indigo and gold a precursor to a second thunderclap stealing my words.

"There is a need to go further back," I continued. "I must start with my parents for they are the root cause of most of my life experiences. They were scientists. You may or may not know that. It was they that developed the theory of our sun's death. I should not say theory though for that implies a possibility of error, and I can assure you there was, and is, none. They gathered evidence from both history and their present and formulated a calculation as to when said event would occur. Their calculation was indisputable, accurate to within a few centuries; nothing to an Eternal. They presented their findings to the Hierarchy, but, like all people faced with obliteration, they are also faced with a choice: fight, or capitulate. Eternal society, as you and I knew it, was over, finished, and capitulation its decision. My parents thought, at first, it was due to shock. It was not. Eternals, and in particular the Hierarchy, were unable to face the realisation that not only were they inferior to the by then extinct humans technologically, living off the scraps of their leftover inventions, but were also subject to their same demise: death."

"Do you follow me so far?" I queried with an intensity of gaze that startled poor Aurora.

"Yes," her succinct reply.

"Death was a concept the Eternals had rarely been troubled with. Yes, an immortal could have their lives, or to be more exact, their non-lives, taken away by force, but one never expects it. The thought of not being long for this world hit them hard. They chose disbelief because accepting thoughts of mortality was an anathema to them. Most still won't accept it. But, as one after another of the ranks of power took their own lives before having them forcibly removed, the message started to sink in. That was the last bit of control those people would ever have and they exercised it. Those who remained chose to live it up, so to speak, whilst still they could. High society gathered to waltz their way into oblivion, hoping the apocalypse might somehow pass them by."

"I get ahead of myself," I said, wiping the rainwater from my face.

"Where did Walter come into all this?"

"Ah, ever to the point, dear girl. Let me explain."

"When my parents and a few select others broke the news that everything would end, they were mocked. Their science was pooh-poohed as hokum. So what, you might say. And so what was how my parents took it. But, as they persevered, pressed their points, the mockery turned to an absolute dismembering of their social and intellectual statuses. At first, they fought back, through me. I had always been a hot-head, and the opportunity to vent my frustrations for the non-life I'd been born to came as welcome respite. I savoured *persuading* our kind to accept the truth. Whilst doing so, I garnered quite a reputation for violence. Actually, that's not entirely true, extreme violence would be more accurate."

"It was during one particular escapade in some nameless noble's home that I met Walter. As I turned my hand to disrupting one overly dramatic party throwing mostly men here there and everywhere, Walter reclined upon a chaise lounge applauding. I think he may have regretted doing so in the aftermath, I made quite the mess. The treatment my mother and father received, my heroes, made me indignant, and it drove me to wild excess. I could not help myself. Walter did not aid me, but made it crystal clear, he believed my parents' findings. I accepted his cold comfort in good faith. Perhaps, I was wrong to? He was indifferent to Eternal society even then, Aurora, much as I."

"After that episode, we ran into each other in similar fashions several times more before my parents and I realised it only made matters worse."

"It was about then, whilst wandering the streets of New Washington, I inadvertently met my future wife Alba. As of that moment, any handiwork on behalf of my parents ended. I was lost to love. Alba was everything I had never had. Her beauty ensnared. Her kindness, an intoxicant I was unable to refuse. I drowned in her eyes and knew nothing but she. I was even happy for a time."

"Losing me to another, even if it love, was the final straw for my parents. There was nothing left for them on a world they knew would soon consume them. They became so disillusioned that they took their own lives. They left me nothing but a note to explain it."

"I am sorry, Jean. That must have been hard for you."

"It was," I said turning away from her in shame at my show of emotion. "It affected me greatly, still does."

"How did they do so?"

"Do what?"

"Take their own lives."

"They wished to see the sun. The two of them decided on an irreversible course of action: they stepped into the light of day. All the Hierarchy found was their clothing and the aforementioned suicide note addressed to their son."

"The sun?" she said, a little surprised.

"Yes, the sun," I repeated in a huff.

"But the sun does not kill."

And like that first drip of blood down one's throat after too long an absence, realisation struck. How could I have remained blinded to the fact after my own enlightenment? My parents could not have perished in that fashion. My head whirled. A universe of stars twirled above me, disparate constellations melding together into one ever-brightening point. The cosmos congealed into a single blazing orb that banished the darkness and the dullard I'd been.

"Murdered," I mumbled.

"Pardon?"

"Murdered," I said again, more to myself than my companion. "My parents were murdered. I did not see it." I punched the step in frustration splintering the wood. "What a fool, Aurora! What an imbecile I've been! I have accepted what I wanted rather than sought the truth. I have taken the easy way out."

"How could you have known? You cannot blame yourself, my friend."

"But, I do."

Like a parasitic ivy clambering for life, I hauled myself to my feet and paced the drive. A booming clap of thunder echoed my mood. Saturated, my cloak wrapped itself about my wet frame like the huddled wings of the raven I resembled. What remained of my world unpicked at the seams.

"The Hierarchy hated my parents, despised them even. Almost any of them could have done it," I ranted. "My parents' words had upset aeons of Eternal life. Who wouldn't have wanted them silenced? Permanently," I added. "I have allowed my disenchanted heart to believe what was simplest to accept. How they all must have laughed at the vagabond son!" I bellowed into the rain. "How they must have shared secret smiles as the one person who would've dared rock the boat, sank with it. They have laughed at me for decades as I've drowned in their lies."

"But you have resurfaced, Jean," Aurora said, rising and walking to my side. "You have learned to swim. No more floundering for you, my friend. Now you can remedy the past, right those wrongs. You can be that which they feared. My people had a belief that in time immemorial the raven would escort the souls of the dead to the afterlife. Perhaps, that is your purpose? Perhaps, you are the eternal darkness that those in power feared, not the blazing fires of light from a dying sun? At least, you could be."

I looked into those ice-blue eyes, unblinking, non-judgemental, and knew I could.

* * *

I mulled Aurora's words, my mood dire, wrestled with the demons of a past I'd sought to cage. Could they ever truly be silenced? Pacing back and forth across the crunching gravel, Aurora fixed on my every move, I made a decision I should have made the instant my parents passed away. I would kill them all and tear apart the Earth to do so.

A sound dispersed my anger with an incessant buzz like a bee trapped in a bottle. Something Aurora held in her palm awakened: Merryweather called.

Chapter 13

Brown

"Answer it then."

"I do not know how."

"What do you mean, you don't know how?"

"Walter did not show me." Aurora held the metallic object at arm's-length as though it would turn on her at any moment. "Walter." She tried speaking to the thing. "Walter, can you hear me?" There was no response until the thing buzzed again.

I snatched the metal rectangle from Aurora's outstretched hand and shook it: nothing. I tried yelling at it myself, then prodding it with my finger.

"About bloody time!" came an incorporeal, exasperated voice.

"Merryweather, is that you?"

"This is the ghost of your dead brother."

"I don't have a brother, idiot."

"Hmm, it was the best I could do on the spur of the moment."

"Where are you?" I blurted.

"Oh, that's charming, that is! I risk life and limb on your behalf and that's the greeting I get. Not even a lovely to hear from you."

"Walter."

"What?"

"It's lovely to hear from you. Now, where are you?"

"That's more like it but keep your voice down, will you. I'm in a rather delicate situation."

"I'm sorry about that, but can't you just answer the question?"

"I'm trying. God, how I'm trying."

"Try harder!"

"Shh. I am currently heading north."

"Well, that's brilliant. At least I know not to head in either of the other three directions."

"Put me on to Aurora, you're driving me insane," he hissed.

"Me, driving you insane, that's rich!"

"Just do it," Merryweather whined.

I passed Aurora the device. She held the thing as though it contagious like supporting a dead rat.

"Walter," she whispered, "Aurora here."

"Ooh, this is all very clandestine."

I had to restrain myself from snatching the thing back and trying to throttle the life out of it. Fortunately, Walter decided to get on with it.

"As I tried to explain to that grumbling crow, I'm heading north."

"From what point did you set off?" Aurora asked.

"That's more like it, what a sensible question. I'm glad I'm talking to you and not, Jean."

"You'll be talking to my fists in a minute!" I called out.

"Will you tell him to pipe down, I'm in a rather delicate situation here," he whispered back.

"Where are you?" Aurora asked again.

"As I am trying to say, I'm heading north. Currently, and you'll just have to take my word for this, I'm hidden in a very large sack full of bags of blood."

"Do you expect me to believe that?" I called out again.

"Aurora," Merryweather hissed. "Will you please tell him to shut up. I really am where I say, heading north, as I say, in the back of some sort of uncomfortable horse-drawn trailer. I would like to add that it is all for his bene…"

The miniature device fell silent all except for an incessant background buzz. Aurora looked most perplexed by it and offered me the metallic speaker. I took it with a grimace and gave it a slight shake. "Walter, are you there?" I whispered. No response was forthcoming. I tried again. "Walter?"

A few more shakes without an answer persuaded me to put the damn thing down before I vented my frustration upon it. The device sat hushed, motionless on the wooden step between myself and my albino companion like a pebble thrown too far from the beach. We took turns in giving it prods, several hard stares and a shaken fist or two before ultimately becoming bored with the thing. The infuriating buzz continued but nothing else. Aurora draped the edge of her cloak over the speaker device to protect it from the rain, but I was already well past caring.

"Do you think that's it?" she asked.

"Who knows?"

"Did we learn anything?"

"No," my curt reply.

"Hmm, I thought it might just have been me."

"It wasn't."

"What now?"

"This," I said, picking the thing back up. I was about to hurl the infernal device into my overgrown jungle of a garden when the voice from the aether returned.

"Aurora?"

"Yes, Walter, I'm here," she replied, snatching the thing out of my hand.

"Can't talk, but in answer to your question, the north we set off from was Vladivar's castle, and we've picked up guests. Follow as soon as you can. Merryweather, over and out," he added with a girlish giggle. The device cut to a buzz before Merryweather returned from his momentary sojourn. "I've always wanted to say that. Don't take too long because I'm developing ice in places a man really doesn't wish it. Oh, and Aurora?"

"Yes, Walter."

"Please hurry, my back's killing me."

The device went mute at that point. The buzzing sound faded away like a regretful sigh, then disappeared altogether.

Aurora gave the speaker a quizzical look, raised one sculpted eyebrow, then dried it off on her sleeve and inserted it back within her clothing.

"What do you make of all that?" I asked.

"I believe Walter to be within a large sack, whilst travelling north with many people."

"Yes, I gathered that much. What I meant was do you believe him?"

"Why would he lie?"

"It's his nature."

"I think he is misunderstood."

"That's one way of putting it."

"I think he tells the truth just in his own unique way. We should follow him and be quick about it."

"I agree. I just wish I knew if the Marquis was with him."

"He said they'd gained people, not lessened. We can presume the Marquis is therefore still with them."

"He won't be far from someone who'll protect him, I know that much."

"A coward," Aurora suggested.

"The worst kind, a coward with means."

"I do not understand?"

"The Marquis is a man of science in the mould of my parents, and a one-time collaborator with them. He possesses the keys to secrets nobody else on the planet understands."

"Not even you?" Aurora asked.

"No, my dear," I laughed into the downpour. "I am definitely no scientist even though I took more than a passing interest in it when younger. I know enough to get by, but that is all."

"I see," Aurora replied running her fingers through her sodden hair. "And this Marquis holds the secrets to your recent situation?"

"I believe if anybody does, it is he. But if he's found an ally in Raphael, as well as the other ties I suspect him of, then we have problems. Although, to be honest, I'm still shocked my erstwhile brother-in-law ran away."

"He did not run away because of my harming him," Aurora stated.

"He did not!" I said surprised.

"He ran away through shame, Jean. He was a beaten man from the moment he realised I was not this Alba. I do not believe I have ever seen such sadness, nor ever will again."

"Then you suspect the next time we meet that will not be the case."

"Most certainly, I would think quite the opposite. A man does not like to be bested by a woman no matter how powerful she is. Grella is testament to that."

"Grella?"

"He wishes to be King, Jean. He has wished it for a long time. He desires the ruby necklace, the mark of our people, with a passion barely contained. But he could never destroy our mother in combat, she is far too powerful. He is ashamed of that fact. I saw a glimpse of that selfsame shame before the weaker sex in Raphael's eyes."

"You see a lot," I commented.

"I see only what is there to be seen."

"I doubt anyone would deem you as weaker than a man, though."

She cocked her head to one side in her beguiling way and considered my words. "It would be inadvisable," she eventually said, and almost smiled.

"Well, either way, finding Merryweather is our most pressing concern. Locate him and other issues shall fall into place. At least, we must hope they will."

"Agreed," Aurora declared, rising majestically from her place on the steps.

"Good. Now where's that flying machine?"

* * *

Merryweather had concealed the flying platform in the rear garden, which by then was more labyrinthine forest than pruned perfection. He and Aurora had covered it in broken branches, much to my annoyance at having to remove them and the thorns which proliferated. Once cleared, we both mounted the machine. Aurora stood poised and ready to fly, whilst I busied myself extracting said thorns from more places than I cared for. I waited for Aurora to set everything in motion and waited and waited. The look she cast when nothing happened did not reassure me of her ability to do so.

"And…"

"He said to press the red button," Aurora replied.

"Then, do so, dear girl."

"That did not work well for you."

"I suspect if Merryweather said it would, then it will."

Aurora reached out towards the aforementioned red button with an outstretched index and gave it a tentative push. The machine reacted in instantaneous levitation, tossing off the remains of the strewn flora, and shooting straight up into the sky. Aurora grasped for the handlebar contraption whereas I, with nothing solid within reach, fell pinioned to the floor like a rag doll stood upon by some giant's boot. However, there was no arguing with results, we were well and truly off. Up and up the machine shot through the dark rain clouds like a lightning bolt reversed. We rose until coming to a juddering pause several hundred feet from the ground, made a full turn, as previously, then rocketed off in a direction I sensed to be north-east. My stomach headed in another direction altogether, as from the look of it, so did Aurora's.

"Well done, Aurora, I knew you could do it," I declared.

"I did nothing," she replied hair streaming out behind her like flowing, white satin. "Are we headed in the correct direction?"

"Depends on your definition of correct. If it means, where Merryweather stemmed from, then yes. If it means, the right way to be headed, I would give a resounding no."

"I take it this Vladivar is not a man you favour."

"Do you not know of him at all?"

"I don't know of anybody other than my family and my mother's people."

"You say your mother's with disdain. Do you feel no affinity with your Nordic kin?"

"Yes, and no."

"You sound just like Merryweather," I laughed. "No offence meant," I added hastily.

"None taken."

Aurora stared off into the horizon. I took it as a please don't ask again type situation. It was of no concern, as I, too, lost myself in the view. We had risen so rapidly that the mountains we should have had to clear were left as nothing more than geological markings on a map. In fact, we had gained such altitude, I was rather glad being an Eternal meant not requiring breath, unless it did? I was never very good with such things.

A landscape of snow-white crags atop grey rock stretched out before us. I thought it would have been beautiful if I'd known it to contain hidden life, but there was something depressing about a landscape devoid of such things.

With nothing left to distract me, I took to brooding, a speciality of mine. Knowing that over some distant northern horizon Linka was perhaps looking southward to me was hard to accept. Had I done the right thing in deserting her? Would those that sought my manipulation simply not dispose of Serena themselves and in doing so Linka, too? The questions flitted through my mind as though snowflakes in a breeze. I had few if any answers, and none definitive. My brain insisted I'd done the right thing; my rocklike heart disagreed. Perhaps, given the opportunity of being able to steer our metallic steed, I should have done so and shot off to seek her. But, as per usual, I had no choice in the matter and resigned myself to instead tracking down Merryweather, and via he, the Marquis, the man I felt pivotal to my situation. Every moment that fattest of foes remained beyond my reach increased my anger toward him. Our day of reckoning, which would come, would be most unpleasant, for him, that I promised myself.

"What is that, Jean?"

Consumed by my musings as I was, Aurora's question took me by surprise. I peeped over the railing to where she indicated to see the writhing ugliness of the Volga/Tigris conjoined rivers. Like a varicose vein, the waterway pulsed in angry resistance to the world around it. How I abhorred it.

"That is the demarcation between the waltzers and the warriors," I replied after some thought.

"Pardon."

"East and West, an overt longing for life on one side and death on the other, or it was."

"Was?"

"Our friend, Vladivar and his accursed bride."

"Ah, the mists disperse."

"Good, you can explain how the hell it all happened then."

"I do not believe I can do that," she said shaking her head.

"I was being sarcastic, Aurora."

"A trait you share with Walter."

"I suppose so, it's all we've got in our joint fight against the fashionable and foolish."

"We've?"

"I meant me really, but I'd admit to Merryweather not fitting either of the other two categories."

"And, this Vladivar?"

"Oh, he's no fool, and he's most definitely not foolish."

"Then, what?"

"Megalomaniac fits best."

"Perhaps it would be best if we avoided him and his bride."

Aurora gave a sage nod to emphasise her point. I had to smile.

"Has anyone ever told you, you ask a lot of questions?" I chuckled.

"Yes, you. And as I stated, I have had no one to talk to."

"But you're a princess."

"In name," came an iced response.

"I'm sorry, Aurora, truly I am. I prefer my own company and seek my own counsel by choice. Having that choice stripped from me would be hard to take." Aurora shrugged her shoulders, which seemed her way of accepting things. "Do none of your family spend time with you?" I asked somewhat gentler.

"On occasion, if the others are away, then Narina will, but only she, and only then."

"Then, when I am done with all those who darken this world, you must stay with Linka and I. It might not be for long, though," I added.

"You have accepted this world will die?" she asked without inflexion.

"It is an undeniable truth. The sun shall soon set forever, and on that day, the planet will die."

"I agree."

"And you are always right."

"Yes," she laughed. "You remembered."

Her laughter was beautiful. A sound reminiscent of the blooms Linka had planted, her voice rang like small bells chiming in the north wind. My glazed eyes must have given my feelings away.

"You miss her, don't you?"

"Is it that obvious?"

"Yes," she laughed again, and the pain in my chest lightened a touch. "You are a good man, Jean. You do not realise it, but you are. And thank you for your kind offer."

"I could insist," I said,

"You could try, my friend, you could try."

I was about to give a witty riposte when Aurora's hair blew from her face to reveal a countenance a shade paler than pale. I knew what she regarded without even looking.

"That does not look a happy place, and I am an expert in unhappiness," Aurora spoke with chilling honesty.

"That, my dear girl, is the rusting blimp of a palace that is the home to my most hated of foes."

"Seeing you have so many that cannot be good."

"On this occasion, I would agree. It is not good at all."

"Are we not heading a touch too close for comfort, Jean?" Aurora asked. She leaned away from the handlebar contraption as though the extra two feet it attained would save her.

I turned to see the pinprick spires of Vladivar's castle fortress reflecting the first of the dawn's morning light. Perhaps it was the fact we headed toward that unholiest of places, but I couldn't have imagined being happier to see the sun.

"What is that?" Aurora asked, pointing way down into the cleft valley below.

"That, my dear, is the Marquis' portable blood bank. It looks like dear old Walter was telling the truth. They must be down there."

"Should we not be moving towards it, Jean?" Aurora said. A touch of panic tainted her usual ice-cool demeanour.

"Merryweather must be down there and not in the castle. We have deciphered that much, so I'm positive we shall turn from Vladivar."

But we didn't.

"Why are we dropping, Jean?"

"I do not know, Aurora."

I jumped to the controls and prodded the red button. It had no effect on anything, so I writhed at the handlebar controls as Merryweather once had. They did not budge. I tried again, only this time harder to the perturbing crack of fractured metal.

"That's not good."

"You think!" I growled in frustration.

The flying platform came to a steady halt above the castle, then slowly, ever so slowly, as if to draw out the pain, descended.

"Aurora!" I barked. "You must conceal yourself."

"I will not leave you," she replied.

"I'm not asking you to. Please, for me, though, disappear for now. You can follow incognito. It will do no good for us both to be caught. This will be unpleasant."

"I will do so, for you," she stated. Her hands moved to the cowl of her cloak, then she vanished.

I gave a cursory glance below, straightened out my wind-dried cuffs and swept strands of long, dark hair from my face. If I was to be slain, it would be as a well-groomed victim.

* * *

The metallic clank of the flying platform landing on the castle courtyard synchronised to perfection with the sun's rays reflecting off the burnished walls of Vladivar's domain. The whole place filled with ruby light, and for a time, we were safe.

Chapter 14

Rust

"Should you not be being brutalised?"

The disembodied voice washed over and through me as though carried on a gentle breeze from Arctic shores. I resisted the urge to turn to it, instead, replying out of the side of my mouth – thank God Merryweather was not there to see it.

"Shh! It's the sunlight, Aurora, they fear it. They cannot harm us whilst we remain outside." I said it more for my reassurance than hers.

"If the flyer brought us here, then Walter cannot be far away. I shall see."

"Aurora!" I hissed, but like the wind, she'd drifted away.

There was nowhere for her to go – not that she knew it – so I turned to that which stretched out before me. My shadow lay there steady and set. I had of course seen it before, but not without the flickering extremities of candlelight or weak castings of the moon. A unique experience, I marvelled in my other self's dark complexity. If the thing had grown wings, I should have looked complete in raven attire, either that, or a dark angel. On reflection, perhaps not the latter.

So enthralled with my new plaything was I, that when a voice whispered in my ear, I almost jumped out of the courtyard.

"I see no one but us, so can only presume Walter is inside."

"I'm not so certain, Aurora? That sounds logical, but why say he was moving north if he was still here?"

"They could have doubled back."

"They could, but that is not the way of those we follow. I think the flying platform was meant to come here."

"Preprogrammed," Aurora suggested.

"If that is the word used for such things, then yes."

"What should we do?" she whispered.

"I'm not sure"

"That is most unlike you."

"This whole situation troubles me. Something seems askew, but I cannot put my finger on what."

"You are sure we are undetected?"

"Whether we are, were, or not, they cannot do anything about it now. Whilst sunlight remains, we are safe." I cast my eyes up to the many-windowed upper tiers of the castle; there was nothing to disprove my assumptions. Like spider's eyes, the myriad glass portals stared down, aware but unfocused.

"Then, might I make a suggestion?"

"What?" I said as I cogitated a million uninspired ideas of my own.

"I could scout around inside and check."

"No," I said, too abruptly. "I will go. I am not about to risk losing you, too."

"You have no say in the matter. It is by far the most sensible option. We need to know who is, or is not, here. I will not be long, I promise." Her apparitional voice drifted away on Stygian currents.

"Aurora!" I hissed. "Aurora! Goddamn it, twice in as many minutes." I cast my eyes across the courtyard like a fool. What was the point in searching for that which could not be seen?

Exasperated by her impetuousness, I bumbled one way then the other, unsure of where to head. Each point of the compass seemed equally uninviting. It was the click of a lifted latch which drew my attention to the courtyard's concealed door. If not for my previous encounters in Vladivar's domain, I would still not have known where to look. Not only had Aurora found the thing, she'd forced it open. The girl was so much stronger than she looked, so deceptive. Yet, no matter how well concealed, nor how singularly powerful I knew her to be, I suspected she would not fair long against Vladivar's horde. I set off in pursuit.

"Aurora," I risked. There was no response. I reached out hoping to brush against her, but she was long gone, or so it seemed. One more step and the false night of the corridor enveloped me in darkening shades of pitch. It felt odd to be stood fumbling in the darkness, waiting for my eyes to readjust from the dawn light. Aeons of sunless existence were hard to compensate for in so brief a time. However, after a few moments, and much hushed cursing, I saw again and made my stealthy way towards the throne room.

Vladivar's home had never been anything other than intimidating, not that I'd allowed it to show, but the absolute silence of the place furthered the feeling. Nothing stirred, not a whisper in the hallways, not a moth in the rafters, it was almost as though the place were swept clean of all but the stubbornest memories. A pity the same attention had not been applied to the stench. An awful stink as of decaying matter, or blood unrefrigerated and allowed to fester in pools, assailed my olfactory senses.

The thought of stubborn presences made me grit my teeth at Aurora's hot-headedness. She meant well, possibly to the point of over-protection, but I was sure she'd never dealt with anyone like Vladivar. The man was a throwback to the time of the vampires where ferocity bordered on the archaic. There was no place for him in any time let alone one that least required dominating.

I was so engrossed in feral thoughts, I almost missed the rasped whisper as of an asthmatic mouse, for I could think of nothing else it could be. The sound was so faint as to be almost unheard. That forced breath would have evaded most ears, but not mine. I slowed my steps, twisted my head like an owl seeking its prey and listened. Both auditory units told the same tale; the sound came from up ahead.

So, it was with more than a modicum of shock that I peered around a final wall and into Vladivar's most desperate of chambers to regard the unimaginable. The stone floor was littered with blood bags in various states of depletion. A crimson jigsaw, its pieces strewn about in careless abandon, the scene did not fit.

I fought the urge to sate myself and allowed my eyes to follow the haphazard trail across the chamber to the throne itself. If I'd said the seat occupied it would have been a gross overstatement. There was something in it, possibly sat, possibly propped, but it was impossible to say what. Bored with hiding, I did the only thing I could, the only way I knew how; I strode purposefully over to it.

"Noooo," the thing wheezed.

"So, you are human," I quipped, although uncertain what I quipped to.

The thing was not unlike a human, but drained of all life essence, a shrunken husk adorned in an iron armour that swamped it. A blood bag hung from a hook that scragged the bear's head that backed the throne. The bag, via a tube of crimson filled liquid shoved brutally into what I guessed the creature's arm, fed the thing.

The creature, as though sensing my nearness, opened two obsidian slits I took for its eyes. They regarded me, and I knew the thing for what it was: Vladivar, or what was left of him.

"Good Lord," I said, taking an impromptu step away from the desiccated figure. "What the hell happened to you?" I was too taken aback to even mock.

The thing tried to raise its head, but failed; tried to whisper, but could only rasp; tried to weep, eyelids creaked shut, but did not possess the ocular fluids to do so.

"Vladivar, can it be you?"

There was no response.

"Can you hear me? Do you know me?"

The abomination's lips, rotted dried up slugs of things, pursed together, but could not achieve speech.

I took a lungful of stale air, then wished I hadn't, and offered my ear to the thing. Still nothing but the steady drip-drip of its portable blood supply.

Collecting a blood bag from the floor, I slit the thing open with a single, razor-sharp talon and poured about half of the contents over the thing's shrivelled face.

I'd seen many disgusting sights in my time from blood filled rivers to blood strewn corpses, and much worse, but nothing had ever sickened me as much as the grey tongue that shovelled forth sandpaper-like from between those ruined lips. The tongue thrashed in the slowest of slow motions, reddening, becoming just slick enough for that which was once Vladivar to speak.

"Have you come to…gloat?" The words seemed filtered through the afterlife and back again.

"I think the time for gloating is long past." The desiccated thing shivered at that, emitting a crinkling rustle. Only when I saw the chest plate rise and fall did I realise it laughed. "Who did this to you?" I demanded.

"My…wife."

"Chantelle, when?"

"As you…escaped." The tongue thing flapped about loosely, so I poured the rest of the bag over it.

"Are you saying you've been here like this since then?"

"Yessss."

"And your people?"

"Those left are now hers."

"Why?" I said looking deep into those dark eyes, Vladivar's sole identifiable feature.

"I cannot say."

"Cannot, or will not?" I pressed.

"Both," he wheezed. "More blood."

"Oh, no, not until you tell me everything."

"She…will kill me."

"You underestimate me if you think I will not."

"Her death…would…be worse." Vladivar struggled to form the words as he dried out again.

I sliced a second bag apart, offered it to him, then snatched it away and took a long, deep swill of the stuff myself.

"Noooo," Vladivar wheezed.

"Shall we try again? Why did Chantelle do this to you, and where has she gone? I presume I'm right in saying she's not here?"

"Gone."

"Where?"

"Blood," he implored, but I was losing patience and ignored his lolling tongue.

"Where?" I allowed my anger to show.

"North." Vladivar's eyes lusted for what little crimson remained sloshing in the bag. The pain therein was tangible when I cast it to one side, the contents spilling all over the stone floor.

"I know she and the rest have gone north. The information I require is where north?"

Something akin to surprise flickered across Vladivar's eyes. The skin of his once taut cheeks sucked in like hollowed out caves, then loosened again. A panic set in, sending ripples of death billowing through his features. This was Vladivar's passage to death, one I would sooner have forgotten.

"Ah! You see, I do know more than you suspected. That, my once fearsome foe, is because I am closing in on the truth. I shall soon know everything and eliminate those who are responsible for the deceptions. You're currently top of the list, or second, depending on my mood, so I'd cough up some answers if I was you."

But all Vladivar did was cough up gobs of black ooze, which pooled over once imposing armour. The gloop ran down his breastplate onto shrivelled, toothpick legs, then slopped to the floor near my feet.

"Urgh! That's disgusting although manners never were your forte. Now, how about those answers?" I picked up two discarded bags and tossed them at his shrunken head. "Where have Chantelle and the others gone?"

The thing eyed me. He shot me such a look of evil, such contempt, I felt a desire to end his suffering right there and then. It would have been wasted, though, he wasn't going to say anything. Fear is a terrible weapon and Vladivar feared his wife more than I. Then again, what man didn't?

I scratched my head, slit open another bag and drank of it, whilst trying to formulate a better plan, when the strangest thing happened. Two of the blood bags levitated from the floor. First one, then the other slit itself open and loosed their contents into thin air. I was shocked. The effect on Vladivar was greater. His desiccated husk creaked and moaned as it tried to push back into the throne; it failed miserably. He strove to rid himself of the vision before him, but could not. My own apparent shock caused him even more unrest as his tongue rasped around his pumice stone mouth. When another bag raised from the floor and floated towards him it reaped more positive results.

"They… seek… the… monks."

"Why?" I roared. "The Marquis stated he only needed the original Sunyin, their father. The others were of no supposed consequence."

"He is dying." The creature's deflated form gasped at that, and I realised he found it humorous.

"So, the Marquis is panicked," I mused, running my fingers through my hair. I did my best to disguise my inner turmoil, but whether or not I succeeded, I could not tell. The withered figure's eyes glared at me with the same venomous intent.

"They use him to track his children," Vladivar continued. "The Marquis knows he does not have long," the thing rasped, a terrible parody of its wife.

"And what do the monks seek?" I growled, as the third bag split open and spewed forth its contents onto the floor.

"Youuuu!" Vladivar screamed, the call of a thing long since dead. His eyes opened wider and wider until I thought they should pop from their sockets, his jaws meeting so violently, they sliced his black and red tongue in twain. The twitching appendage fell to the floor like a gigantic slug and writhed at his deformed feet.

I took an involuntary step back as a voice materialised out of the aether.

"The Sunyins," came cool, crisp Nordic tones.

"Yes, Aurora," I replied to my invisible friend realising it she who was again our saviour. "Our enemies seek to reclaim what they believe their own."

The Vladivar thing's eyes looked on in amazement. When Aurora threw back her cowl to reveal her luminescent splendour, he visibly quaked. She lighted the room, a goddess amongst lesser beings.

"You look like you've seen a ghost, Vlad, old boy." He did not reply.

"We should go," Aurora stated.

"Yes, we should," I agreed. "But I need to ask Vladivar one more thing." The dried up creature's eyes turned to me then. "There're so many things I wish I could ask you, Vlad, old bean, but in the circumstances, I shall narrow it down to one."

Aurora looked on puzzled as I strode over to him and unhooked the blood bag's supports from the back of the throne.

"Do you remember when you allowed the monks to be massacred in your courtyard, tovarisch?"

Vladivar's eyes flicked between his guests. "Sssss," the thing hissed.

"So do I," I snarled, as I ripped the tubing from his arm and threw the rig against the far wall.

Aurora looked shocked at my outburst before inclining her elegant head. She stooped to collect the best of the blood bags from the floor, and then glided away. I followed.

* * *

I didn't look back. I'd seen quite enough of the thing who'd once been my mortal enemy. I was glad he would die as he deserved: badly.

Chapter 15

Bloodshot

"Did he deserve that?" Aurora asked as we walked out into the carmine light.

"And more."

"I see," she pondered.

"No, Aurora, you cannot."

"I sometimes think those most deserving are worth the least effort."

"I do not," I replied.

"Do you feel better now this Vladivar is dead?"

I stopped, inhaled of the morning, and gazed at the ruby orb. The solar object rose into a bloodshot sky in a bittersweet parody of the blue it should've swum amongst. "No, I do not," I said after some thought.

"Then, killing him has achieved nothing."

"Au contraire, my dear girl, it has achieved much."

"Please explain," Aurora insisted.

I was about to launch into a tirade regarding her contrary attitude, but one glance at her puzzled features revealed she meant nothing other than to understand my actions. I calmed myself and made it a point not to make such harsh judgements of her. Yet a look to the sky and the smouldering wrongness of the sun somehow inflamed my passions still further.

"He represented all that was, is, and ever has been flawed with our kind. His actions caused the deaths of some of the best men I ever knew. No, the best," I corrected. "What Chantelle did to him was dramatic, I'll agree to that, even sick, but it was less than he deserved."

"And, now?"

"Still less, but if nothing else, I feel as though I've laid the Sunyins' memory to rest."

"Then, I apologise for my questioning you." Aurora inclined her head, a waterfall of milk-white satin cascading through the space between us.

"There is no need. I am a man of dubious morals, some would say hypocritical in my reaction, but I am trying to do the right thing. It is difficult, Aurora, but I strive to be a better man. Ending that monster's life was part of a process I intend to complete."

"If that is so, then I am proud to be a part of it."

"Really," I laughed. "Am I your new role-model, Aurora? I have never been one before, so you shall have to let me know how I do."

"I shall," she stated.

"How do I rate so far?" I asked pouncing onto the flying platform. Aurora followed and watched with amusement at my prodding of the red button; there was no response from it or the craft.

"It is hard to say, you vary."

"Oh, do I now."

"Yes."

"How, may I ask?"

Aurora stood there, tapping the craft's perimeter rail, her pale skin transfused to red, her blue eyes twin pools lost in a blood-shot ocean, considering, just considering. Twice her lips parted about to say something before she rethought her position.

"Ah, I see you are unsure as to whether saving me from those Arctic depths was wise, or not."

She smiled at that.

"That is it, that is exactly how I feel."

"What do you mean, that's exactly how you feel? I was being sarcastic."

"I think saving your life was the best thing I have ever done, yet the worst for others. Nevertheless, I should gladly do so again if required."

"Very reassuring," I said. "But I can assure you, I have no intentions of ever becoming resubmerged."

"My brothers shall certainly think twice before casting you in."

"I'm sure they will."

"They will never forgive you for their humiliation, never forget the sleight to their statuses."

"I'm sure they won't."

"You do not seem concerned."

"Should I be?"

Aurora stood and thought again before replying. "Not whilst I stand with you, Jean. I believe it would make them very foolish indeed."

"That is a rather certain assumption."

"As I told you, I am always right."

I said nothing, but the mischievous glint in her eye only made her porcelain beauty all the more endearing.

* * *

Giving the flying platform a final kick of frustration, we left Vladivar to his personal tomb and set off down the mountainside on foot. I had removed my cloak, piled as many blood bags into it as it could hold, and lofted the thing over my shoulder like a makeshift sack. Aurora had offered her assistance, but I had declined her help stating the task unbefitting of her royal status. Content in each other's company, we began our descent in a silence that did not last.

"I dislike these steps, Jean."

"I thought you of all people would be used to steps."

"It is the drop they abut," she said backing away from what even I considered a frightening plunge.

"Try looking straight ahead," I suggested. "Keep your eyes on the horizon."

"I have been, but I still see the valley. The Marquis' ship draws my eye."

"Turn away."

"I have tried."

"Does it bother you so?"

"Yes," came an iced reply.

"Is it vertigo?"

"What is vertigo?"

"A fear of heights."

"This is the first time I have ever been this elevated, so I cannot be sure."

"You seemed all right on the flying platform."

"That was beyond my control, this is not."

Aurora huddled as close to the rock side of the stairway as possible trembling with fear. The poor girl looked petrified. So, I did the only thing I could to comfort her and offered Aurora my hand. She looked at it, then me with wide-eyed fear.

"Take it," I insisted. "I promise I shall not let you fall."

"You promise."

"You have my word," I said and took her alabaster digits in my own.

I led her away down one step at a time, all the while making quite sure to stay on her outside. That seemed to appease the princess, but not completely, so I tried another tact.

"Tell me more of your home."

"I thought you hated it."

"I was hasty."

"You were not," she replied attempting a smile.

"Then, tell me what you like about it."

"I like the peace found on the ice. I like to watch the ocean and the sun burning upon its surface."

"Why, Aurora, why exactly?"

"The colours, Jean, I love the colours."

"More so than the blues of the city walls."

"I hate blue. Blue is a lesser stage of black. I much prefer the ruby of the sun, how it transfuses my soul, warms me. Hvit is so stark, cold and uninviting. I would spend every waking minute in the light if mother did not forbid it."

"I thought you already did."

"Shush," she whispered offering a finger to her lips. "That is our little secret."

"And, did I hear you right? Did you just say you felt its warmth?"

"I don't really feel it, silly," she giggled. "I imagine it."

"I wish I could."

"One day, you shall."

"I doubt it," I argued.

"You never know, it's nice to dream. In dreams, our hearts soar and minds travel without boundary or demand."

"I envy you as my dreams are... disturbing. Until recently I did not dream, but now I am less certain. I do not remember them, nor can I prove I've even had them, as I thought an Eternal couldn't, but on waking, the residual terror remains. I can explain it no other way. Not so long ago, I almost perished. During the madness that ensued, I thought I dreamt of the sun, or perhaps witnessed a vision, something almost tangible, but not of this sun, a golden one. That is all I have ever wanted, Aurora, to walk in the golden light of day and feel its warmth suffuse this pallid skin. Do you know what it did?"

"No," Aurora said transfixed.

"It burned."

"I am sorry."

"No need to be. If I do tread the dust between stars, those silvered pathways in the darkness, then we've just cleared one of them. My journey can only ever run smoother now Vladivar's evil is extinguished."

"Good," she stated.

"What would you dream of, Aurora? What is it that you want more than anything else?" I asked, whilst she still seemed inclined to smile rather than frown.

"I thought you knew."

"I do not believe so."

"Why, this of course."

"What?"

"Freedom. You have made my wildest dreams come true."

I stopped at that and looked deep into those ice-blue eyes of hers. There was no hint of jest, no sarcasm, Aurora meant every word. Rendered speechless, I continued in my escorting her down the staircase.

"Jean," she said as we wound around a rocky outcrop, the valley floor opening out before us like a savage wolf's maw, revealing a vicious yet blessed end to our descent.

"Yes, Aurora."

"Do you trust my family?"

"No." I answered without a second thought.

"Then, why would you leave your beloved with them?"

"I had no choice."

"One always has a choice."

"Did you not have the choice to leave Hvit?" I returned like a testy child.

"I had nowhere to go. I had never been more than a swim away from its entrance and always accompanied."

"I apologise, my reply was rash."

"You do not need to," she smiled.

"I have been the subject of blackmail, as you know; they wished me to murder your mother."

"You would not be able," her cool riposte.

"Able, or not, that's what my manipulators requested."

"I do not see why. My mother never leaves Hvit other than to hunt."

"Perhaps, they seek to exterminate all the Hierarchy, all those who might oppose them? Maybe they want me dead and thought I should end up so if I did as they commanded? I cared not of those things, but their threat was against Linka, so I chose to desert her in the hope those who play me will reveal themselves."

"Do you have any idea who they are?"

"I didn't, although now I believe it tied to my parents' murder. Someone seeks to wipe their perceived venom from this world and me along with it."

"Does Walter have any idea?"

"I have never discussed it with him. I have had no reason to."

"You should," replied Aurora, releasing my hand and running her fingers through her hair. "He has much knowledge."

"He knows far more than he lets on, always has. I made the mistake of believing Merryweather an idiot, as he regularly acts it, but the truth is, he is far from one. I even regret having almost killed him. Such misunderstandings colour future judgements."

"You tried to kill him?" Aurora looked shocked. "I presumed you spoke metaphorically."

"He deceived me, dear girl, still is, I believe."

"How?"

"I left him strung up ready to be turned to ash by the sun, but as you can guess it did not work out that way."

"My mother claimed only we Nordics held the truth about the sun. I always thought she exaggerated."

"She did not. I wasted far too many years of my life blissfully unaware of that salient detail. I cowered in the dark when I could have lived in the light."

"That is a shame, Jean," she said, as we made the bottom of the staircase and stepped onto the dusty valley floor.

"More than you could ever imagine," I replied.

"Should we examine the Marquis' ship?" Aurora asked pointing to the grottier than normal mobile blood bank.

The craft was almost unrecognisable covered in the loose dusts of the valley floor its metallic sheen dampened to a dull grey. It looked less magnificent when not reflecting the cosmos.

"He would be long gone if he saw me descending the mountain. I think it best we move on."

"Does he fear you so?" Aurora asked.

"I'm glad to say he does, and he has every right to. I shall kill him, Aurora, you do realise that don't you? I shall kill them all."

"Yes," her succinct answer.

"Good, I'm glad we understand each other. Anyway, less doom and gloom, and back to business. Now we've got you down safe and sound, I think it best we hurry. I cannot be certain how far ahead our adversaries are, but judging by the tracks in the ground I would surmise they are on horseback. We are not."

"Indeed," Aurora replied in all seriousness.

"And it looks like Walter was telling the truth. Look, in the dirt, cart tracks." I pointed to the unmistakable ridges left by at least one heavy, wheeled object.

"Will they all be on horseback, do you think?"

"The Marquis will that's for sure. He wouldn't make it out of the valley otherwise."

"Are there no horses for us?"

"I have no idea where to look if there are. Vladivar once attacked me in a craft the size of a palace. If he could conceal that behemoth without my seeing it, I don't suppose horses would be a problem."

"Technology can amaze if you understand it."

"Do you understand it?" I asked.

"No," she laughed, the valley echoing to her tinkling tones.

"I suspect that for all the Marquis' technological trickery, he depends on Sunyin sniffing out his kin. I believe the old monk is essential to locating his sons, but that he can only do so if in close contact to where they've passed. He senses their presence, their thoughts if you will. The Sunyins are interlinked, in many ways a single entity. I have borne witness to it on numerous occasions. The old monk would sooner die than seek them intentionally, but in his current enfeebled state, he wouldn't even realise he was doing it."

"You admire him greatly, don't you."

"If it comes to it, Aurora, I admire him enough to die for him."

"But what of Linka if that was to happen?"

"Let us hope it doesn't," I replied in upbeat fashion. "I have no intention of succumbing to the Marquis, less so to Chantelle, and even less than that to Raphael Santini bastard that he is. Excuse my language."

"Then, might I make a suggestion?" Aurora said without batting an eye.

"Of course."

"We should run. If they believe what you say about the sun, they will not have got too far ahead. The sun is up therefore they must be sleeping."

"I like your thinking."

"Thank you," she said, looking very pleased with herself.

Bu by then, I was already twenty yards ahead.

* * *

We sped across the valley floor, I with the bags of blood bashing off my back, Aurora keeping pace with annoying elegance and ease. We ran without words, both lost to our thoughts. In a strange way, I enjoyed those hours. The company I kept was perfect; Aurora was honest, and quiet, two of my favourite qualities. I couldn't have asked for a better person to be with even if it not for a reason of my choosing.

The sun had long past its zenith, no more than a winking eye atop the western peaks, when I realised the light to have lessened. The shimmering spectre of Aurora's passage grew brighter and more awe inspiring with each incremental fading of ruby to black. Every glance to her became a bedazzling mixture of grace and terror for the set of her eyes was one of intensity. If ever she tired, she did not show it. If she sought to complain, she did not voice it. Aurora was a hunter on the hunt, a predator par excellence and born to it.

"Does it feel good to stretch your legs, dear girl?" I asked the ghost at my side.

"Unbelievably."

"Then why so quiet?"

"I'm savouring the moment."

"Which one?" I quipped as a grin swept over the far side of my face.

"Every one."

"Touché, my dear."

"But, I would appreciate a pause if we could."

"Of course, you only needed to say." I slowed to a steadying halt, placed my cloak on the floor, passed a bag of blood to Aurora, then took one for myself. "Are you tiring?"

"No."

"Thirsty?"

"Not really."

"Then, why stop?"

"I wondered what it would be like to see that smile span both sides of your face."

It took a moment to realise what she alluded to, but when I did, I could do nothing except break into the beam she desired.

"Is that not better?" she winked.

"You shouldn't do that, you know."

"Do what?"

"Wink at old men."

"We're about the same age, and I don't believe I did."

"You certainly did, young lady."

"You shouldn't do that, you know."

"Do what?"

"Joke flirtatiously with young women, especially princesses."

"I wasn't, it's my natural charm."

"Does it work?"

"When required."

"Is that often?"

"Not any more, I've retired it on all but Linka, and even then, I only use it to antagonise her."

"Is that what love does to people?" Aurora asked, cocking her head to one side inquisitively.

"It affects everybody differently."

"I wouldn't know."

"I shouldn't let it disturb you. Love is overrated. So many people think themselves to be party to it when in fact they lust over minor infatuations."

"You understand such things?"

"An unfortunate by-product of my misspent centuries."

"Do you regret them, Jean?" Aurora asked it with such a sad, sympathetic look, I pitied her, not me.

"I didn't, but I have of late. I believe it was my father who once told me of automatons, devices that resembled humanity, yet were without soul or true thought. They were hollow creatures without hope or future only servitude. I believe when my parents died, I became one. Only when I met Linka did this automaton develop the innards to transform it once again into a man."

"Has she such power over you, Jean, such control?"

"Yes," I replied, and for possibly the first time realised just how much.

"Howoooo!"

I had no time to dwell on it, as at that moment, the howl of a wolf reminded us other night dwellers roamed the evening, too.

"Sounds like our good friend Vladivar released the wolves with his dying breath."

"Good friend?"

"Figure of speech."

"I see," replied Aurora. She gave one of her best pondering looks and brushed a stray lock from her cheek.

"I think it would be best if we recommenced our pursuit. The last time I met with Vladivar's wolf pack it did not end well for them. I took no pleasure in killing animals and would do so even less a second time."

"Howoooo!" came a second even louder howl.

Aurora cocked her head again, as was her way, and listened with an intensity bordering on the palpable until the beast's echoes vanished into the oncoming evening. "That is not the sound of Vladivar's wolves," she said when all became hushed.

"How can you be sure?"

"I am always sure."

"And right," I added.

"Always," said she. "And it is not difficult to recognise such things."

"What things?" I enquired.

"The sounds of the Arctic. The calls of my mother's wolves."

"Your mother's!"

"She has sent them to hunt me down, Jean. For this, I apologise."

"No need, I'm sure we can handle a few mangy mongrels between us."

"So am I, but it is not they I apologise for."

"Then what, my most cryptic of associates?"

Aurora sniffed at that and smiled. She then took the deepest breath I thought I'd ever seen, closed her eyes, and flicked a pool of milk-white hair from her shoulders.

"They hunt for my mother under the stewardship of others: Grella, Ragnar, and the twins are nearing."

"Damn!"

Chapter 16

Green

"We should go," Aurora suggested.

"Any particular direction?"

"My brothers will find me sooner or later, so we may as well resume our pursuit. There is a chance we will catch up to those who hold Sunyin before my brothers reach us. That may cause confusion all-around."

"Is that the best you can do?" I sniffed.

"I am not used to making decisions, I've been following you."

"Hmm, you have a wicked sense of humour, dear girl, it crops up every now and again."

"Really, I've never noticed."

"If I had a drum, I would roll on it."

"I don't see how rolling a drum will help?"

"If we make it through this day alive, I shall try to demonstrate."

"Thank you," Aurora replied politely, "I shall look forward to it. Now, Jean…"

"What?"

"Run." She threw back her milk-white hair and vanished into the evening, a slipstream of stardust for a wake.

I shook my head, collected our food from the floor, and took off in pursuit.

We hurtled through valley after unending, barren valley. No sooner did I think we should have reached the end of one than we charged through another. Our world was one of rock, dust and steep-sided imprisonment. But no matter how fast we travelled, I could not shake the feeling we ran through a trap. I was unused to being preyed upon and didn't savour how it felt.

Another pained howl disrupted my morbid thoughts. The sound appeared no closer than before, but neither had we distanced ourselves from it. Someone kept pace with disturbing ease, which caused considerable frustration. I couldn't have run any faster if I'd tried. Aurora, on the other hand, appeared lost to the freedom of the wind. Elemental, devastating of form, almost feral in the way she skimmed the ground with only a passing concern for gravity, Aurora knew no bounds. If the girl's clothing had concealed her white-booted feet, I should have said she flew.

"Jean, this valley is a dead end," she called across the space between us, indicating ahead with a gesture of her elegant chin.

"Then we have no option but to climb, my dear."

"I wasn't sure if you could manage it, old man," she returned. The moon glinted in sharp reflection off her sapphire eyes, captured forever in those bluest depths. A blink and it sank without trace.

"Oh, I wouldn't want you going easy on me just because I'm doing all the work," I joked, the moon having returned to the sky where it belonged.

"I offered to help."

"I know, but I can see what state you are in even without baggage. You should struggle to make the incline if burdened. I see my decision as more a necessity than a charitable gesture."

"Really." She grinned the toothy smile of a she-wolf.

Before I knew what had happened, Aurora had swept me aside, snatched the makeshift sack from my tiring fingers and redoubled her pace. I was left in her proverbial dust as a white blur streaked up the mountainside. She appeared as an avalanche reversed, not falling, but climbing, devastating and unstoppable. I'd have watched in awe if not for our howling, canine pursuers. Somewhere to our rear, the wolves gathered. I redoubled my efforts.

By the time I attained the top of the valley slopes having skidded my way over an infuriating amount of loose gravel, Aurora already stood there resplendent gleaming like a settled star.

"All right, you've proven your poi…"

"Shhh!" she said cutting me off mid-spiel.

Aurora turned a slow three hundred and sixty-degree rotation, paused, then signalled simultaneously in two opposite directions. Her left hand pointed north. I followed its indication, squinting my eyes to focus past the near vertical plunge of our position to a flattened landscape of twisted and grotesque forest that spread inexorably out far below. There, way off in the distance was the unmistakeable sight of a flickering fire. Smoke rose like an apparition contorting in and out of view in the clear night sky. That was the last thing I'd expected to see, as Eternals did not require heat. I put it down to some kind of false comfort on Chantelle's behalf, although it appeared stationary and I should have thought her to be making greater haste. I then spun to where Aurora's right hand still pointed directly in our wake.

"They close," her words ominous in their cold delivery. "We lost track of our quarries back in the last valley, but our hunters have not lost track of us."

"That cannot be," I protested.

"No wheeled carriage could have made that incline, Jean. I do not know where or how we lost them, but we did. Now, my brothers approach and we have no place to hide."

"But, I see nothing, Aurora."

"Look closer, Jean, follow my line."

Aurora pulled me uncomfortably close, so I looked straight down her outstretched arm all the way to the tip of her forefinger. I concentrated, steadied turbulent emotions, focused my mind, and there they were. There was no mistaking the sight of fast moving wolves and behind them a quartet of glistening shooting stars.

"Damn it!"

"You say that a lot."

"It's appropriate," I grumbled.

"Any thoughts?"

"You must hide. That's all I can suggest at the minute." I made to lift her cowl, but Aurora waved me away.

"It is too late. If I see them, then I can assure you they see me."

"They won't once we start our descent."

"Descent! We cannot, it is too steep even for such as us. Our only option is to retreat."

"Oh, Aurora, still so much to learn."

"I do not see this as a time for jesting," she retorted.

"Neither do I, we *shall* descend."

"It is impossible," she declared.

"As impossible as it was for me to defeat the twins?"

"I... I do not know?" And for the first time, Aurora looked the young girl I knew her to be, relatively speaking, lost in the big wide world.

"Just follow me, my dear, we shall descend with grace, or fall with style."

"Easy as that, then."

"Easy as that," I agreed and raised her cowl. She vanished into the night, eclipsed.

The cloak full of blood bags remained hovering five feet from the ground – not the best thing to be seen drifting down the mountainside – so I tied the top in a tight knot, took it from Aurora's hand and slung it down into the forested abyss.

"I presume you can still hear me even though I cannot see you," I said, as I lowered myself over the rock face.

"I can, but I suspect you already knew that," Aurora replied from below.

"Ah, so you've already gained on me. Well, just remember, my friend of the secret smile, I can fall past you anytime I choose."

"Can you try not to?"

"I can't promise."

"Well, if you have to, at least refrain from falling on me?"

"I shall do my best, dear girl. I shall do my best."

I would have said more but for the fact I concentrated so hard in digging my fingernails into the granite, polished to a glasslike finish by northern winds, that if I hadn't, I would have been doing so right there and then. My task was hampered further by the sharp updraft that seemed determined to wrest me from my grip. Yet it is amazing how the prospect of extermination can push one's limits. The thought of a Nordic's hands wrapped around my precious throat caused an imperturbable tranquillity to fall upon my mind. Where I should have wandered in a daydream, I remained calmly focused on the task at hand.

We spent too long on that perilous descent. The moon's ethereal light passed from left shoulder to right long before we'd attained even half the required distance. I had climbed upwards against ridiculous odds on all too many occasions, but the strain of that wicked descent was beyond any comprehension of pain I'd ever experienced. I had lost the feeling in my fingers after minutes, my arms soon after that. Thereafter, I judged only if I maintained a grip by the metronomic disappearance of my blood strewn fingertips into the rock wall.

By the time I felt the first grasping branch of a tree strike my ankle, I had had enough, and simply let go. The fall was still some distance, I cared not. I landed in an exhausted heap amongst the loosened chunks of our own descent.

"Jean, are you hurt?" came my companion's clipped voice.

"Only my pride."

"Look at your fingers!" Aurora sounded shocked.

I stared at my hands, or rather, the shredded remains of them. A mangled mess of blood, shards of nail and loose skin hung in tatters from my finger ends.

"This might help," came the voice of my guardian angel from somewhere within the arboreal gloom. Her voice trailed away to be replaced by a gentle rustling as of someone, or something, walking over the crisp undergrowth. The next thing I knew a porcelain hand emerged from the dark carrying a blood bag which ripped open before my eyes and thrust itself over my extended right hand.

"Can I add nurse to your many talents?" I asked.

"If this works, yes."

A witty reply was cut short by the deep-throated howling of a hunter who knew its quarries lost. "I think that shall have to do, Aurora," was all I managed.

"I will carry our sustenance from now on, you can keep one hand at a time submerged in the blood."

"But…"

"No buts, Jean, we need to move and move quickly. You will be a hindrance to yourself and therefore me if you lag with our supplies."

"If I think you're smiling under that shadow of night, I shall not be amused."

"I would never smile at your infirmities, nor mock them."

"My what?" But Aurora's footsteps already moved off into that excuse for a forest, the cloak full of our liquid food bouncing off her unseen back. I followed in grumbling protest.

The trees, if they could truly be called that for they were closer in resemblance to the twisted bodies of the dead just larger, crowded over Aurora and I. Those contorted representations of a glorious past grasped and tore at us. Within minutes, my shirt was in tatters, the skin below shredded and raw. On the plus side, my fingers felt much better for the few minutes each had spent submerged. It was whilst looking at the repair job I noticed Aurora's burden had suffered the same shredding as I. The bundle of blood, lacerated right through my cloak's fabric, disgorged its contents over the forest floor. Accordingly, I bent to collect the fallen packets.

"Leave them," my companion said.

"I'm quite able to carry them in my bare hands."

"Leave them, Jean."

"We're safe you know; nobody would attempt the descent we just made."

"Wouldn't they?" came her querying voice as I felt a hand rest upon my shoulder and spin me slowly around. "Look up," she instructed.

I did, but wished I hadn't.

At first, I saw nothing, so thick was the decaying tangle of limbs, but as had become uncomfortably frequent, I was very wrong.

"Do you see?"

Her words frosted my ear, crystalline and cool, each vowel, each consonant taking flight into the night. My eyes followed their trajectory, watched them gather high in the air, then fall again as four Eternal-sized snowflakes.

"Yes, I see them, Aurora. We may not have lost your brothers, but at least we've thrown off their wolves."

"They will find another route."

"You really are a barrel of laughs."

"I am honest, nothing more."

"Brutally, dear girl."

"I suggest haste."

"I concur."

"Then follow, if you can."

At first, I thought Aurora mocked me that she chose her words to chasten. She did not. The retied sack was hoisted over an invisible shoulder, then shot off through the gnarled landscape at such speed I was indeed hard-pressed to keep up. If I knew things would not end well if they caught us, Aurora knew it more so.

Secretly, I chastised myself for not realising the true implications of Aurora's desertion sooner. The Nordics were never going to allow her to leave without permission. In not doing more to return her whence she'd came, even if an innocent party in her escape, I had doomed us both. Yet still I ran forever hoping for a miracle. And despite the razor-sharp branches, bare of foliage, arthritic fingers grasping and reaching for the two of us, we swept all aside. If our hunters had reached the forest floor, who knew, but I felt sure even such as they could not have snuck up on us through so dense a setting.

"Howoooo!" was the answer to those thoughts.

"How the hell have they got down so quick?" I asked the nothingness.

"They are Arctic wolves, Jean, bred to hunt, to kill."

"I didn't think there was anything left to kill!" I huffed.

"Not much, but some. When our kind hunt the orca the wolves will wait by the ice fringes and attack the whales the moment my people drag the leviathans ashore. If it were not for they, I fear our ranks would be more depleted than they are. I have even known the largest wolves to leap into the ocean after their keepers."

"You speak as though proud of the canines."

"I am. They are magnificent creatures."

"How the hell can you talk so calmly after the descent we've just made, never mind the fact we've been running non-stop for hours on end?"

"Good breeding."

"If you said that with a smile, I may well feed you to those wolves," I panted.

"Let us hope that will be unnecessary."

"I hope so, too," I agreed. My hushed words were lost as we burst into a clearing and the smouldering remains of a fire. "Damn it!" I cursed before realising how loud I'd been.

"Maybe it's just not meant to be, Jean."

I don't know why I reacted as I did, but Aurora's words sounded so despondent, so resigned to their fate, I lost my usual composure under pressure.

I ripped the makeshift sack from my unseen companion's grip and was about to tell her just how wrong she was when I realised us watched. A dozen or so pairs of eyes gleamed in the remains of the firelight. The things lurked beyond the clearing's perimeter, unblinking and watchful. At first, I thought the wolves had caught and somehow overtaken us, but not even the Arctic canines stood so high from the floor? There were too many sets of eyes for it to be Aurora's brothers, so who?

The mystery was solved when a flash of russet garb revealed the identity of those we'd stumbled across. It was not the Marquis, nor Chantelle and her cohorts, but the Sunyins. I rushed over to the outstretched hand of one of the identical brothers.

"It is a great pleasure to see you again, Jean," said the beaming monk.

"As it is you, my small friend."

"Will you not introduce us to your companion?"

"How the? She's invisible!" I gasped.

"Sacks do not float in thin air, and I do not remember you as a man who would refer to himself in the second person."

"Plus, you already knew."

"Ah, you still surprise us, my friend." The monk inclined his head. The momentary gleams of reflected light suggested the others did too.

"Well, you always seem to know everything before I, why not the fact I travel with another."

"Not any other, Jean, but a princess."

As if on cue, the crack of a twig and sudden luminescent revealing of Aurora's stunning self proved the monk right.

"I am very pleased to meet you and your brothers, Sunyin."

"The honour is ours, Princess."

"My friends call me Aurora."

"We understood you to be a princess without friends?"

Aurora cocked her head to one side, puzzled over how the monks could know such things, then responded, "I now have many."

"It feels good, does it not?"

"It feels very good."

"I hate to cut in, but was there not more of you the last time I saw you."

"Yes, Jean."

"And…"

"And, they have split up," Aurora interjected. The man who I took to be the Sunyins' newly adopted head brother nodded once in agreement.

"Then they are in grave danger and so are you. We must all hurry."

The words had barely left my mouth when the unmistakable scent of lavender washed over the clearing. Aurora's brothers swept from the forest in an avalanche of white. All four were there, they eyed us.

"Aurora, I want you to lead the monks away," I growled, turning to the girl who looked an even whiter shade of dead.

"I cannot leave you, Jean."

"You *will* leave me!" I commanded in my most uncompromising voice. A quick look to Sunyin and an acknowledged lowering of his head was all the confirmation I required. The little monk glanced to his brothers who melted away into the night. He, in turn, took Aurora's hand in his own.

"Jean is correct. Your brothers cannot defeat him. He has a greater destiny."

Aurora looked disconsolate. I thought she might burst into tears at any given moment. Her eyes took me in, bluer than the polished gems they resembled, overflowing with grief, the hand that touched my face trembling with the same. "I'm sorry, Jean," her only words. But she did not argue just allowed herself to be led away.

I turned back to the four snow-white princes; they had not moved an inch. They had no need to chase after their sister, she was already theirs, and they knew it. It was Grella, resplendent in his glowing attire, despite its rather more ragged appearance than normal, that took the lead, as was his birthright. It was Grella who spoke first.

"My apologies, Jean, but it is your time to die."

Chapter 17

Black

"Have to is such an uncompromising declaration, it leaves no room for bargaining. There are so many other options to consider: might; should; possibly; could, they would have at least presented some flicker of hope."

"An incorrect one," Ragnar growled from his older brother's side.

Grella gave him the briefest glacial glance that chilled even my lost soul. It was with a look of gentle reservation that he set his gaze back upon me. "I have no wish to kill you, Jean, despite what you may think. However, taking Aurora from us was a mistake, an unforgivable mistake."

"What makes you think I took her?"

"The fact that you now defend her, the cold reality of her having left and everything in between."

"I see. Almost a whole week of reasons, then."

"There or thereabouts," Grella spoke in measured tones as if to a child.

"Is there anything I can say that might prevent my imminent demise?"

"I doubt it, Jean. Regardless of whether you can, or cannot, our mother has decreed it and thus it must be."

"Serena sent you?" Caught off guard, I allowed my thoughts to show.

"Enough!" Ragnar roared. "Let us have his head and be done with it."

"You will do nothing until I command it," Grella returned, the embodiment of calm authority.

"Ouch, what a put-down. Does it burn, Ragnar, that you must do as you're told? If a Nordic can be burned that is?" I added, scratching at my chin. "I'm sure someone as powerful as you must take great offence to such things."

"You have a fast mouth, vagabond prince."

"That's the second time one of your kind has called me that. It's not that I'm ungrateful, don't get me wrong, it's nice to be recognised, but you really should just call me Jean. I am no prince and would not wish to be if it meant acting like you."

"I'll call you it whilst I rip your head from your shoulders," Ragnar rumbled.

I thought the very mountains about to cast themselves upon me in an avalanche of rage such was his demeanour, but I was not about to let him know it. "You can try. It didn't do the twins much good, though, did it, boys?" The two skulked in the shade of their elder brothers. I thought an additional long, slow wink to each a particularly nice touch in my efforts to irritate.

"I am not they," Ragnar continued under the withering glare of both the twins and Grella.

"Thank goodness you're not. Twins are bad enough, but triplets! Doesn't bear thinking about. Having to sully my hands once instead of thrice would be a bonus, though. Come to think of it, I didn't sully my hands, did I, boys?" The twins looked fit to explode, their brilliant white visages touched by a hint of rose. The advantage was mine. "Dem bones, and all that, eh," I sniffed. The button pressed, I awaited a reaction.

The twins knew their place; Ragnar did not. He was not about to let my words go unpunished.

I braced myself, my taunting having achieved its purpose in driving them to strike without care or consideration. More pertinent to my cause, to act as individuals and not a group.

Ragnar was a blur of sparkling snowflakes, a maelstrom in the making; Grella was faster. He caught his brother by the arm before he'd closed half the distance between us, and thrown him to the ground with devastating ease. The impact was earthshattering. An explosion of debris, soil and rock flew into the air to rain back down as a rebuilt landscape. All that remained to show Ragnar had even stood there was a crater of epic proportions. The whole episode carried my mind back to Vladivar's bombing of Rudolph's palace, the parallels in sheer power almost beyond comprehension. The fact I bore witness to mere strength of arm and not technology almost drew a shiver.

My mouth hung agape as I struggled against the urge to step back. I knew not to show fear, weakness in the face of the Nordic princes, but the thought preyed on my mind.

"You will not touch him," Grella growled into the pit of his own creation.

Personally, I didn't know why he bothered, as nobody could have retained consciousness after such a blow. I was wrong.

A white hand on the end of a massive, muscular arm rose from the hole like a great, albino spider. Fingers thick as tree branches clawed at the ground for purchase. Ragnar's digits drove into the rock with piledriver power dragging his fearsome frame out once implanted. The largest prince spoiled for a fight. He shook his head twice, bashed at his right ear, then closed on his sibling, a look of such rage plastered across his features I felt Grella must cower before it.

"You've just made a big mistake, brother!" he boomed.

"The mistake is yours, Ragnar. Your lack of respect is inexcusable and I shall not stand for it."

"I do not care. I'm sick of this dying planet, sick of this life, and most of all, Grella, I'm sick of you."

The titan fumed, his fist raised to attack, towering over Grella like a frost giant of legend. The would-be king didn't bat an eye. It was Ragnar's first and last controlled movement. For in Grella, a far slighter man, I saw a master in the art of war. He was upon Ragnar in an instant, the bigger man a lamb to the slaughter. Grella took him by the throat with one hand, bent him over toward the ground, then squeezed and crushed and contorted. Ragnar's arms flailed as though willow tendrils in a breeze, but Grella's form moved like candlelight flicking from one position to the next in a blur of phosphorescence. Ragnar never got close.

In that instant of brother on brother infighting, I had my one chance to strike and took it.

The twins never knew what hit them. I snatched a branch from the forest floor and smashed it over the first then struck an uppercut to the gobsmacked second, which sent him flying into the trees. Faster than drawing blood from an innocent's neck, I'd laid both out senseless. So swift was my attack, I thought none could have reacted to it. But, as I rolled from one action to the next in fluid motion, Grella was already behind me. I was at his mercy. There was nothing I could have done and knew it. He did not strike?

"You claim you did not encourage Aurora to leave. That is not what my mother said." Grella spoke as though nothing untoward had occurred.

"If I said your mother lied would you believe me?" I spun to see the puzzled eyes of the one true prince of the Nordics.

"I… I might," he stuttered.

Grella struggled with his inner demons, almost as much as me.

"Prince Grella," I said standing tall and proud. "I am many things, and have been many more, but a liar is not one of them. I am not proud of my life, that is to say quite ashamed of most of it, yet I possess honour. Whether you are aware of my past, I am uncertain, but I can assure you, I have never been partial to untruths, and never shall be. If I said I knew nothing of Aurora's departure, I did not."

I watched the fissures in Grella's polar visage ease a little. The fjords of the prince's troubled face widened until expanding to a sea of serenity.

"I believe you."

"Good. But make no mistake, Grella, I will not allow you to return her against her will."

"You have no choice," he replied.

"I have the choice of a free man, a man without restraints. I do not succumb to the commands of others. Not even you, Prince Grella. I mean what I say, you shall have to kill me to get to her."

"I do not wish to kill you, but I cannot disobey our mother."

"You can do whatever you wish, my friend."

"I cannot."

Grella's fists clenched and unclenched, his brows furrowed. The man's albinism had never looked more acute than at that moment thrust as he was into an alien environment. He tried to subdue the power he held, quell it beneath his pallid exterior, but he was losing the battle.

"Has Serena so much sway over her children, they cannot perceive when she wrongs them? Can you not blame Aurora, a princess of your people, for wishing to leave? I barely know the girl, yet it is blatantly obvious she is unloved."

I did not see his strike, only felt it. By the time I sat up rubbing at my jaw, I was at the opposite side of the clearing. Grella stood twenty yards away, impassive, still as a midnight shadow, brooding.

"Did I hit a sore spot?" I asked not wishing to look weak, nor in any particular hurry to return his strike.

"She is loved," Grella whispered.

"What?" I asked straining to hear him.

"Aurora is my sister and I would do anything for her if she but asked. It is not I that see her as an outcast, yet I am powerless to do anything about it."

He stood there close to tears that mightiest of men. I truly believed Grella would have wept if not for the slight stirrings of one of the two twins. He whipped around to regard either Serstra or Verstra, for I could never tell the two apart, with such venom, I thought he might set upon him. He didn't though, his self-control returned.

The apparition that was Grella stared back across the distance between us, ghostlike, barely there. Those few yards couldn't have felt greater even if he'd stood at the North Pole itself.

I said nothing, only returned his look and pondered on the icicle which built at the corner of his eye. The thing lengthened like a stalactite with centuries of growth crammed into moments. Then the strangest thing happened. The tiny icicle quivered, vibrated, then shattered its minuscule mass across Grella's snow-white cheek. I thought myself dreaming, that I had witnessed the impossible, but the tremors that had affected it also struck me. The ground beneath my feet shook with some unseen yet mighty force. Branches from nearby trees cracked under the strain and snapped like twigs from their trunks crashing to the ground in twisted piles of destroyed life.

Grella appeared even more surprised than I. He looked this way and that in utter bemusement as the shakes took a hold of his legs, then torso, then right up to his long hair, which quivered like a white, shaken sheet.

The world trembled as I had read it did in the long distant past. The ground cracked and lifted. Rocks plunged both up and down, the trees wrenched from their anchored mornings, weightless, before crashing back to the ground. Through all the upheaval Grella moved as though in his own personal nightmare. The Nordic heaved the twins from the floor, each flung over a shoulder. He then whirled between the destruction like one of the waltzers of Europa's ballrooms until he reached Ragnar. With the loyalty only family can produce, Grella gathered his brother in his arms like firewood. With all three safe, he turned to watch me leave. I saw it all over my shoulder as he charted my flight through stern eyes. He looked so confused, a man who bore the weight of the world rather than that of his siblings. He stood there motionless as the ground beneath his feet surged upwards and my own collapsed down. The last thing I saw as we went our separate ways was a profound sadness in his eyes, then they, too, vanished in a rain of broken forest.

There was no time to dwell on the Nordics' fates, my own of more imperative importance. I leapt from one point to another, my feet dancing across the crumbling scenery avoiding one gaping hole after another. It felt as though ancient giants manipulated the landscape. In a way, I supposed they did. There was no mistaking the great earth-moving abilities of humanities' machines. Those earth shakers worked at fullest capacity, the planet creaking in protest. But that should not have been? No lesser person than my father had once told me the great landscape changers of mankind, those of such vastness as to manipulate the earth's tectonic structure could not operate whilst the living, or even non-living, such as ourselves, still moved upon them: safeguards, or some such mumbo-jumbo. What occurred should have been impossible, but that did not change the fact it did.

I stopped looking up to the hundreds of feet of new cliff that had separated me from the Nordics, instead, turned and ran. I ran as if my non-life depended on it, which it sort of did. I ran with a speed I never knew myself capable of as that disfigured forest crashed around me. I ran towards a looming chasm of total blackness, an intersection between two fractured landscapes. Like a hurricane given human form, I swept towards the vastness and launched myself into the air with all the might at my disposal. It was not enough. I landed on the cusp of the far bank clawing at the turf for dear life. Thank God I'd taken Aurora's advice. If I'd not soaked my hands in blood as instructed, I should have died. But, my talons, regrown, although not at their sharpest, dug into the earth, rock and whatever else they could gain purchase on and secured me. I clung in desperation as I shot into the air, no more than a speck of dust in a storm, but did not let go. Higher and higher, the shelf rose upwards. I thought it should never stop. When it did, it was with such a jolt it hurled me up and over the ledge to land on my back with a sickening thud.

I lay that way, chest heaving in protest, unable to believe what had happened for longer than I should. When at last I rolled onto my front to look whence I'd came, I found myself on one side of the deepest, darkest canyons I'd ever seen. A vertigo-inducing glance over the edge showed nought but littered rubble on the distant floor, a floor I'd almost partaken of. I'd risen so high that a sanguine dawn simmered on the horizon; the old desire to flee before the sun felt as strong as ever. Somewhere out there, Chantelle and her party would have sought shelter, but where was another thing altogether.

It was the howling of distant wolves that snapped me back into the real world. I wondered if they pined for lost masters, or in joy at their renewed pairing. Such things were hard to be sure of.

With only a passing glance at the broken distance, I set about continuing north with the hope the Sunyins and Aurora had fared better than I.

Chapter 18

Snowflake

I smelled the blood in the air, an alluring intoxicant. That odour of a forgotten past drew me to the chaos that was the monks long before I saw them. When I walked into the clearing they occupied it was as if a war had taken place. The Sunyins had lost more of their kind in the violence, too many. I felt their pain like walking into a wall, an almost tangible solidity in the rising dawn. Those that remained bore the blooded signs of struggle; lacerations and worse covered each of them. Their leaking life essences overpowered my senses, the beast within straining at its leash.

The monks were not alone in their suffering. The mangled carcasses of half a dozen great, grey wolves lay in various states of contorted death. Those beasts had died badly.

Aurora sat on a rock some distance from the others scratching behind the ear of one gigantic canine, her coat a perfect snowflake white. The wolf whimpered into her left palm, as it lay sprawled across her thighs. If she shared any of the ancestral vampire urges to sate I did, her calm demeanour showed no signs of it. Perhaps, she had other things on her mind? The crystal tears that pooled at the corner of her sapphire eyes alluded so.

One monk shuffled over head bowed. If it was the one who'd appeared to be their leader earlier, I could not be sure, identical as they were, but I did not have the heart to ask.

"It is good to see you again, Jean. We feared you lost or worse. Are you hurt, my friend?"

"I think it is I who should ask that question. I see your brothers have lessened since we parted. There are no words at my disposal to express my bitter regret at that saddening fact, so I shall not even try."

"These things are a test of our faith, and our faith is strong."

"You take such news better than I."

"We all have our ways, Jean. We should have lost far more if not for your beautiful companion. Aurora saved us from the wolves you see scattered all around. We would have wished for no deaths, but they left her no choice." Sunyin brushed the scene with saddened eyes.

"Needs must," I replied.

"I gather the Nordics' hairy contingent made it across the new divide before their masters."

"I know only what you see before you. However, I must excuse myself whilst I aid those who require it." The little monk bowed, I returned the gesture, then he shuffled his way back over to the closest of his brothers who dabbed at a deep gash on his arm.

I turned my attention to Aurora.

"This one was my own," she said without even looking up.

"She is magnificent, Aurora."

"You have met her before."

"I have?"

"Yes, outside Hvit."

"She looks so different now."

"Out of place."

"Yes, out of place."

"She is called Nordvind, my companion since a pup. She could have traced me to the ends of the earth and almost did." Aurora wept into the wolf's luxuriant fur as its breaths became shallower. "She was as incapable of obeying me as my brothers were of she that set the pack upon us."

"Your mother?"

"Yes," a terse reply.

"I am sorry, Aurora."

"It is too late for sorry."

"Yes," I replied not knowing what else to say. Instead, I sat on the ground by her side and looked into the faltering eyes of the beast she tended to. "Nordvind," I whispered. "You are as beautiful as your mistress." But the words had barely left my mouth when the she-wolf's chest heaved one last time.

"Was beautiful," Aurora said, as her tears flowed like the Arctic Ocean they stemmed from.

There was something innately wrong about seeing one so beautiful as she stricken by grief. If there was a realm beyond our own, a place beyond the dark curtains of eternity, then I hoped it not populated by angels as sad as she, for my long-lost soul could not have borne it.

"We must bury her, Jean. I cannot, no, will not, allow other predators to feast upon her flesh."

"Do we have time?" I returned without due care.

Aurora locked me with her piercing blue eyes and replied, "We make time."

I was not about to argue.

* * *

Aurora and I dug the hole with our bare hands, the dead ground no match for our steel talons. The little monks tried their best to assist us even though I begged them to rest and save their energies. Only when we reached a depth sufficient to accommodate every wolf's carcass did the monks ask if we might make it deeper so they could bury their own with the animals. I thought it sick; they thought it fate.

When we had finished and refilled the makeshift grave the monks stood around its perimeter and chanted words of kindness to all those lost souls. In the eyes of the monks all were equal, and I felt shame at my prior indignation. Aurora joined them holding the hands of two shaven-haired Sunyins in solemn respect, whilst I stood quietly to one side.

I pitied them in a way the old me never would. Yet, through it all, all that loss, all the loved ones mourned, I thought only of Linka. How I yearned to be with her again. How I wished I could have turned back time and done things differently. But I couldn't. And despite all the sadness, all the pain that overflowed from that small clearing, I felt only anger, it consumed me.

The monks' ceremony went on too long for my liking, but I kept my thoughts to myself. Instead, I continued my vigil, rolling stones beneath my boots, as Eternal and human mourned together in harmony. What had happened all those many millennia ago to upset such a perfect balance? Then I remembered: blood.

I presumed the sun heard my thoughts for at that moment it deigned to reveal itself from behind its cumulous covers casting a haze of ruby light over the proceedings. It was odd to look up to that which I'd wished to see for so long with nothing but hatred. I might even have said I despised it.

A strange buzzing sound drew me from my introversion. Like a demented insect, the noise persisted with ferocious urgency. It was a sound I recognised but couldn't place. Not until a polite nod of the head signalled Aurora's release from the chanting circle did I realise its source. She glided over, once more herself, reached into her robes and passed me the offending object. The moment she did, it ceased its infernal racket, as if awaiting my words.

"This is not a good time, Merryweather," I growled in complaint. There was no answer, so I gave the thing a shake and tried again. "Walter, can you hear me?" Again, silence, all except a slight rasping, which I put down to interference. I cast Aurora a perplexed look. The Nordic remained impassive.

"Bonjour," a single, sleepy reply that cut through the silence like the licking of blood from one's lips after a feast. "Do you hear me, Jean? Are you not pleased to hear from your one true love?"

"You were never my love," I bit back.

"Non! I thought I wassss," she scraped. "Your losssss."

"Where's Merryweather?" I growled, unable to contain the animosity that swelled from within.

"How wassss my husband?" she asked ignoring my question.

"He…was," my reply.

"Ah, so you killed him."

"You killed him, I just helped hurry him along."

"Jean, Jean, Jean," she purred, the voice of death. "Alwayssss so heroic. Alwayssss so predictable. Alwayssss so…you," she settled on.

"I'll remember that when I rip your heart from your chest and crush it into black powder. If I can find it that is."

"Non, you were doing so well. Why must you alwayssss resort to violence? Life is too precioussss to waste on anger, surely you would have learnt that after your parentssss' death."

Before I could vent my fury upon Chantelle, Aurora snatched the communication device from my hand. She held the thing in her palm and spoke with a chill that rivalled Chantelle's own.

"I am Princess Aurora of the Nordic clan." There was a silence at that, and I wondered what played through Chantelle's warped mind. "Your reticence says you know of me."

"I do now, madame," Chantelle replied. "I thought the Nordic-ssss a myth until they arrived at my wedding."

The twitch I gave told Aurora what my lips were unable to communicate.

"Then, it was not you that requested our presence?"

A something not unlike the last choking breaths of a perforated larynx echoed across the clearing. Chantelle laughed, whilst I almost baulked.

"Why would I seek the likessss of you? Only Duke Gorgon wassss supposed to attend, bald-headed ignoramussss that he issss. Hissss signature would've made the wedding legal in the eyessss of the other Hierarchy memberssss, not that I needed it. But, you came, or your kind did to be exact. I wonder why you did not, dearest Aurora?"

Aurora flushed a tint of blue, but held her tongue with a self-restraint I envied.

"I believe Jean asked where Walter was but did not receive a reply. I would like to hear that question answered."

"Please," hissed Chantelle.

"If you please," Aurora responded.

"Ah, you ask so nicely, how can I refuse so divine a request. In answer, Sir Walter ran away."

"Ran away!" Aurora snapped.

"Yessss. He is an expert at it. Walter hassss been running away for yearssss and yearssss and yearssss. He dropped thissss in hissss hurry to escape."

"Did you harm him?"

"Is that concern I hear?"

"Did you harm him?"

A glacier cracked asunder, Aurora's voice containing all the forces of her homeland. I felt the intake of Chantelle's breath just as I did my own.

"No," came the eventual reply.

"That is fortunate for you," Aurora replied coolly.

"And unfortunate for him. He has fled into the day assss I and my compatriotssss have returned to the eternal rest of our dark coffinssss. I imagine Walter will be nought but ash by now. Perhapssss, it is for the best, he wasn't very good for anything other than annoying Jean. I only wish I'd had a chance to bid him bonne journée."

There was a pause in the conversation as the two women weighed each other up. I thought the device Aurora held might crack and break such was her intensity. I offered my palm to her then; she tipped the communicator in as if it deceased.

"Chantelle."

"Ah, Jean, you could not stay away. I'm glad, I dislike that girl. I prefer to talk to you. If only you were here with me, I do so tire. We could hold each other assss we once did."

"I would love to hold you, too."

"Really?"

"How else could I be certain I'd killed you?"

"You cannot kill me, silly boy, you have already tried so hard."

"I can always try harder."

"Alassss you will never get the chance. It wassss not meant to be. Now, we must sleep. We have thingssss to plan, placessss to go, people to kill."

"We?"

"Yessss, we."

"Might I ask who that encompasses?"

"How could I refuse so polite a request?"

"Indeed," I replied trying very hard to keep a lid on my volatile emotions. Chantelle appeared not to notice as she blathered on.

"There is, of course, the Marquisssss."

"Of course," I concurred.

"It appearsssss he requiresssss the other Sunyinssss' blood rather more than he first presumed. The one you left behind doesn't seem up to much, an aged and poor specimen. He doessss have a nose for his kin, though, and that'ssss all that really matterssss. The changessss to the landscape have hampered thingssss, but we shall soon pick up the scent once more."

"Then, that was not your doing?" The thought had been going around my mind, so I thought I might as well just ask it. Chantelle seemed so much more direct than she used to, less guarded in her decrepit shell.

"Oh, Jean, my once love, you know so little. I would love to take you in my armssss and comfort your innocence away."

The accompanying sound as of broken bellows did nothing to lessen my disgust for the woman. However, I had another question ticked off my list, so she could hiss and huff all she wanted.

"Then, there is your brother-in-law, the tanned and handsome Raphael. How issss Alba by the way?"

I slammed the speaking device down so hard it shattered into tiny, metal pieces. Aurora looked on with the expression of an exasperated mother.

"Sorry, I couldn't help myself, it was the next best thing to her head."

"So, what now?"

"Choices," I cogitated.

"We have choices?"

"Possibly," I said in a sudden burst of inspiration.

Aurora arced a sculptured eyebrow, as was her way.

"Sunyin," I called to the little monk, who had kept a polite distance during our conversation.

"Yes, Jean."

"Why were you heading north?"

"We searched for you."

"How did you know I was there?"

"We sensed it."

"But I left almost a week ago."

"You shall return."

"Really?"

"North is where both our destinies lie."

"If you can sense such things, why did you not seek out your own and Shangri-La? In my opinion, that would be your safest and most logical retreat."

"We know precisely where Shangri-La resides, but that is not what we wish."

"Why, Sunyin, what do you wish for?"

"We wish to be reunited with our brothers and through them our father. We wish for the family we have never had. We wish to be complete."

"So why come to me?"

Sunyin looked between Aurora and I, then set me with such a look of calm intensity, I almost fell off my rock.

"Because you are the only one who can help us, Jean. You are the only one who ever has. We know our destiny to be intertwined with your own, it is our shared fate."

"But, I'm just an ordinary man, nothing more, nothing less. I have no army, no way of doing what you wish of me."

Sunyin shuffled over to stand before me, his feet pitter-pattering in the loose sands. He came to rest a few feet before me, smiled a smile of such contentment the like of which I knew I should never smile myself, and spoke.

"You are so much more than you know, my friend. Before long you will realise what we have known since first we met you."

"And what is that, Sunyin?" I huffed, shaking my head with frustration.

"That when the time comes, when the sun bleeds into the horizon and all is cold, when the world as we know it ends and time resets, you will be the one left standing; you will set things right."

"You have great confidence in a man who seems to be a master of only one trait."

"And that is?" Sunyin's unblinking eyes moved a little closer to my own.

"To kill. I am a killer, and that is all I know."

"No, my friend, you are so very wrong." Sunyin placed his hand upon my head and I felt a sensation that was un-cold, something I should never have felt. "It is not your mastery of death that will save us, but the desire to overcome it through love. No force is more powerful than love, Jean. Nothing."

Sunyin removed his hand only for the sensation to diminish leaving me once more the cold Eternal I had always been. He stepped away, his residual kindness ebbing with each footfall, then looked back once more.

"In answer to the questions you would ask, yes, we can sense where our brothers are, and our father."

"And where is that, Sunyin."

"Why, North, of course."

Sunyin gave a polite bow, then moved off to where his brothers still amassed about the communal grave. I waited for him to reach them before moving to Aurora's side.

"How does it feel to be the saviour of so many?" she asked with a renewed sparkle in her eye.

"Underwhelming," I replied.

"You do not relish the task?"

"All I wish is to be back holding Linka in a place and world where I can do so in peace."

"And to achieve this?" Aurora asked. "What are you going to do, Jean? What do you need from me?"

"Oh, it's simple really."

"Really!"

"Indeed."

"How so?"

"I need your help in killing every single person who looks to prevent it."

"Simple as that."

"Simple as that."

"And what of Walter, he seems to have slipped through the cracks, yet again?"

"I fear Merryweather will have to fare for himself, for now. I suspect he will find us when he needs us."

"Yes," Aurora nodded. "I have that selfsame suspicion."

"And you, Aura? I mean, Alba. I mean, Aurora. Oh, good grief, I'm a mess."

"Aura?"

"Sorry, a slip of the tongue, I think all this disruption has affected me more than I care to admit." No sooner had disruption slipped from my lips than I wanted to throttle myself for such a poor choice of words. Once again, Aurora chose to excuse me.

"I like it."

"Like what?"

"Aura."

"You do?"

"Yes."

"Then Aura it is," I beamed, "after all, you do gleam." She smiled at that. "Now, you ask of others but never of yourself, so I ask you, Aura, what would a Nordic princess wish? What is it that you need?"

"As always, my friend, I wish only to follow you, if necessary, to the end of eternity and back again. My needs are your needs, nothing more, nothing less."

Aurora touched my shoulder with a kindness I did not deserve and swept away to assist the others.

Chapter 19

Charcoal

"Jean, might I make a suggestion?"

"Of course, Aura."

"You need blood."

"Do I look that bad?"

"Worse."

"I appreciate your honesty."

"You're welcome."

"And, you?"

"I would prefer not to."

"Not quite orca blood, eh," I chuckled.

"Not quite."

"I don't want you going all weak on me."

"That will not happen."

"That was a very definite answer."

"It is a simple fact. I owe it to Nordvind."

"I am not sure vengeance is a dish that suits you, dear girl. Such things fester and twist, strive to rob you of that which sets you apart."

"Which is?"

"Innocence, Aura. It is a rare gift, one I would not be so hasty to lose. I know I was and deeply regret it."

"Innocence is a quality I was robbed of at birth."

I didn't get a chance to respond. Aurora had thrown me a blood bag, pirouetted, her hair spiralling out in creamy waves, then glided away without my ever having chance to say thank you.

* * *

Our passage, although a simple one for Aurora and myself, proved to be far from so for the monks. Whether debilitated from the loss of six of their brothers, or even less capable of physical expenditure than I'd imagined, who knew, but their struggles were etched into the contours of their no longer calm facades. Furrowed brows clashed with grimaces of pain, shuffling steps became trips and falls, and I for one grew more and more concerned for their wellbeing. To their credit, not one complained of the pace we set, nor asked for help. The little fellows formed a line caterpillar-like, the way I saw them do from high atop Vladivar's castle walls, and shuffled ever on. They were taciturn and determined in a way I'd never been and didn't suppose I ever would.

The dismal landscape we journeyed through was unlike anything I'd seen on my travels. Death was something one became used to beyond the false boundaries that the Hierarchy built about themselves, but desolation on so sweeping a scale as in that wasteland was almost unbelievable. There was simply no life, nothing. A vista of bare rock in various sizes, from gravelled shale to black, mountainous mounds filled my vision. Not even the gnarled and twisted excuses for trees we'd past earlier lived in that world of stone. It felt like a taster of how the planet would one day be, a sorry excuse at best.

We walked for hours, the ruby sun spluttering high into a pastiche sky, a mockery of the blue it should've been. By the time the tired orb reached its pathetic zenith, the monks were little more than husks, yet still our strange group stumbled on.

As usual, Aurora shone incrementally brighter as the night grew closer, first rivalling, then surpassing the day's tepid glow. The monks strove not to show it, but their fractional glances revealed how they marvelled at her. Who wouldn't have? She, in turn, marched with purpose, but one detached from ours. She brooded with a passion that rivalled my own, her malaise an infection, which I knew from experience as hard to clear. I considered approaching her several times, but somehow could never think of the right words, or so I told myself. Instead, I traipsed on, the leader of our disparate group, my mood darkening by the second.

Our passage was torturous by Eternal standards, but the monks could not have travelled faster even if their lives depended on it. I hoped they did not. Our pace did, however, provide an opportunity for a painstaking scouring of the scenery for any sign of Chantelle's passing. My senses worked overtime, scent, sight and mind striving to identify any proof we drew closer to our quarries. They revealed nothing. It was not that I disbelieved what Sunyin had said, not at all, just I lacked the same faith as he, and required visual confirmation. Unfortunately, it was not forthcoming. If Chantelle, Raphael and the Marquis had taken the same route, then they had done so without stirring the ground. There was not one trace of anything other than the planet's lingering death.

* * *

"Jean," Sunyin said with a gentle tug at my shirt sleeve.

"Yes, my friend."

"We feel drawn to the mountain ahead. We do not know why, but we feel we should go over it, not around."

"Are you sure?" I looked to the monstrous lump of chiselled granite looming before us. "I mean no offence, but it looks an ascent you and your brothers are incapable of making."

"Thank you for your concern, but I think you will find us a hardy band."

"There is a difference between hardy and foolhardy." The words escaped my mouth in my usual – speak before thinking fashion – but if my faux pas offended the little monk, he did not let it show. For that small mercy, I was grateful.

"If you do not wish it, Jean, we shall understand."

"I apologise, my friend, I was merely concerned the extra time and energy involved would be better spent conserved. If that is the way you wish to proceed, then that is the way we shall."

"We do not wish it, we feel it."

"I wish I could say the same."

"You do just in different ways. Time means less to an Eternal. You do not heed the instincts of old because you need not act upon them."

"And, you do?"

"Yes, my brothers and I have a set amount of time in this world, so the desire to understand what our minds tell us is of great importance." Sunyin nodded at his own words as if reconfirming them.

"But I thought you incapable of…"

"Death from natural causes," he interjected.

"Yes," I agreed, glad he had said it and not I.

"We are bound to our genetic code much as you, if not more so. Did you think death beyond us?"

"I presumed, what with the monks populating the monastery for so long and I dare say Shangri-La the same."

"No, we are shackled by the same terms of existence humanity always is," he continued.

"Was," I corrected.

"If you prefer. I thought you would have realised this when you saw our older brother die."

"You know about that, how?" I said surprised.

"We sensed it."

"How so?" I pressed, intrigued by the monks' biologies.

"Imagine having three fingers on one hand, four on the other, knowing you lacked one even though you had never possessed it. That is the only way I can explain it. We feel a loss, a lessening of ourselves. As the years have progressed, and the Marquis has generated less and less of us, the feeling has become ever more apparent. Our shared memories dwindle much the same as the sun."

"Then he is truly responsible for all your lives?"

"To an extent, yes, as much as anyone could be, anyway."

"So how do you know so much of those who have passed before you?" I grabbed Sunyin by the elbow as he looked to stumble.

"Thank you, Jean," he smiled. "And in answer to your question, we feel it, just as we do everything else. The universe is composed of energy. This energy swirls and moves between the living, the dead, and the places in between; we are a part of this as are you. It is only that we feel its movement, whereas you have forgotten how, that marks us as different."

"I see," I said scratching my chin even though I didn't.

Sunyin burst into a shrill laughter that ran throughout the monks like a river to the sea. At first, I was a touch angered by their amusement at my expense, but it was contagious, and I soon joined them in their hysterics.

"You sound so much like another we knew," he said once their mirth had subsided.

"Do I?" I laughed. "Have I a brother of my own?" The look Sunyin gave silenced my laughter, and the lowering of his head told me he would say no more.

* * *

We walked on until the approaching mountain dominated the night horizon, then consumed it. By the time we started up those barren slopes there was nothing before us except a wall of rock.

The mountain rose like a dark, blistering bunion into a maddened charcoal sky, a swathe of bulbous clouds having consumed the night. The whole landscape was one of inhospitable solids, its unholy nature compounded by the cloying smell of charcoal. Loose dust soon coated us in ever-blackening suits, although the effect was somewhat lost on me compared to the others. Yet, despite all that grot, I thought the subtlest aroma, as of a sweet floral nature, punctured the staleness on occasion. It was bizarre for there was nothing on that desolate rock but ourselves. I put it down to an overly vivid imagination and dispelled the notion.

Up and up we climbed, Aurora and I assisting the little ones where we could. Most of the time they refused our help, on others, they had no option but to accept. Our steady rise was almost proportional to that of the infrequent moon. The whole experience had a strange symmetry to it that I thought the monks would've enjoyed explaining if they'd had the energy to do so.

The climb became an arduous obsession for the little ones. I saw how they struggled. However, not once did they complain, nor fall back. My admiration grew exponentially for them during those arduous hours.

When Aurora broke from our wards, apparently content they could manage on their own, I was more than a little surprised when she drew close. We had remained distanced throughout the evening's onset and hadn't spoken since we'd left the burial ground.

"I have been thinking about what you said." Aurora's iced tones cut through the deadened silence like the first crack of an Alpine storm.

"About what?" I replied, having quite forgotten.

"About vengeance."

"In what way?"

The girl that looked to me appeared strangely aged to she who I'd spoken to last. Aurora looked troubled, desperate even, and I pitied her in her less than pristine robes. She looked more ordinary, it did not suit so angelic a creature.

"I do not like vengeance. I have mused on it these past hours and am uncomfortable with the feeling. It sits like a stone in my gullet that won't allow anything good to pass."

"I feel that way all the time," I jested, then apologised for my ill manners.

"Does it not consume you, Jean? Do you not wish things could have been different?"

"Indeed, I do, Aura. I wish for nothing more for it gnaws at my very soul, or whatever we Eternals have in place of one. I would have everything in my life redone if I could."

"Do you blame any one person for your unease?"

"I have blamed many people, but none more so than myself."

"Why?" she asked, cocking her head to one side in her usual way. The moon appeared over the mountaintop at that moment, slipped between the cloud, and reflected in those deepest pools of blue that were her eyes. She looked once more the goddess in those seconds. I wished I could've taken away her pain, but I could not.

"Because when it boils down to it, dear girl, I could have said no, and didn't. At any second in my centuries of life, I might have chosen a different path, my own, but instead, I blindly stumbled from one instant to the next."

"Do I have that choice to make, Jean?"

She looked at me, her eyes pleading. I couldn't imagine the loneliness Aurora must have felt in her lifetime and did the only thing I could think to lessen her anguish.

"I believe you have made that choice in asking the question. I believe you will be just fine."

"Do you, Jean, do you really?" she all but begged.

"Please forgive me, I do not mean to have listened in on your conversation," Sunyin said wandering over, "but, if I may?"

"You may," I replied, somewhat relieved by his intervention.

"My brothers and I know of your life, sweetest child."

"You do!" Aurora said startled.

"Yes, we do. We have meditated on your place in this world as we have our own, and even Jean's." Sunyin bowed to me, and I returned it. "We believe your loneliness will soon end. There will be a time in the near future when you will know the happiness you have thus far never felt."

"Honestly?" Aurora said with tears in her beautiful eyes.

"We are as incapable of lying, as you are of looking anything less than sublime." Sunyin bowed to his questioner, lowered his bald head and continued his climb. But within a few steps, it became evident that he, and the rest of us, did not have to climb any more.

"The summit!" I exclaimed as a subtle scent assailed my senses once more.

"You smell it too," Aurora said, as the Sunyins staggered onto the level surface in various stages of exhaustion.

"I know it, dislike it, but cannot place it."

"It is lavender, the very faintest whiff," she replied. "My brothers close on us." She spoke the words without intonation, it simply was, and that was how she saw it.

"That is not good," I replied straining to see back to the horizon we'd left behind.

"But that is," said Sunyin. He pointed in the opposite direction where the faintest flicker glowed against a lightening background: fire.

"What should we do?" Aurora asked. "We dare not leave the monks to chase down the others."

"No, I agreed," sucking in a great intake of un-required air.

"May we rest a short while, Jean?" Sunyin asked. "The sight of our brothers has settled our hearts and the distance will close sooner if we are recuperated even a touch."

"I agree," I said.

"I too," Aurora concurred.

"Thank you," was all Sunyin managed. The monk turned back to his brothers almost collapsing in the process.

Aurora tugged at my arm, drawing me away before I had a chance to aid he or his fellows. I followed her a slight distance from the others where she pulled me in conspiratorially.

"Jean, if these Sunyins sense their brothers' proximity and strive to reunite with them, why do the others not? And how is it that one party has gained such distance on the other?"

"I don't know, but you're only voicing concerns that have troubled my own thoughts."

"It does not feel right," she added.

"I agree. I expected to come across the others long ago."

"It is a puzzle," Aurora noted.

"It is suspicious," I corrected. "I think it best if we both keep a vigilant eye out. If your brothers catch up to us, I doubt they will allow themselves to be stalled twice."

"They will not. But we need not keep a lookout."

"Why?" I replied.

"I see them," said she, pointing to a white glow on the boundaries of our southern vision.

"Oh, great," I bemoaned.

Chapter 20

Luminous

Grella's apparent reluctance to harm me was a dilemma. I would have said kill, but it was such a harsh choice of word. Whether to share the fact with Aurora was one I postponed until more certain he didn't.

Any conversation concerning Aurora's family was one that required careful consideration. She had alluded to her family's disdain for herself several times, and although I suspected there more to it, I understood only too well the pain of a certain mind being challenged. Yet, Grella's hints at none of it being his choice had altered the situation dramatically. So many what ifs to be deliberated over, too many, in truth. For better or worse, I chose the path of silence.

"You look to ponder when action is required," Aurora snapped, quite out of character.

"I am pondering over what action to take, dear girl: we cannot resist them, we cannot stall them, and with the monks in tow, we shall never outrun them."

"Then, you must leave us," came Sunyin's level-headed response having risen once more. His ashen pallor suggested he might not have managed it again.

"I will not," I said.

"You must. Aurora's Nordic brethren do not wish harm upon us, not as I interpret it. They seek their sister's return, not our capture. You should go ahead, reach our brothers, and then ask them to wait. We shall follow with all the haste our mortal frames allow."

"I will not. I will not be driven from what I know to be right, not again." I stamped on the ground like a petulant child.

"He is correct, Jean, it is our only choice. We have completed half of what we set out to do. Now that we know these monks are safe, we must make sure of the others." Aurora regarded me coolly, too coolly for my liking.

"How the hell can you say that!" I exploded. "Your brother's set their goddamn wolves upon them last time."

"They were sent for me, not the monks, and even then to track and delay, not harm. It was not the wolves' fault that nature drove them to kill. Besides, they have no more wolves with which to do so again. Thanks to me," she added with a look of such hurt that my anger subsided that instant.

"That is not true."

"It is."

"Aura, I'm telling you, I heard another wolf when last I departed your brothers. I quite forgot about it until now, but I did." I spoke with a tempered rationale, my anger stabilised.

"Strange," she said puzzled. "They always hunt in packs of ten and that is how many I killed."

She cringed at the word ten. I visualised her thoughts then, they were written all over her porcelain features. Memories of Nordvind running over the Arctic ice to be with her, her only companion, two souls drawn together in a world of almost perpetual snow. Poor girl, how desperate she must have been. How much her kind had to answer for. Almost as much as my own.

"Well, they have either changed those rules, or we will have Vladivar's own hounds to deal with at some point. Either way, the monks are not safe."

"They will not be safe until those that track them are dealt with. We have not overtaken Chantelle, therefore, she must be ahead of us. That again indicates we must proceed to the others."

"I... I do not feel...comfortable with that," I stammered.

"It is the only course of action, my friend." Sunyin lay a steadying hand upon my arm.

I shook it off and walked a few paces from my companions, leant against the mountain's very pinnacle and sighed. "Will I never make a choice of my own free will?" I punched the rock in frustration, hung my head to hide my temper.

When I deemed myself calm enough, I turned to see Sunyin's smile and Aurora's look of concern. I warranted neither. The disgust I felt at my inability to finish anything I started rankled deep within my gut.

"We must leave, Jean, every second counts."

"All right, Aura, as you wish it. We shall go, but I will not pretend to hide my thoughts on the matter."

"I understand," she acknowledged with a polite inclination of her head. She then paced back to the makeshift blood sack where she discarded all but a few of its contents.

"And what should I say to you, my small friend?" I asked Sunyin.

"You do not have to say anything, but I would like to say something to you."

"Hm, and what would that be?"

"Please save our father. I, my brothers, and all those who still reside within Shangri-La want nothing else. We would give our lives freely to save his. We would not have lives at all if not for he."

"Is that not a touch dramatic?" I sneered, then instantly regretted it. "I'm sorry, Sunyin, old habits," I apologised.

"You are frustrated that is all. We understand the reasons why and believe that someday soon you shall be free of them."

"If you say so."

"I do, or rather, we do. There is not one iota of doubt in our belief that through you we shall find that which we both seek."

"And that is?"

"Freedom, Jean."

"I have my freedom," I replied.

"Have you, dear friend? Have you?"

The little monk gave a shallow bow and returned to his brothers in meditative contemplation. Aurora stood beside them awaiting me.

I had no choice but to do as the others wished, but still chanced a surreptitious glance to Aurora's brothers. A halo of white light shimmered on my vision's peripheries. There was, however, no mistaking the fact the white fog would not remain there for long.

With nothing more than a nod to the monks, we set off. I had never liked goodbyes.

Down the mountainside we sped. So fast my companion and I travelled, that should we have created a rockslide by the force of our passage, we should have outrun it. We descended at such a pace the distant fires of the second party of Sunyins soon vanished into the night. Rather sooner than I would have preferred, we were very much alone.

* * *

We'd been running for about twenty minutes, silent passengers on the same road, when the clouds that had obscured the night sky disgorged their bellies upon us, and how.

"You didn't see this one coming," I attempted a poor joke.

"I did not have the heart to tell you," Aurora replied, her cloak streaming out behind her into the whitewashed night.

"We'll struggle to find each other in this never mind those we seek!" I balled into the now blizzard.

Aurora just smiled despite the abundant snowflakes which sought to obliterate her beautiful visage. It was odd to see her do so when I myself struggled so much. It was almost as though she came alive in the storm, a Nordic goddess. If the girl's cloak had been of falcon feathers, I would have said her Freyja reborn on our dying world, but I doubted even myths and legends could've had such piercing, blue eyes. She ran unimpeded, a force of nature. I stared across at her, rubbed the ice from my eyes, and marvelled, for that was all one could do.

Perhaps in response to my concerns, Aurora stretched out a slender arm through the maelstrom and took my hand in her own.

"We shall not lose each other now, Jean." She hurled the words through the weather although they felt whispered in my ear. "And do not worry, I have the fire's scent, we shall not lose your friends."

"You can smell the fire even in this?"

"With ease, my friend. I have lived in these conditions for too long to not thrive in them."

"Can you sense your brothers, too?"

"I can."

"And?"

"They close," her flat response.

"How long do we have?"

"How fast can you run?"

"I was going slow for you," I winked, the gesture made incomplete as my eyelid froze in closed mode. It took several fierce rubs before the thing unlocked of its own accord.

Aurora responded with a laugh that made light of our situation. Despite carrying the cloak of blood bags, she redoubled her efforts almost pulling my arm from its socket in the process.

How Aurora navigated the whiteout who knew, but she sped on through the elements with utter disdain for everything they hurled at us. Occasionally, she would veer to one side or the other allowing enough latitude for me to avoid whatever materialised out of the gloom be it the deformed shapes of solitary trees, boulders, or worse. Never once did she break stride. Never once did I doubt her.

After a time, instinct took over. My body allowed Aurora to tow it through the night, as, in turn, my mind wandered back to the mountaintop. I feared for the Sunyins. Even if the Nordic princes circumnavigated their pinnacled resting place, I doubted they'd survive the storm we ran through. My knowledge of human anatomy was rudimentary, gleaned from the scraps of information my parents had stashed in the books they so cherished, but one thing I knew for sure was such extremes of exposure were beyond them. If tears could have fallen in the temperatures we hurtled through, my pale face should have been encased in them, an ice mask for my melancholy. The little men had exposed a part of me I never knew I possessed. From my first encounter with them in Shangri-La, to the brutal slaughter of he who would always be, to my mind, the one true Sunyin, at the hands of Scott's Zeppelin crew, those most honourable of men had shown life was not to be scoffed at, belittled, or scorned, but treasured. One day I would, too, I was determined to, but I doubted they themselves would ever see it.

"Jean," Aurora's whispering snapped me back into the tempest.

"What?" I shouted back.

"We have arrived."

She came to a skidded stop, me along with her.

"I see nothing, Aura. There is only snow, ever more of it at that."

"Beneath the snow."

At that, Aurora released my hand, dropped the cloak to the ground and clawed at the foot-deep snow. I joined her, although I knew not what she sought until like ebony jewels set in a porcelain crown, we uncovered the charred remains of a fire.

Aurora put her hand to the burnt offerings, then shook her regal head.

"What do you sense?" I asked, raising my arm against the ferocious weather.

"Nothing. That's the problem. I had hoped for a clue as to how long ago they departed."

"But you have none, I take it."

"None at all," she replied. "Help me, Jean."

Aurora swept the snow aside with a speed that testified to her desperation. I joined her, hoping to uncover something, anything. When I did, it was not what I'd wished for.

"Is this what I think it is?"

Aurora rushed over, shook her head, and sucked in her cheeks.

"Yes," she grimaced. "Chantelle's carriage tracks."

Twin sets of deep ruts sat pressed into the dark ground.

"Then, Chantelle and the others have them."

"I assume the same."

"But the sun will be up soon," I said with a hint of desperation.

"True, but if they have the monks, then they can drive on through the day."

"Damn it!" I bellowed into the storm. The wind swallowed my words, but I felt better for their release. "Why the hell would they keep going north if they already have the monks?"

"My mother," Aurora said standing and facing the accused direction. The wind tore at her clothes, the snow sought to encase her in an iced tomb. Aurora faced it with a determination that burned in those bluest eyes. Even the wind abated before her in apparent fear of her rage. As for me, she inspired.

"Come on, this is good news, not bad. We now know who, what and where we chase down."

"Yes, we do," Aurora said fixing me with a penetrating glare. "Let us leave."

And before I could respond she had retaken my hand and set off at a rate of knots unparalleled, so swiftly we sliced through the maelstrom.

* * *

We'd raced for perhaps another hour when, as all our kind could, I sensed somewhere behind the curtain of winter the ruby sun to rise. I only prayed it slowed those we hunted.

If Aurora thought the same, she did not express it. In fact, I would have said her expressionless. She ran as though in a trance and I worried for what went through that elegant mind. Aurora moved as one with the elements, eyes closed, head flung back, long hair streaming out behind whipping against her shoulders to an ominous rhythm. She sashayed through the winter's violence in direct opposition to my battle against it. Then, as abruptly as she'd commenced her sprint, she ceased and released my hand.

A tsunami of snow pushed forward under the force of Aurora's sliding feet and she ducked to the ground like a predator of old. One hand touched to the snow, the other twisted in the wind. Her alabaster fingers twirled amongst the snowflakes, sought something in the midst of that elemental barrage, something that disturbed her. I remained silent not wishing to break her concentration.

"Something's wrong, Jean. Do you not feel it, a vibration?"

I ducked down beside her as the snowfall abated a fraction. I placed my hand on the ground and was about to reply in the negative when a cry of such magnitude split the dawn I almost fell on my behind.

"AAAUUURRRROOOORRRRAAAA!"

"That does not sound good," I growled.

My royal companion paid it no heed. Both her hands felt at the ground, whilst I searched the night. The snow lessened dramatically then, and I thought I saw the distant outline of the Nordics, but couldn't be sure.

"Aura, we must go," I hissed. The princess looked up wide-eyed, then flung herself forward grabbing my arm in one fluid motion, dragging me with her. The ground split asunder behind us with a crack that heaven would've heard if there was one. We scrambled forward through the deepening snow as the crack behind us became a fissure, then gulf, then void.

"AAAUUURRRROOOORRRRAAAA!"

"The twins."

"Unfortunately," she agreed, climbing to her feet.

I pulled her a few steps further back as the single landscape became a very definite two.

"There," she said pointing to the unmistakeable forms of her snowflake-like kin. Her forefinger stabbed south.

"They're not going to be happy about this."

Aurora arced one perfect eyebrow.

It was difficult to tell who was who in the ever-growing distance. The snow had again trickled back into downward motion after its respite falling into the chasm like flour in a bowl.

"I'm sure the distance is too great even for your brothers to span."

"Not yet it isn't," she replied, staring across to the diminishing ledge.

"No man can make that leap," I insisted. It didn't stop my apprehension, though, as I stood there trying to convince myself of that salient fact. "Look," I said, somewhat relieved, "they slow."

"Three do," she replied. "One does not."

I knew what she intimated, but thought her mad to even contemplate it, as the impassive face of Grella materialised out of the murk.

"No, don't do it," I heard myself voice. The words were as lost on me as they were anyone else. It was clear Grella attempted the impossible.

I watched beside my Nordic princess as three brothers slid to a triumvirate of stops in their older brother's wake. Grella paid them no heed as he reached a speed I thought impossible for any living being. He shot towards the chasm, arrow-like, not for a second slowing his pace, never wavering, then leapt. He sailed into the air, a hawk to its prey. Even then I thought he'd fall. The Nordic prince had other ideas.

My companion swept an entangled cloak from her arms and tensed. I tensed with her. For right before my eyes, the impossible became the possible, the miracle jump achieved. Grella landed in a crouch with the effortless grace of an ancient panther.

I was so shocked that he'd made it, I was rendered temporarily immobile. I wanted to say something humorous, something devastatingly witty, before he ripped me apart, but stood dumbstruck. All I did was marvel as Grella rose from the ground, spun, and bowed to his brothers in one elegant, luminous movement.

By the time he'd adjusted his cloak, goggles and shirtsleeves, I felt as prepared for those final moments of my Eternal life as anyone could.

The prince of the Nordics turned to his prey, us, ruby eyes gleaming, opened his mouth and said, "Good morning, Aurora. Good morning, Jean."

I almost reeled back into the void.

Chapter 21

Blood

"Aurora, I am here to escort you home." Grella offered his sister an outstretched hand.

"I do not want to go home."

"You must, Mother wishes it."

"I do not care, I am staying with Jean."

"You are young, so I shall forgive your petulance, but you are going. I have already had this same discussion with Jean."

"It was hardly a discussion," I chipped in.

Grella, unimpressed by my words, took a step closer to his sister, who in turn took a step back.

"It is unfair to embroil a stranger in the workings of our family, my sister."

"Oh, I wouldn't let it bother you. I have no family of my own, so it's nice to be a part of one even if it's just to disrupt it."

Grella's fingers were around my throat in a blur of white movement, snowflakes lifting in his wake to kiss their brethren halfway down their descent. His grip crushed, although he held back, or I wouldn't have had a throat with which him to do so.

I had no chance to react for Aurora was upon him in a flash of white lightning. She ripped his fingers away, and then swung the hapless prince around by his cloak releasing him to a distance of thirty feet or more.

"Do you think your jump scared me, brother?" she hissed, feral and uncontainable.

"It was not meant to," Grella replied, already back on his feet. "I do not wish to hurt you, Aurora." In less time than it took him to speak her name, he stood before us.

"Then let me be," Aurora replied unmoved, determined to not back down.

Polar opposites, they stood apart, separated by nothing more than the shade of an eye.

"I must do as our mother commands. It is a son's duty to obey."

"I am not a son."

"No, you are not," Grella replied with a shake of the head.

"Do I bore you?"

"Never that, dear sister."

"You're killing me, Grella, just tell her what you told me. Before you hit me hard enough to level a small mountain," I added, placatory palms raised.

"What did you tell, Jean?" Aurora demanded.

"I…"

"That you hate me!"

"I…"

"That you despise my half-breed self!"

"I…"

"That you have never loved this sister like you do your others! That you wished I was dead!"

Aurora spewed one verbal tirade after another.

"I…"

"I thought so."

"Give him chance, Aura," I said.

Grella gave an astonished look as I spoke her name. I let him stew on it.

"Go on then, thrall me," Aurora huffed.

I didn't think it possible for a man who was quite probably thousands of years old to look so uncomfortable. He mopped his brow as the snow, having begun to fall heavily again, collected on his cold shoulders like white epaulettes. Separated from his distant brothers, already obscured by the storm, Grella appeared even more isolated a figure. It was like he thought for himself without anybody looking over his shoulder or offering advice for the first time in his life, and the strain told. He shuffled from one foot to the other like a naughty child, his regal face set with a hint of desperation. He stared to where his brothers should have stood, then back to his sister. Whether Aurora's unblinking gaze unnerved him, or he was just uncomfortable expressing his true feelings, I was unsure, but he had two inches of snow piled atop him before he spoke again.

"I told Jean that I love you."

His words were uttered so softly that Aurora leant in to hear them said again.

"I love you, sister. How our mother has treated you has been a constant source of unrest; it has torn my soul asunder. I wish things could have been different. I wish them with all of what heart I possess, as I have every single day since your miraculous birth."

"I… I…"

"Well, answer him," I laughed.

"Thank you," Aurora said.

They were just two little words, but they were important ones. To see the Nordic prince take his younger sister in his arms and hug her touched even someone as cold as I.

I'd have stepped away and left them to their private moment if not for the chasm at my back and the silence shattered by Ragnar's deep, growling voice.

"You have just forfeited your position, brother!" he bellowed across the fractured landscape.

I saw none of the three brothers through the storm, obscured as they were, but it appeared at least one of them saw us.

"Ignore him." Grella released his sister and brushed himself clear of deposited snow.

"Don't I always?" she replied.

"Hmm."

"Was that a, hmm, of disapproval?"

"Reluctant acceptance."

"Did your brother just crack a joke?" I asked, faking amazement.

"I can spare one," he said with a shake of his head. "So, dear sister, now you know you are not the straggler you imagined, will you not permit me to escort you home?"

"No, but I will let you help us."

"In what way?" he said, raising a quizzical eyebrow.

"We seek the rest of the Sunyin monks, their father, and those that hold them captive."

"And who is that?"

"Princess Chantelle."

"Queen Chantelle of all Europa," I corrected.

The cracking of Grella's clenched knuckles sounded like thunder in an electric storm. Having been hit by them, I knew the similarity to be well observed.

"Chantelle," he rumbled with a voice like an oceanic swell.

"Yes," replied Aurora.

"Unfortunately," said I.

"That woman, if she can be termed such, is a disgrace to all I stand for."

"You were not pleased to attend her wedding?" I inserted into the conversation.

"I had no choice, none of us did."

"Why?"

"Mother commanded us to attend."

"Do you always do as she says?"

"Of course, as my brothers and sisters shall one day do for me."

"I sense Ragnar may struggle with that."

"He may, but it will do him no good." Grella straightened and gave a cursory look to his stranded kin.

I pressed home my advantage. "Why did your mother force you to go?"

"She did not force."

"Ask then!" I exclaimed, then apologised. "I'm sorry, Grella, I grow tired of the games others play. They are never in my best interest."

"Ours is not to question why?" he said solemnly.

"Don't you think it's about time you did? We did?" I implored.

"You are so young, Jean. When you are as old as I, you will find that respect counts for much. I respect the Hierarchy and what they hold as their values."

"The Hierarchy didn't even know you existed. I can assure you, much as I hate her, it was not Chantelle, nor her accursed husband who requested you attend their wedding."

"But?"

"Now do you see, brother? There is far more to all this than meets the eye." Aurora placed a hand on the shoulder of the puzzled prince.

"I trust our mother with my life," he eventually said. His look was less convincing.

"We both know that is not the entire truth," said Aurora and fixed him with her sparkling eyes.

Grella looked at me, his expression pain-filled, then to Aurora, and back again to the extinguished horizon containing his brothers.

"What would you have me do?" he said, his head hung low.

I bowed and replied, "Only what you believe to be right. I would never ask for more. I think, and I say this with the greatest of respect, that I trust you, Grella. This may not sound like much, but I can assure you, I trust very few besides myself and even then the trust is sketchy." I thrust my hand to the prince, who looked at it askew, then took and shook it.

"If, and I say if, I opposed my mother's wishes, what would I be doing it for?"

"I can say with some certainty that Chantelle and her band of fools wish above all else for just one thing."

"And, that is?" his deep voice enquired.

"That before the sun dies, and with it this world, she shall be Queen of all, not just the Rhineland, nor Europa, but everything including your homeland."

"That is madness!" Grella roared.

"That is the truth, brother," Aurora intervened.

"And you think mother is party to her own downfall. I cannot believe that. I will not believe that."

"I do not believe she knows it, but she is," I replied. "Your mother is being manipulated, although, I can only surmise by whom."

"But all we want is to be left alone, to hunt, to know peace."

And just like that, another piece of the puzzle slipped into place.

"What is it, Jean?" Aurora enquired sensing my epiphany.

"Blood."

"Blood," Grella said. "What has blood to do with anything?"

"Chantelle needs it, she craves it, they all do."

"All Eternals do, there is nothing unusual in that."

"There are all kinds of blood, Grella: false, orca, human."

"Humans are no more, and orca blood is for the Nordics alone."

"Who says?" said I.

"To which?"

"To both."

"It is a simple fact," he said crossing strong arms across his broad chest.

"Well, I'll grant you there aren't many humans, but the monks we spoke of are some. Their father, the oldest of their kind, was the key to the Marquis de Rhineland's production of false plasma, in one form or another, or so I've concluded. He is a friend, a good friend," I added. "He and his sons have been mistreated to the extent they no longer offer the Marquis and his Hierarchy clientele the resources they have become accustomed to. I could be wrong, but I fancy Chantelle has taken it upon herself to guarantee a new source of said life-giving liquid. She seeks to secure it and her futures."

Grella placed his arms behind his back and paced around in the ever-deepening snow. I did not stop him.

Aurora watched her brother's every step with an intensity that bordered on frightening. She hoped he'd aid us, it was written all over her face, but Grella was ever unpredictable.

All the talk of blood had made me thirsty, though, so I crouched down to our makeshift sack, took a blood bag for myself and handed one to Aurora. The contents were more slush than liquid, but it satisfied my needs to a degree.

When I raised my eyes again, I saw Grella had stopped to watch, so I offered him one too. The prince looked at the bag of crimson content with disdain before a taloned finger sliced it open. The face he pulled whilst he partook of the semi-fluid said it all.

"Not quite orca blood, eh?"

"Not nearly," he replied. Grella stooped for a handful of snow and used it to clean his hands and face.

"I agree," said Aurora. "Having drunk nothing but orca blood since birth, I believe I would be upset bordering on hysteric if robbed of it."

"Or promised it," I added realising what she planned.

Grella listened to our dialogue cocking his head to one side in symmetry to his sister. I watched his albino face shift to an ashen grey, and thought he might keel over, so ill did he look. But the seeds of Aurora's words were sown, and he knew we spoke sense.

"Which way have they gone?" he asked after some deliberation.

"All roads lead north," I replied.

"Are they far ahead?"

"Far enough," said Aurora, as a broad smile broke out over her beautiful, pale face. The change suited her.

"Then, I hope you can run, Jean?" Grella bowed at that, a sweeping thing of ancient elegance, then took off.

Aurora collected what remained of our sustenance sack from the snow and shot off after her brother, leaving me coughing in a spray of loose flakes.

However, I still dallied a few moments longer glad of those seconds of calm. It had seemed a lifetime since I'd had a moment to myself. I allowed the falling snow to engulf me and for a certain peace to settle over my world. But time was ever against me. A glance across the canyon confirmed what I already sensed; no one was there. The Nordic princes had departed who knew where, not that I cared. So, I set off in pursuit of my speeding companions and allowed the fierce northerly to purge what troubled thoughts remained.

* * *

I had still to reach the others when the howl of a great wolf cut through the dawning day. It stopped me dead in my tracks, the wail of the lupine stoking my inner demon, a sharp pressure, uncomfortable, which left me wondering who still stalked us? I strained my every auditory sense, peered into the snow with narrowed eyes, but the call never sounded again. It left me wondering if I'd imagined it, a ghost of the slaughtered many. But, much as I might've wished it, I hadn't. So, despite the shiver that crept up my spine, I renewed my pursuit of the others a tad more chilled than an Eternal should ever have felt.

Chapter 22

Crimson

I had thought Aurora to be a miracle of nature in her grace, poise, perfection, but Grella was something else. Containing the Nordic prince was akin to bottling the wind. He was a beast uncaged, a force unparalleled. Grella moved as though unburdened by conditions, racing along within a separate reality, a space in time where he and the elements were one. The snowflakes that bombarded my frame fell by the wayside before he, unable to lay a single, cold touch upon him. I trailed that man in both awe and respect basking in the subtle scent of lavender that emanated from his person. If I'd been Nordic by birth, I should have served him to the end of eternity without question or complaint. But I wasn't Nordic, and I served no man.

Aurora ran beside Grella an almost exact female representation of her brother. For the first time since meeting her, she exuded pleasure. I could not see her smiling, running in her wake as I was, but I perceived it in my person. She radiated joy, and the world was happier for it. I believed that for the first time in her life, Aurora felt more than just an unwanted mistake. The fact she did, I thought the saddest thing in all creation and that it somehow redressed the cosmic balance.

* * *

Seconds became minutes, minutes became hours, and the snow fell inexorably on. The world was silent but for my crunched footfalls; the Nordics made none. I thought once, I should have been happy to run through that limbo forever, but my mind was not what it was. Despite the peaceful calm, the gentle kiss of snowflake on skin, I worried: I worried for the Sunyins, both before and behind, and the cold they must have felt; I worried for their father and whether I should ever see that best of men again, and if I did in what state; but most of all I worried for the girl I loved above all else, the emerald-eyed beauty that was my Linka. I knew I closed the distance between us with each passing moment, but it did little to appease my rocklike heart. I missed her with a passion, a passion I thought would consume me. To have been with her again in blissful touch, I would have done anything to anyone, and that worried me most of all. For her, I should've torn down the sky, ripped up the world and forsaken all else. If it had meant turning my back on those who'd befriended me, I would have. I prayed that choice would not have to be made because it would not have been one.

* * *

Drawn from my inner ramblings by the sound of tinkling bells, I realised Aurora laughed again. It was only the second time I had heard her quite so exuberant. Unfortunately, both times had taken me back to Rudolph's palace and the flowers Linka had planted within its grounds. That saddened me further.

"What's the matter, Jean?" asked Aurora peering over her shoulder, a broad smile splitting the lines of her perfect face. She never even broke stride. "Are you growing tired, can't you keep up?" She laughed again, joy infusing her face with a subtle shade of powder blue.

"Luckily for you I have a broken leg, or I should be well ahead by now."

Grella stopped dead to a tsunami of snowflakes. I almost ran straight into his back. Only a quick swerve, a loss of balance and a face-first plunge into the snow halted my momentum.

"My apologies, Jean, I had not realised you were injured. I would have carried you if I'd known. You had but to ask."

Grella sounded so formal that his newly stationary sister burst into joyous giggles once more. I took the gloved hand he offered and allowed the prince to help me to my feet.

"I am quite well, thank you," I replied.

"He was joking, brother. Jean is a master in the subtleties of both sarcasm and wit."

"Should I have laughed?" Grella asked with a sincerity others would have lacked.

"No, you shouldn't, my friend. But I can show you something that will bring guaranteed joy to those serene features of yours."

"Really, I can't remember the last time I laughed. Do you think I will have forgotten how?"

"Let's see," I said, collecting a dollop of snow, forming it into a perfect ball, and tossing it at his sister's head. Unluckily for Aurora, it caught her completely off guard. She turned into the missile as it splattered across her angelic features. The look of shock that shot across her face was matched only by the metamorphosis of her brother's own. Like the granite facade of the mightiest mountain cracking open to the seismic power of an earthquake, his features transformed from dour, to quizzical, to fun. His roar of laughter was akin to the roar of the avalanche that had engulfed me near New Washington. I was equally shocked, too.

I didn't have time to dwell on the matter as a snowball smacked right into the end of Grella's nose, and then another into my cheek.

"I've wanted to do that for years." Aurora grinned at her brother, then turned to me. "It's felt like that with you, too."

"Was that another joke?" I replied as Aurora ducked below a snowball larger than her head. "I'm not sure that's quite how it's done, Grella."

"You could be right," he laughed, as he jumped on top of his sister only to be kicked off into the snowdrift he'd created.

Aurora rounded on her brother sending a torrent of quickly formed snowballs against his back. Grella, for his part, stood motionless before the barrage. I wondered if he'd forgotten you were supposed to duck. It took another blitz to spur Grella into a simple raising of one hand. Aurora stopped that instant.

I was unsure what occurred between the two and gazed at Aurora with a blank expression. She had returned to her normal taciturn self, as still as that pause before death.

"What is it?" I asked nobody in particular.

Grella responded by clawing away some of the heaped snow at his feet, grasping something, then pulling it free of its white covering in one fluid motion. He dropped it again almost as fast.

Time stood still as the object fell rigid to the ground. With the soundless slump of a fallen moth, the thing settled in the snow. It left me inspecting the frozen corpse of a small, bald, tunic-clad figure: a Sunyin. I could have accepted that except for the crimson puncture wounds to his neck. My mind imbalanced, I screamed.

"BASTARDS!"

Grella ignored my outburst. Already the prince searched for more. I joined him in a frenzy of black motion, clawing, kicking, and shovelling snow to one side. However, it was the quietest of the three of us that made a second grisly discovery as Aurora called us men to her.

"I am sorry, Jean, truly I am."

She stood there holding a blue, frozen hand in her own, the hand itself long since detached from the arm it belonged: Chantelle sought to stall us. An exchange of glances was all it took to reinvigorate our searching.

Despite burrowing through to the parched earth in a radius of fifty feet or more, there was nothing else to be found. Only a frozen pool of crimson blood where Aurora had discovered the missing limb marked the monks' passage. Much to my shame that blood called to me, but I covered it over, buried it one might have said, and stepped away. I could not bury the memory of its owner so easily.

The passage from mirth to madness had never fallen so rapidly. Even Grella shrank from my rage. He did well to, for in those moments, as I realised the full implications of what we'd found, I descended into a red mist I had hoped to have left in my past.

"It is never easy to lose those you care for, Jean," Grella said putting an arm about his silent sister.

"They did not deserve it." I shook with uncontrolled rage.

"The innocent seldom do."

"The…the…monks would never hurt anyone," I stammered.

"Such is the way of the world. The strong dominate, the weak used as fodder in greater schemes."

"I am sick of scheming, Prince Grella. I am sick of innocents being used in these so-called grand designs. I am sick of secrets, lies and deceptions. But most of all, I am sick of myself."

"You do not mean that, my friend," Aurora spoke in hushed tones. "Your heart is good. You do not realise it, Jean, but it is."

"You sound like a Sunyin."

"If I do it is because we both speak the truth."

"The truth!" I spat. "There is only one truth, and that is that all this," I gestured to the landscape, "all this, will soon be gone. There will be no more world to squabble over; no more power to lust over. All gone!"

"You are so certain?" Grella asked cocking his head to one side.

"I know it the truth. When the ruby sun ceases to rise all that I had hoped to see will end: no more animals, no more plants, no more life, just rock, ruin, and whispered memories. The least loss of them all, no more damned Eternals."

"If that is true, then why does this Chantelle and her lackeys go to the lengths they do."

"I do not know," I answered honestly.

"There must be more to it," he persisted. "There has to be."

"If there is, then I am unaware of it, but being that I have been unaware of everything, seemingly, that does not say much."

"That is not your fault, Jean," Aurora tried to reassure me.

"I can't help thinking it is."

"How can it? You are as caught up in these events as myself and my brother now are."

"You would not have been if not for me."

"It was we that came to you, Jean, not the other way around," Grella's deep voice corrected.

"Perhaps, friend? Perhaps, not? But I can't help feeling my inadequacies contributed to it greatly."

"Inadequacies! What inadequacies? I have never met someone so resourceful. Who else could've found so many uses for a whalebone?"

"Was that another joke?"

"Possibly?" replied Grella scratching his cheek.

"I'm sorry about that by the way."

"Are you?"

"No, but I thought it polite to say."

"You should never apologise for doing right. It was you they wronged, Jean. Mother had no option but to allow you the opportunity for recompense."

"I got the feeling it was because of she the twins acted as they did. I believe your mother wanted rid of me, still does. I am a nuisance, a hindrance. Linka alone was meant to be saved. My salvation was your doing."

"I do not regret it," said Grella.

And I realised in that moment that he meant it. Prince Grella was as much a puppet in the schemes of others as I, if not more so. At least I had a measure of choice in my actions whereas he had none. Grella was bound by a pact older than time. Eternal law, which stretched right back to our vampire ancestry, may have been unwritten, but it was understood by all, and until his mother died, Grella would forever be bound by it. He was too honourable a son, too decent a man for his own good.

"Do you wish to continue searching for others?" Aurora asked.

"It would do no good if we found them. As far as I understand it, dead is dead where humans are concerned."

"If only it was with us," Grella replied somewhat cryptically, then turned away to look into the snow-filled north.

"We should go then," Aurora insisted. "I am as ready as you to deal with this Chantelle."

"I'm glad to hear that, dear girl. I will need all the help I can get to deal with her. What say you, Grella?" I enquired, but he had sprinted off some distance away.

By the time Aurora and I reached his side, he had turned over a body that had lain prostrate in the snow, only visible in part from above. The figure was female and tanned.

Grella said nothing just cocked his head one way then the other bepuzzled.

"One of the Hispanics," Aurora suggested.

"It appears the Marquis' genetic dabbling has left Raphael's people susceptible to the cold. Let us hope my brother-in-law is also so stricken."

"I… I do not understand what has happened here?" Grella sounded bemused to the point of delirium. He pulled the body free of the snow, cradled the once beautiful woman in his arms. His albino hand shook as he examined the teeth that poked from behind blue, once luscious lips. The fangs that sneered back at him provided all the confirmation he needed.

"The Marquis de Rhineland seeks to make us human. He seeks to make our kind able to withstand the sun," I said.

"Why, would he do such a thing?"

"For the same reasons I wished: an unqualified desire to stand in its light just once before I died."

Grella shook his head at that and mumbled.

"What, what is it, brother?" Aurora asked stepping to his side.

"I did not believe it. For all my aeons of life, I have thought mother exaggerated about the sun. I thought she tried to scare us into remaining safe, secluded."

"On this one, I can assure you, she did not," I interjected.

"Do they really not know, Jean?" he asked. "Does the sun truly frighten them so?"

"More than it is physically possible to believe."

"Then, when you stood before it in the Zeppelin, you feared death?"

"I did, but I would trust Linka with my life."

"Then you are a greater man than I imagined," he said, kneeling before me and inclining his regal head.

"You should not bow to a foolhardy coward such as I, Prince Grella."

"You are never that," he replied.

Just as he took his sister's aid in standing, the world trembled. The snow shook so much that it lifted from the floor to clash with its falling brethren in cascades of solid white.

Aurora looked most unhappy about the whole situation and offered her free hand to me, which I took. We stood there, a triumvirate of contrasting white and black-clad immortals, as the world heaved around us. There was nowhere to run. Rock surged into the air to form hills, then mountains, then plateaus, whilst we looked on in awe. The very ground beneath our feet lifted as the three of us held firm together rising like birds must once have into the sky. So high were we thrust that snow, then cloud, then gloom fell from us like a dropped cloak and we stood atop the world with nothing to see but a clear, ruby sky. I marvelled at it. I had waited so long for the like that even amongst the apocalypse I admired it.

We stood there, all eyes to the sun, Grella having donned his ruby goggles, unwilling to believe the tremors to have ended until every last rock and stone lay impassive on the new plateau. It was I who broke the silence.

"Damn whoever's doing this."

"Doing what?" asked Grella.

"This," I said, spreading my arms to encapsulate the whole planet.

"Why do you say that?"

"Because it's the truth," I replied, surprised by his demeanour.

"You believe that *this* is being controlled."

"Of course."

"By who?" Grella enquired, whilst his sister looked on.

"By the Hierarchy, the powers that be."

"I can assure you, Jean, this is not the Hierarchy's doing."

"Then, who?" It was my turn to be surprised.

"It is the planet just as you said. We near the end of all."

"But I was told the Hierarchy manipulated the earth, moved mountains, altered the course of rivers and in turn the oceans. We inherited humanity's earth moving machines for just such purposes."

"No, my friend, that is untrue. It never has been," he added, with a look of such pity, his sincerity was in no doubt. "Who led you to believe such untruths?" he asked.

"Does it matter?"

"I believe so."

Grella spoke with quiet authority. And despite my rising anger, I knew he did not seek to bait, but aid me. However, I still found it hard to give a straight answer.

"It is a well-known fact," I blustered.

"According to whom?"

"To everyone."

"Not to me, nor my sister."

"That is because you are removed from society."

"Perhaps so, all the more reason to explain who has proliferated such lies."

"Just people." I watched as Aurora turned away to stare into the bleak distance. She could not bear to look.

"Due to whom, Jean?" Grella pressed, placing an albino hand upon my shoulder.

I looked to the sun, the newly formed mountains, the rock-strewn desolation, trying desperately to disperse the tears that welled in my eyes. "My parents," I whispered. "It was my parents."

Chapter 23

Dark

There are times in a man's life when he must face hard truths. He must look into the mirror, past the veneer, past the disdain, and judge himself: what he is, where he is, who he is, and how he got there. That time was upon me. I had come to many difficult realisations over those past short weeks; they had changed me. I had accepted Alba's death, although deeply regretted it. My having left Linka was the lesser of several unthinkable scenarios, a necessary evil. The Sunyins and the fact that humans, of a form, existed, had been acknowledged even if it still seemed fantastical. But coming to terms with my parents' murder, with so many manipulated falsities, and worse, was beyond my capabilities. Everything I was and everything I knew had formed from their teachings. It beggared the question: had my whole life been one of untruths? I needed answers for I had none.

* * *

My head whirled with a million new thoughts. I'd have put it down to the altitude once, the set of the stars, palmed it off as madness, but lies were lies and I could no longer live with them.

Aurora stood stock-still, her cloak flapping in the breeze like an angel hovering above the earth. She looked contemplative, a troubled goddess looking down from atop Mount Olympus. The ruby sun lighted her features in blooded hues she did not warrant, nor suit. But, like the oceanic tides sweeping in from unknown origins, her features softened, and she spoke. "Do you know what I think?"

"What is that, sister?" Grella answered.

"I think we all know less than we thought, but more than we did."

"Very succinct," he replied, the sun dripping in his goggles.

"We all have questions we want answered, not just Jean. So I suggest we take advantage of the storm's cessation and make haste north."

"I could not agree more," Grella nodded.

"Has the storm ceased?" I managed, finding my voice.

"It has. Look down, Jean, all becomes clear."

Despite feeling like nothing was any clearer, I did as Aurora requested.

The clouds had dissipated, the storm departed, the still distant path to Hvit marked by a line of snow and ice.

"You see?" her voice tinkled across the heavens.

"I do."

"Then, you agree."

"Oh, indeed I do, dear girl. And I can assure you, I would have it no other way. Lead on."

* * *

We sprung across the newly formed plateau as though on springs, or at least my companions did, jumping over rocks, leaping over fissures, dicing with death as though it a friend. Aurora led the way, something I found surprising, but her brother appeared not to care. He followed behind the shooting star that was his sister throwing occasional cursory glances my way.

I trailed the two through ruby tinged morning, the sun never seeming to attain its zenith, an untouched glass of half full blood. That weakest of celestial objects highlighted my deficiencies favouring the gleaming Nordics rather than the dark shadow that was me, an embarrassing stain on the pure white landscape. Where I found the way a necessary evil, a step in achieving my desired goal, they thrived in it. Where long shadows cast in ruby light sought to trip and hinder me, they cut through them in a blaze of diamond light. Where I ran, leapt, climbed, head down and at the limits of concentration, they threw their own back and dared the world to constrain them. I was so much less than them, so small a person.

After a time of self-degradation, I was the first to break the silence of our passing.

"Grella!" I called to the blur that sped before me. The light coalesced back to the form of he who was heir to the Nordic throne. He dropped into a loping run beside me.

"You seem troubled," he said.

"I am troubled."

"Your parents?"

"You see much, Prince Grella."

"It is not hard to see," he said, as he leapt over a rock of some twenty feet landing back at my side with graceful ease. "You wish to know who has used them, but I cannot answer that."

"Cannot, or will not?"

A flicker of something akin to anger crossed his face, but quickly subsided.

"I cannot. I am as much a pawn in this as you. My people, or rather, my mother's, left Europa long ago to avoid such petty machinations. We sought only to live in peace, to see out our time in quiet solitude. I believe to an extent, we did."

"Did?"

"Do you pick up on every misplaced word?" Grella rumbled.

"I do now."

"And that would be my answer to you, Jean. The present and the past have become defined by the actions of the current few."

"But not you?"

"No."

"Yet, you seem as troubled as I if not more so?"

"I will feel happier once home."

"And your brothers?"

"They can look after themselves."

"And you can look after them."

"Yes, if required, but I feel my attention has been drawn from where it should have focused."

"Sorry."

"Why?"

"That's due to me."

"Indirectly. You are not to blame, Jean."

"Can I remind you of that if it turns out I am?"

"You may."

Grella laughed then, his voice rumbling across the plateau, a manmade thunder.

Aurora, hearing her brother's outburst glanced back to us. Her eyes gleamed bright like a summer sky should've, her smile so pure it would have settled almost any soul. It did nothing for mine. Although, when she turned away, the loss I felt suggested it had.

We ran for hours, Aurora always ahead, Grella running beside me or just between us in silence, each of us lost to our musings. Until, that was, Aurora came to a sudden and violent skidded stop at the rim of the plateau.

"Damn it!" she cursed.

"I thought I was the one who cursed, not you," I said.

"I am sorry, Jean."

"For swearing! You needn't be."

"Not for that, for that."

Aurora pointed out over the almost perfectly flat landscape before us. There was nothing, the world a barren, monotonous vista.

"For what?" I queried.

"Exactly," she huffed.

"I believe what my sister is trying to expound is that she expected to see those we pursue."

"Exactly," she huffed again.

"I had almost forgotten them," I admitted. "I have been lost within myself."

"I saw," she replied and forced a smile. "Sometimes we find a peace, a freedom in unimpeded movement, we would otherwise not. Then again, there are other times when it does not help at all. I suspect this is one of those other times."

"I suspect you are right," I agreed, squinting into the distance. "Is it me?" I asked frowning. "Or has the sun not moved?"

"It does, but so minutely as to go unnoticed. That is how we know we close on Hvit. The sun will only move in accordance to our own direction," Grella confirmed. "Do you see far into the horizon, there is a balance between dark and light?"

"I think so," I said, straining to see where the prince indicated.

"That is our destination. I pray we shall find signs of Chantelle along the way. I fear that if we do not, she will have attained Hvit before us."

"But you said Hvit could only be found by the Nordics?"

"It could, or can, but I gather from our discussions those we follow are rather more resourceful than most."

"When you put it like that," I replied.

"I do."

"The ice seems to go on forever." Aurora's exhalation was more a deflation than breath, and I remembered it was not only me on their first Arctic journey.

"It is magnificent is it not, dear sister? Even covered by the snow as the Arctic is there is something primordial about it. The world as it was before mankind and how it will be ever after."

"Yes," was all she mustered.

"So much ice," said I.

"It was not always this way. The lessening power of the sun, that which has granted our freedom, has also been responsible for the ice fields doubling in comparison to what they once were. In other parts, it has swallowed both ocean and land. Mountains can be seen to pierce the ice in places, as do the various seas at times, but nothing can match the power of what our ancestors once called the cold."

I had to agree. The plain of ice, smothered in a layer of soft snow, stretching as it did into forever and tinged by the ruby glow of the sun, was magical in its way. I could not see it, but knew where the ocean lapped between day and night, Linka awaited. How I missed her. How I yearned for her.

We paused there and partook of the final three blood bags. Aurora offered them around with a sense of decorum I found unnecessary. Grella took his with reluctance turning his back on us as though ashamed at drinking the false sustenance. I, however, was famished and gorged myself. Aurora seemed likewise in need of refreshment, yet still drank without spilling a drop upon her already ruby lips. I would even have said if it was possible for an albino to colour, she did. By the time she'd finished and collected the empty bags, she looked decidedly more her normal self.

"Throw those over the edge, sister," Grella demanded.

"Why?" I asked.

Grella regarded me with a hint of anger unused to being questioned, but on seeing my expression, his stern features softened. "They mark our passing."

"You are concerned," I said.

A simple nod was all I received in return.

"Here, you'll look more refined with your cloak back in place."

Aurora shook my less than pristine accoutrement and tied the black material around my neck and shoulders.

"Thank you," I replied.

"Wouldn't want anyone getting the impression you were a rogue."

"Like who?" I laughed.

"Anyone at all. First impressions count, you know."

"And yours would be, Princess?"

"That you were a rogue regardless of apparel."

"Hm, I'm glad we've cleared that up."

The piercing depth of a wolf's howl cut short any further frivolity. The thing came from behind us, which accounted for Grella's sudden about face, dropping to one knee and placing a hand to the ground.

"Can you sense them?" Aurora asked.

A raised hand was his response as Grella cocked his head one way then the other. He tasted the air like a true hunter.

Two more howls of lupine origin choked the atmosphere. Grella didn't need to say anything as Aurora and I exchanged glances. The wolves were closer than before, though I knew not how. Grella had obviously been aware of them for some time.

The pace we'd travelled at had been akin to flying. I wouldn't have believed any beings of earthly origin able to have sustained the same, but they had.

"We should go," Grella spoke in calm authority, as he strode past us and stepped off the edge of the cliff. I watched his cloak vanish beneath us like the setting moon. He hadn't even looked.

Aurora approached the edge with more care than her brother, but skipped off into nowhere after a smile my way, a sure sign it was safe to follow.

Descending from such magnitude was easier than I'd imagined. The sudden upsurge in the landscape had created ledge after ledge of makeshift steps, and we used them to the full. Leaps of thirty feet at a time were as nothing to us, Grella leaping double that, but to each their own. I had experienced enough sudden plummets in my recent past to be warier than the others. When all was said and done, I no longer made such descents for myself. The race was afoot from both before and behind and I for one had no intention of becoming hunted when born a hunter.

When Aurora and I landed as one by the side of her albino brother, he was already touching the ice with a delicacy I would have said beyond him.

"This ice is weak," he stated.

"How can you tell?" Aurora asked.

"I can hear them."

. "Oh."

"Oh, what?" I asked, quite at a loss as to what the two referred.

"Look closer, Jean." Grella indicated to where he'd cleared the snow from underfoot.

"Water. I really don't care for water," I said, sucking in my cheeks.

"Yes, water," he agreed. "We are at the tip of where the sea ice radiates to. I can assure you, if we can see the water here, then there will be places where the ice is so thin there will be breaks in it that reach to the liquid ocean beneath."

"Then, we should tread with care," I suggested.

"You do not fully appreciate what I seek to imply."

"If you are concerned for my flailing self's safety, I would not be. With Aurora and your good self as my guides, I can be assured of being rescued should I go through. Not that I would wish to," I added.

"He does not refer to the water, Jean."

Aurora's tone was grim, her ashen face more so.

"Then, what?" I asked puzzled by the two Nordic royals' seriousness. What troubled two beings with enough raw power at their disposal to have brought down armies? What made them frown so?

"Orca," the two said as one.

Chapter 24

Obsidian

I had witnessed first-hand the slaughter of both the orcas and Nordic species; they were equally matched. When the battle that rages is for your life these things have a way of evening themselves out. Experience had taught me as much. A mother defending her child is more tenacious an opponent than any battle-hardened war veteran, a fact I observed many times over during my days of reckless rampaging. The children may have been older than me, their parents immensely, but that instinct was there. I had done many bad things in the name of my parents, none more so than those. And there it was, no matter what situation I found myself in, my thoughts always returned to life before my parents' death. The realisation that others had manipulated them as much as I lessened the hurt not one jot, in fact, they made my misdeeds doubly terrible. I had performed like an organ grinder's monkey, skipped and played to some unseen master's tune. One day they would step into the light and I would be there waiting. That, I vowed.

Those thoughts grated as I followed the Nordics across the ice plain. In truth, it was far from the barren sheet of white it had appeared from our eagle's eyrie. The landscape was nowhere near level. The sea ice undulated like the liquid surface it covered, criss-crossed with a lattice of still flowing waters. Fortunately, we had encountered none of any great significance and nothing beyond a single bound, but Grella treated each break in the ice with a respect I found bewildering. He would approach with caution looking both up and down the channels before making his leap. Aurora would follow likewise circumspect. Eager to be moving at a faster gait, I grew more and more frustrated at the laborious nature of our progress. I would hurl myself over the breaks, even leaping beyond my companions, at times, much to their chagrin, and then have an anxious wait for them to catch up.

"You should be careful, Jean," Aurora reprimanded.

"Why?" I sounded like a spoiled child but was getting quite past myself.

"Beasts lurk below the ice. The water channels allow them a view; a view allows them a potential meal: we are that meal."

"So you have said, but I have seen no evidence of it."

"The fact the water is revealed, the channels flowing unimpaired is evidence enough."

"I don't understand?"

"Only those who spend their lives on the ice, or under it, ever could," Aurora said stony-faced.

"But every moment we waste allows Chantelle to pull further from us and the wolves at our backs to draw closer."

"I have no concerns over land wolves, it is the sea variety we must be wary of," Grella interjected. "It is they that keep the water flowing, they that prevent the ice from freezing over."

I said nothing, but my look must have given me away.

"You should listen to what my brother says, Jean. It is for all our sakes he checks the way."

"If you say so."

"I do," Grella said stern and determined, his face carved from marble. "I can assure you, I wish to reach our prey before they reach Hvit, but better to reach it alive than to not reach it all."

"Well, I suppose so. You seem to know what you're on about."

"You can be a most infuriating man!" Aurora said in exasperated fashion.

"I'd normally be glad of that, but not today."

"Sometimes, I think Walter was right in what he told me of you."

"Oh, and just what might that have been?" I rounded on her.

"It does not matter," Aurora retaliated.

"It does to me."

"You don't need to know."

"Every time you say that it makes me want to know even more."

"Really?"

"Yes, really."

"In that case, it was that you are and always have been quite a trial, or words to that effect."

"How the hell would he know," I replied, more than a touch perturbed.

"I don't know, but he's right. Why can't you accept you have friends who wish to help you, and in so doing must trust them as they trust you?"

"I've never had any friends," I said.

"No need to pout about it, neither have I," Aurora replied.

"Must you two make so much noise," Grella chastised.

"We don't have to," Aurora responded.

"No, but we may want to," I said stamping my foot on the ground.

Only when the ice cracked like the splitting of heaven did I realise what I'd done. A hairline fracture opened at my feet, which became a fissure and I fell through it into the ruby-tinged waters below. My head was under the surface before I even knew what had happened, my windmilling arms flailing about me as water surged into my mouth.

For a few moments, I felt the fear which always happened upon me where water was concerned. And it was in those few seconds I realised my own flapping vibrations were not the only ones to avail my ears. There was the creaking and cracking of the ice, the surging of the ocean, but also a strange wailing as of dark, desperate angels. I'd heard the sounds before, but in my panic couldn't place them.

I had no time to dwell on the fact, as two strong hands gripped my wrists and yanked me clear of the water, clear of the ice, and right over he who'd saved me. My landing was undignified, but a welcome relief from the sea.

"I told you to be careful!" Grella reprimanded, glaring at me with the ferocity of his full majesty.

My world turned to one of treacle then, a sluggish passage of time. Grella's cloak flapped, paused in mid-air, his trailing, alabaster locks hung in an Arctic updraft as the liquid surface lifted behind him and rose into the air, bulged with some unseen force. I tried to call out as the gloss black facade of nature's servant of death shot from the water and seized him. My words, like the moment, stalled, the look on the prince's face one of utter disbelief. Grella vanished below the churning waters writhing in the grip of the leviathan's jaws. The last flick of an obsidian fluke was all that marked his passing.

I sat in the snow unmoving, shocked, unable to comprehend the visual stimuli I'd witnessed. Aurora was not so incapacitated. She closed the ten yards between her and the point of Grella's abduction in a blur of pale motion and dove into the water without a second thought. An instant later, and there was nothing to mark either of the Nordics' passing other than their memory.

"No!" I screamed into the frigid air, but the words came far too late. I shot to my feet and slid over to the water expecting to see a flash of porcelain skin, a glimmer of reflective black hide, something to prove my two companions survived. There was neither in those cruel depths. I set about sweeping at the ice like a housemaid possessed clearing trail after trail of snow down to the glasslike surface, spreading out from a central hub like the spokes of a wheel. I created a veritable spider's web of trails, but no matter where I looked, it revealed nothing.

Even then, I still hoped. I knew the Nordics could, and did, spend inordinate amounts of time under the water, so sought to convince myself they would return. When they didn't, I took to running up and down the length of the original fissure, which had joined other channels in the ice. It was all in vain. They were gone, and I was alone.

* * *

Our sun mocked me, reluctant as it was to confirm the passage of time. The orb hung in ruby elegance too weak to light beneath the ice, too impassive to offer dipped condolences.

The channel of sea water had iced over despite my repeated attempts to chip away at it. If one hadn't known better, they'd have thought nothing untoward had ever occurred. But I knew, and my impotence haunted me.

I patrolled the area for a short time longer before deciding I had no other option but to continue. My destiny lay North, or so the Sunyin monk had insisted. I owed it to him to at least make the effort. Like a pea in an otherwise empty pod, I stood deserted, separated by many leagues from he and those of his order who Chantelle and her motley assembly had abducted. I would return to Linka as both a coward and a failure, and pray those who taunted me with their infernal letters took pity on the shadow who'd once been feared by all.

If I needed any convincing of my direction, the howling of a wolf confirmed it. The creature seemed no nearer, a constant distance from wherever I stood, but reminder enough to move. Who drove it on, if anyone, was still a mystery, but a mystery I no longer cared for. As if that and all else that had happened wasn't bad enough, it started to snow, and how.

There was nothing but snow tinged with the sun's blood glow, an almost solid curtain of partial death. Head down, I focused on my booted feet and paced my way in carefully placed footsteps over the Arctic snowscape. Every time I came upon one of the sea channels that sliced the ice in twain, I paused, waited and hoped, but never once did the Nordics reveal themselves. A single bound carried me over the obstacles, yet my conscience yearned to be swallowed by them and my misery ended.

Only the promise of being reunited with Linka kept me going through that hellish weather. At least, that's what I told myself. In actuality, my gut burned with such murderous intent, such desire to vent my frustrations on Chantelle and her cronies that I thought I should incinerate the storm. It soon ebbed, though. There was something about the colour of that not-quite-night, not-quite-day, that quashed such devil's thoughts. The loneliness, a thing I thought I should never be troubled by, accentuated the isolation that walking through that non-world brought on. After a time, I could bear it no longer, as the sleepless days told on me, and I fell to the ground and into the slumber an Eternal so desperately craves. The snow was my pillow, my blanket, my balm, and I accepted the bliss of its release with only eternity on my mind.

* * *

How long I'd slept was impossible to judge. Without sun or moon to guide me, my instincts were rendered useless. I might have lain there an hour, a year, or a lifetime. The pile of snow that fell from my rising body suggested the latter.

It appeared my instincts were less affected than I'd first supposed. The howling of a wolf assailed my ears, and I knew what had roused me. A moment or two of clearing the snow from my right ear and a shake of my clothing, which regathered a layer of the still falling white stuff in an instant, and I was back to full working order. A second howl confirmed all I already supposed; the wolf was close.

I was unsure if the beast was a lone hunter tracking down one of the few meals available in a world close to death, or if one of a pack like those which had attacked Aurora. Neither scenario appealed. I didn't wish to harm the creature, but knowing if the wolf or wolves were being driven by some unknown master would have changed the whole complexion of the game.

The only way was forwards, which I judged from presuming the howling still to my rear. I trudged away in delicate fashion each individual foot placed with a care usually reserved for my first advances on the female form. But, just as they would invariably give way to reckless abandon, so did my passage. Ever bored, I soon stomped my way through the ever-thickening surface with such gay abandon as to be misplaced. I could no longer see the waterways, covered as they were by layers of snow, so saw little point in trying to avoid them. If I was to fall, then I might as well do it at pace, as not.

However, the further I pressed the less likely the event seemed. My northwards bearing took me deeper into the heart of the Pole and the security of thicker ice. If that assumption was correct, then I needn't have worried about an orca attack, but more so of those in my wake.

In typical fashion, I soon couldn't have cared less about the attentions of my hunter and although there was no let up in the weather, nor my general malaise, I started to whistle. I wasn't sure why, perhaps nerves had got the better of me, or I sought the intentional distraction of my stalker, either way, the response was almost immediate: a howl of pathetic pain met my sonics head on. Recklessly blasé, I carried on whistling my way through the snowstorm as much as frozen lips allowed.

The serenade between it and I continued for a distance most would have found impossible, but I found frustrating. I made my mind up that when I did eventually find Hvit, I would march down that infernal sub-aquatic city's staircase, snatch Linka from the claws of whoever held her and leave the place with a damning curse. The whole thing played out in my besieged mind like clockwork until I felt so certain I'd perfected it, I could have completed the whole scenario in record time. I was so sure of myself, I became indifferent to being preyed upon and was more than a little shocked when I realised the howling almost upon me. The snow precluded any searching for cover, not that I supposed there was any, so I turned to face my foe. A quick toss of cloak over shoulder to free my arms, an old fighting trick, and a shuffle of both feet to firm their stance and I was ready.

That was how I waited, unmoving, yet restless, as the snow fell all around. I gave an occasional extra whistle just to make sure the wolf did not lose itself when so close to its prey and eyed the storm. It didn't take long, as something emerged from the incessant snowflakes coalescing into a dark, ominous form. One last howl, and I was upon it. I leapt forward striking at the highest part of the darkness with my right fist, but missed. My left followed swiftly, and I grasped for the beast's throat with my next lunge. I got a certain sick satisfaction from my talons closing about the creature's windpipe, its furless throat?

The figure I pulled toward me through that most desperate weather was not that of the lupine kind, but the human kind. The man hung like a rag doll from my vice-like grip offering weak retaliation at best. I drew his eyes to my eyes just to be certain, but there was no mistaking the quaking form of my blond-haired antagonist and sometime friend, sometime enemy, Sir Walter Merryweather.

"Hello, Jean," he gasped.

Chapter 25

Beetroot

"Evening, Jean, or is it morning, I'm really very lost with it all," said Merryweather rubbing at his throat.

"Was that you making all that racket?" I demanded, ignoring his ramblings.

"Of course!"

"What in God's name were you howling for?" I growled, unable to contain my fury.

"I thought that was our secret signal."

"What the hell are you talking about, we don't have a secret signal."

"That's what makes it a secret. Don't you know anything about these things?" he said, shaking his head.

"You are the most infuriating man."

"Look who's talking!" Merryweather interrupted before my rant had begun. "Every time I thought I was about to catch you up, you sped off again. I thought I'd never reach you. If I didn't know better, I'd say you were trying to avoid me."

Walter turned his back on me as he sat there in the accumulating snow.

I had the most intense desire to boot him over the horizon but resisted the temptation. Instead, I stood and fumed in silence.

"Ah, cat got your tongue, has it? Seen the error of your ways?"

"You should be mindful, Merryweather, I am becoming less and less glad of your presence."

"Fine thing, that is. Have you any idea what kind of ordeal I've been through? Hey, have you?"

"No, and I don't want to," I huffed.

"Well, too late, sunshine, I'm telling."

"Do you have to?"

"They tortured me, that's what they did."

"You don't look tortured," I replied giving the dandy the once over.

"Oh, not physically, but the boredom was a terrible ordeal. Truly terrible," he said, putting a pale palm to his head for added effect.

"Really."

"Oh, yes, far worse than being hit."

"I may put that theory to the test if you don't shut up."

"Ha!"

"Who's joking?"

"I don't see why you're in such a grump, I'm the one that's had the hardship."

"What hardship!" I roared rounding on the idiot.

Merryweather cowered in the snow before realising I wasn't quite at the point where I'd rip his head from his velvet-clad shoulders. He offered his hand for assistance, which I snubbed, to his blinked disapproval and tutted disgust.

The pathetic nature of his efforts to stand coupled with his repeated attempts at brushing the snow from his backside only drove me to further annoyance. I tapped the snow in frustration and gritted my teeth. If it bothered him, it did not show.

"Jean, I've been having a think."

"What, in between sitting and standing?"

"Yes, if you must know, and I've decided we need to work on our communicatory skills. I suggest a howling contest in which we choose an auditory tone to be our secret signal. It's not that I'm worried about me, of course."

"Of course," I grumbled before he could finish.

"It's just that with all this snow, and your fear of water, I think it would be best if I stuck close to you. Just in case you need rescuing," he added, with a wink.

My hands were around his throat and lifting him clear of the snow before he had time to un-blink.

"What...what did I say?" he coughed, as I tightened my grip.

"Did you see what happened to the others?" I asked, eyes narrowing to a focused glare.

"What?"

"Did you see me go through the ice?"

"No."

"The prince that saved me getting taken by an orca?"

"No."

"Aurora jumping in after him and not resurfacing?"

"You what!" he gasped.

I released him back onto his posterior to the sound of crunching snow. Even Merryweather was not that good a liar. He seemed mortified by my revelation and sat there combing gloved hands through his mop of unruly hair in bewilderment.

"Dare I ask?" he eventually managed.

"It would be...unwise," I replied.

"Oh, Jean, you've killed them, haven't you. I didn't think even you could pull that off. Aurora was such a charming girl, a real delight. Once she and I got to speaking on the way to Vienna, I mean New Washington, old habits, I thought I'd made a friend for life. And as for Prince Grella, well, as the Nordics go, he was a real gent."

"Merryweather?" I said quizzically catching him mid-babble.

"What?" he said startled at my interruption.

"How did you know I was with Prince Grella?"

"You said."

"No, I didn't," I corrected. "I just said the prince."

"Well, who else could you have meant?"

"Any number of people. The last person one would've assumed should be a Nordic."

"Not when you've seen his brothers wandering around like the proverbial lost sheep. I like that expression by the way even though I don't remember sheep. I think I shall use it more often."

He wandered off then in deep contemplation.

I did not let him get more than a few yards before I had my arm wrapped around his shoulders. "Walter," I said squeezing him like a lemon.

"Yes, Jean."

"How did you know they were Nordics?"

"Er, they were white."

"Albino," I corrected.

"White, albino, deader than dead, it's all the same."

I thought that a strange response, but let it slip, instead, letting my arm do the talking, as I tightened my grip on Merryweather's shoulders to the cracking of his bones. "I'd like to ask you one more thing, Walter," I purred in my best impression of an old-world languid lion.

"Fire away, old boy," he joked.

"Was Ragnar very annoyed at losing me to his brother."

"Oh, he was perfectly seething. Oops!"

"Oops, indeed, dear Walter. Oops, indeed."

I made the mental calculation to not hurt Walter too badly as he seemed to know so much that I didn't. I had every intention, however, of finding out just how much. The question was how to get him to reveal it without having the joy of accidentally murdering him.

I weighed up the pros and cons of the matter whilst sitting on the fop with his face pushed into the snow. Occasionally, I would ruffle his precious hair and prod him in as antagonistic manner as I could. By the time I got off him and turned him over he was red as a beetroot, or as red as an Eternal's pale skin would allow, and had tears streaming down his face.

"Sorry about that, Walter, I was just deciding how best to extract the information I require. I've now decided."

"Are…are you going to hurt me?"

The poor fellow looked so pathetic that even if I had I might possibly not have.

"No."

"No!" He sounded shocked.

"No, I am going to ask you nicely."

"Me!"

"You're the only one here."

"Oh."

"Only an oh?"

"I'm just surprised, that's all." Merryweather wiped at his eyes, brushed the gathered snow from his velvet garments, and smiled. "Thank you," he said.

And, as if in response to our joint turnarounds in character the snow stopped, the clouds peeled back and a ruby glow broke across every surface. The Earth seemed dipped in a glass of claret and I basked in its momentary calm, whilst my insides churned in violent disapproval at my chosen path. I mulled over where to start with Walter's questioning and decided why not at the beginning. So I did, in as surreptitious manner as I could.

"Merryweather, my friend, I believe we have got off on the wrong foot too many times." For once, Walter did not interrupt or offer quick wit, but instead walked quietly beside me as we made our way north over the crisp, new-fallen snow. "I think I've been quick to judge you."

Walter pulled a serious face and said, "Yes, you have."

"Well, here's your chance to set me straight. It took a great deal of resilience on your behalf to escape Chantelle's clutches, as you did, and it's earned you some leeway. By the way, how did she look?"

"Truly terrible," he replied pulling a face.

"How did you manage it?"

"I waited until the sun was up, then wriggled and jiggled my way out of there."

"Where?"

"The machine they drove."

"I thought you were in the back of a cart."

"I was."

"You just admitted you weren't," I said, already losing my temper.

"I was in the cart that they *towed*." He put particular emphasis on the towed. "But, as you should have guessed, they discovered me when I tried to communicate with you. Painfully so," he added.

"Sorry, Walter, forgive me."

"I will this once."

He gave a dramatic arm waving bow at that.

"Do go on."

"Well, they didn't believe my story at first."

"What story?" I interjected.

"Give me a chance, I'm getting there."

"Sorry."

"You should be. Anyway, I showed them the scars on my chest and stomach, told them they were because of you, and how I would do anything to get my revenge. Chantelle believed me from the start. She really hates you, you know," he added with undisguised glee.

"Hmm."

"Anyway, as I was saying, she believed me, but the Marquis most certainly didn't. He asked me all sorts of questions: how I'd found him; how I'd really got the scars; what I knew of the Hierarchy's demise, which I only guessed at, and any manner of other boring trivia. I don't like him, Jean, never have. I'd be rather glad if you disposed of him."

"I intend to," I replied.

"Good, good," he said nodding his head. "I think you and I are finally singing from the same song sheet."

"I'm sure we are, Walter," I said giving him an encouraging pat on the back.

"Yes, I agree. Well, to continue, he wasn't having any of it and communicated his thoughts to the others including Raphael, who I was very surprised to see. The rumour was you'd killed him in that fight you'd had?"

"No, but I won't make the same mistake again."

"I'm sure you won't. By the way, he and his countrymen, and country-whores, mustn't forget the ladies, looked a darker shade of pale than I should have expected."

"They are tanned," I replied.

"Tanned. That's impossible, isn't it?"

"It appears the Marquis has been dabbling in genetics."

Walter, wide-eyed and gawping, just shook his head at that.

"He's trying to make them human," I said, rather more bluntly.

"Why?"

"So they can go out in the light."

"Ha! Ha! Ha!" he screeched. "If only they knew, eh? I was itching to tell them, you know."

"You didn't though, did you, Walter?"

"Do you think I'd be here if I had?"

"Good point."

"So, the Marquis wants us Eternals to be human again," mused Merryweather. "Must have had enough of this world." He scratched at his head. "He's a stupid bugger, always was. I expect that's why your parents hated him so."

"Hang on, go back a minute. What do you mean, be human again?"

"Well, we were once," he said very matter-of-factly.

"And how did you know my parents hated the Marquis?"

"It was common knowledge."

"How common?"

"As in everyone."

"Well, I didn't know," I said, honestly.

"You are still so very young, though, a mere seedling compared to the rest of us."

"Hm, well, I'm catching up fast."

"Do you know what, Jean?" Merryweather said coming to a sudden stop.

"What?"

"I feel like I'm tutoring you, and as such, should be getting paid for it."

"You'd think that," I snarled.

"There, there, only joking."

Merryweather held his hands out placatingly.

"Sorry," I said, sensing my time to strike. "Did you know my parents well?"

"Oh, only in passing. They were really quite moody most of the time...I mean charming," he quickly corrected.

"It's okay, Walter, I realise they had their moments."

"Don't we all," he agreed. "But, like I said, I really didn't know them that well. I knew what they wanted, of course."

"What was that?" I asked.

"To rule."

"What?"

"To rule, Jean. Didn't you know?"

Merryweather stood there, his slim frame stiff as a rod, his expression one of genuine bewilderment. If an orca had cracked through the ice and snatched him away, he couldn't have looked more surprised.

"No, no I didn't," I said.

"I just presumed, what with you committing all those heinous acts on their behalf."

"Believe me, Walter, I did not know."

"It didn't go down well with the rest of the Hierarchy. Personally, though, I couldn't have cared less. One overlord's as bad as the next. Unless they're a desiccated and completely unstable half-zombie princess, that is."

"Queen," I replied somewhat in a daze.

"Queen?"

"She's a queen now she's wed her since-deceased husband."

"Have you killed someone else?" he said, shaking his head.

"Don't worry, there's barely anyone left to kill now."

"True, true," he replied looking overly serious.

"Why did you say, other Hierarchy?"

"How do you mean, dear boy?"

"My parents were scientists, Lords only, not members of the Hierarchy."

"What are you talking about?" Merryweather appeared confused.

"What I say, they were not members of the Hierarchy."

"They most certainly were; they just didn't like it. Old blood, those two, very old blood indeed," he said, with a solemn nod of the head.

I sat down with a crunch. Merryweather's revelations were too much to take in all at once. My parents had lived as virtual recluses for so long I had just thought them private, dedicated to their work. To be told that they were as aloof as those I hated was yet another kick in the teeth. But it made more sense of their murder.

"Have I shocked you, Jean?" Merryweather asked, disrupting my thoughts.

"Yes," my blunt response.

"I didn't mean to."

"It's all right, Walter, really it is. I don't hold it against you. It's all a bit much to comprehend, that's all."

Much to my surprise, Merryweather brushed away some imaginary crumbs from the snow, grimaced, and then sat down beside me.

"Urgh, I hate the wet."

"I thought it was just me."

We looked at each other and burst into hysterical laughter. I quite forgot what I was moping about as we rolled about in the snow. Merryweather beat the ground until tears ran from his eyes and the two of us could laugh no more. We then laid back in the snow like two childish brothers and stared up at the ruby sky.

"Really is beautiful," Walter said.

"Sort of," I whispered back.

"All those years wasted. Such a very long time," he breezed. "If only I'd known this goddamn sun couldn't harm me." Merryweather let out such a sigh as if the weight of the world was balanced on his shoulders. "I'd have done things so very different, Jean, I really would."

"Done what different, Walter?"

"Just things," he said, after a long pause.

"If it's any consolation, I would have too."

"A little," he replied. "What would you have changed?"

"I'd have had a bloody good sit down with my damn parents, that's for sure."

"Anything else?"

"Just Alba, I think. I would have treated her better than I did."

"She loved you, you know," Merryweather said as if speaking to a ghost.

"I wronged that poor girl, and I felt, no feel, terrible about it. I even belittled her attempts to tell me she'd seen the sun."

"I'm sorry, old boy," Merryweather said after a few moments. He spoke with a degree of sincerity that I'd never heard from him. He then reached down, took a handful of snow and crumpled it over his face. "It would be nice to feel it melt, don't you think?"

"Yes."

"I think so, too."

"I've done a lot of bad things, Walter," I confessed, feeling brutal honesty the only ploy left.

"Some of them to me," he replied, but not with intent to provoke.

"More so to the women in my life: my mother, misunderstood; Alba, neglected; Linka, deserted. I have not made the best of things."

"Love will do that to a man," Walter said in hushed tones. "The things we do for love."

"Sorry, Walter," I said, having barely heard him, but sure it was the same words he'd uttered when I'd been on the brink of killing him in the forest.

"All for love," he replied, in the same quiet tones. Then, in a most un-Merryweather-like fashion, he rolled onto his stomach, pushed himself up onto his feet and made a slow amble away in our original direction.

I got to my own feet, realising our conversation had come to an abrupt end, and watched a man who looked every bit as miserable as I sniffle his way into some unknown future.

I had nothing else to say, so straightened out my clothing and set off in pursuit.

Chapter 26

Garnet

Merryweather had revealed so much, yet nothing. I wanted more, thirsted for it, but dared not pressure him. Having seen him willing to die over questions he did not wish to answer, I was not about to push him too far. Not until I had to, anyway. What drove a man such as he, a dandy, a good-for-nothing playboy, a man with nothing to protect but secrets, to act as he did? Merryweather proved more enigmatic by the moment. What tales he'd told of my parents' past were so far beyond my comprehension as to be bordering on the absurd, but nobody could've made up such nonsense and made it so believable, could they? If any other man had told it, I would have killed them without hesitation, but not Merryweather. The more complicated the answers, the closer they held to the truth. After all, a man who lived a life of veneer rarely showed what lay beneath, I appreciated that more than most, and recognised a kindred soul. But it wouldn't prevent me taking his secrets. I had to.

* * *

I paced behind my companion's slouched form at a respectful distance. He seemed too disconsolate to speak to. I was not good with such things anyway, and Merryweather would have seen through it with ease. I was hardly the kind of person to lend a sympathetic ear. When all was said and done, I'd tried to eviscerate him once and doubted he'd have forgiven it. Speaking for myself, I knew I wouldn't have. But despite all of Merryweather's revelations, his very real show of emotion, I felt he still held back. It troubled me.

As was my way, it did not trouble me for long. My mind flitted to those affected by that single bite I'd placed upon the accursed Chantelle's neck. Somewhere, hidden away to the light, she laughed at me, her rasping mirth echoing inside her coffin like a saw through wood. I had been an unwilling pawn in her machinations and it had cost me dearly. She'd disrupted my melancholy life, my morbid waltz towards inevitable death and I judged it unforgivable. Yet without Chantelle's demise would Linka have shown herself? Would Aurora and her Nordic brethren ever have revealed themselves? And there they were, the two thoughts I'd tried to subdue risen once more. Always split down the middle. I imagined a tearful Linka at one side hating the man I had hidden from her, and on the other the vanishing form of Aurora leaping into Arctic waters after her brother. For both, the blame lay at my door. Dark thoughts for a dark raven of a man, a bad man. As if on cue, Merryweather broke our self-enforced silence.

"What's that?"

I followed his trembling finger to a view that matched my mood. "That, my dear Walter, is the demarcation of night and day."

"The what-what?"

"It is the point where light ends and darkness takes over."

"I don't remember it being like that," he mumbled. "It was either night or day with a transitional period in between."

"Pardon."

"Oh, nothing, Jean, I'm just a tad surprised, that's all."

"So was I the first time I saw it."

Merryweather stopped his trudging plight and regarded me. His face held the confusions of a man with something to ask, but unwilling to do so. His mouth twitched, his mind waging war with his gut, as he blurted out the words. "What was it like?"

"What was what like?"

"Hvit." He said the word with a passion he normally reserved for antagonising me.

"You know it?" I asked.

"I… I know of the legends."

"How much do you know, Walter?"

He eyed me before responding. "Only what all those of a certain age have gleaned, that the Nordics left their Scandinavian homelands to move north, ever north. That one day they left the land altogether and moved out over the ocean, then below it, or so the stories told. I think…"

"You think what?" I interrupted.

"If you let me finish, I shall tell you."

"Please do."

"Thank you. To continue, I think it would be quite something to see."

"It was if you like the life sub-aqua."

"Tell me more?" he asked, as we set off again towards the veil of gloom.

"Not much to tell, really. The city was constructed of ice or an ice-like substance. The whole thing was underwater as you said."

"And?" Merryweather asked eager for further information.

"And that was it. I thought it drab, to be honest."

"It doesn't sound drab, it sounds fantastical. How did you find it? Was there an impressive gated entrance guarded by polar bears and wolves with towers of ice and battlements watched over by Nordic warriors?"

"Overstatements aren't the Nordic way."

"You know what I mean," he said in a most agitated manner.

I took great pleasure in being as annoying to him as he usually was to me, and then remembered I was supposed to be staying on his good side. "I'll try and describe it to you."

"I wish you would, as I'm on the verge of falling asleep from your boring repartee." Merryweather feigned a yawn to emphasise his frustrations.

"Well, it was like this, there was a doorway, or really more of a hatch, that opened in the ice."

"Ooh!" said Merryweather in genuine amazement.

"The hatch lay invisible to all just within the light side of the more permanent darkness. I think that was the Nordics' safeguard against other Eternals trying to get in. Not that I have any idea who'd want to," I added.

"Could someone find it?" Merryweather asked, with a stare of such intensity he almost burned my eyes out. "Could a stranger stumble upon it and know it for what it is?"

"They could not."

"Oh," Merryweather hung his head before remembering himself. With great effort, he tried and finally succeeded in meeting my gaze again.

I decided to put the poor fellow out of his misery. "Walter."

"Hm."

"I am not someone."

"Does that mean you can find it?"

"Yes."

"Oh, goody, I'd so like to see it. I bet it's something to behold. It's been so long since I've seen anything new." Merryweather blathered out words in such a hurry I had all on to follow him. He then stopped mid-spew and gave me another one of his intense stares. "How is it you can see it when others can't?"

"I can't see it," I replied.

"You can be most infuriating," he snapped.

"Look who's talking and stop calling me infuriating."

"I can't help it, whereas you do it on purpose."

"I put it down to nerves."

"Do I make you nervous?" he said with a jolt.

"It's the way you dress."

Walter scowled, then continued in a lighter vein, "So, do tell, if you cannot see it how in God's name do you intend to find it?"

"I can smell it," I replied and tapped my nose.

"Smell it!"

"Yes, I have an excellent sense of smell."

"And…"

"And I'm pretty sure that if we follow the line of light and dark, then I will at some point sniff it out."

"Pretty sure. Is that all we're going on to rescue the so-called love of your life, smell?"

I gave Merryweather a flash of annoyance before replying, "I had two guides who could've easily found it, but as you're aware, I haven't now."

"And full circle back to poor Aurora."

"Something like that. But don't worry, I'll find it."

"It must give off a hell of a stink," Merryweather said chuckling to himself. "Poor old smelly Nordics," he sang.

"Not really," I replied with a shake of the head. "Just an overpowering perfume of lavender."

"Lavender!"

"Don't ask me why, but it does. They all do."

"Strange," he pondered, "I never smelled it on Aurora."

"That's a good point, I can't say I did."

"Do you think you could smell it through a snowstorm?"

"Possibly. Why do you ask?"

Merryweather didn't reply, instead, waved the forefinger of his right hand around and around. Realising it was his way of saying look behind you, I did. I wished I hadn't. There, rising like a wall of pure white that eclipsed the insipid, ruby sun, came the snow.

It hit us so fast, I actually lunged for Walter to prevent us losing each other. Rather than recoil from my touch, he grabbed a hold of my shoulder with such ferocity that it quite surprised me. His taloned nails bit deep into my collarbone, but better that than be split up in that most feral blizzard.

"What do we do now?" Merryweather yelled.

At least, I thought he did. I saw his lips move, his face leer through the snowstorm, but heard only the wind.

I tried to signal a reassuring smile, but didn't know who I tried to kid; I was already lost. Only the fact we hadn't moved since grabbing each other gave any indication of which way to go. So, with heads bowed, we set off in what I for one hoped was the right direction like two hamstrung ducks.

On and on we waddled through that white hell, our feet moving without command, our unwilling forms towed in their wake. All sense of forward propulsion was lost to the storm. We might have been stepping on ice, slip-sliding on the spot without ever making progress for all I knew and just prayed we weren't. The only sign we progressed through time at all was judged by the ever-shortening timescale between Merryweather's incessant bleatings.

"Are we there yet?"

"No, Walter!" I'd bellow back.

"Did I just smell lavender?"

"No, Walter!" I yelled.

"I'm sure I sense the sun to our left. I'm worried we've turned about face!" he bellowed without taking a breath.

"We haven't, Walter!" I shouted back.

The last one was actually a lie because I had no such sensations, and could barely tell if we even stood, never mind walked in any given direction.

He would no sooner ask if we'd done such-and-such, then do so again. My right ear felt as though it had become frozen to his lips, so often he called out. A veritable tirade of nonstop worrisome questions spewed from him. In truth, I feared for his mental state.

* * *

To be awake whilst sure you were sleeping was a most peculiar sensation, but that's how it felt. The wind, a cacophony of spectral voices, melded together as one incessant cry of torture. It was as though the planet's pain, a realisation that it would soon be no more, had risen from its core to let out one final torturous scream. I was never a man prone to fear, but for a time, I covered my ears to all that anguish, all that terror. I wondered if I would be the same when my time came, go kicking and screaming into eternity, then realised I'd probably be glad to go if I couldn't be with Linka.

Merryweather, to his credit and my eternal surprise, didn't complain about the conditions. His head remained bowed throughout, his grip vice-like, as he trudged with the metronomic efficiency of an automaton. Once he realised I could not, or would not listen to him, he just got on with the business of walking. If anything it was I who was the first to show signs of weakening. It was a slow process, as the snows piled higher and higher, inhibiting my stride ever further. First to go was sensation. I thought Merryweather had released me and was set to panic until realising my mind played tricks on me. My body was, in fact, going numb. When I turned to my right, the blood that was my life essence sat solidified as flattened gemstones. Small pools of garnet circled the fingers that punctured my clothes and skin, yet I felt nothing. Next to go was sight. I hadn't noticed at first, the scene being one of semi-night, but evening morphed to midnight and I realised my eyes to have frozen shut. I rubbed at them, but there was no heat in those hands to defrost, there never had been. I tugged a little at my eyelashes, tried to blink, but it availed nothing. Even then, I wasn't unduly panicked. An Eternal has many gifts, if they can be called that, and being children of the night, those senses required to hunt are attuned to the task with unequivocal excellence. So, where sight failed, hearing took over, and when that failed, then smell. And that was how the two of us continued. If Merryweather shared my predicament, I couldn't have said, nor cared. Survival was all that mattered, all that concerned, for I had no intention of becoming a tall, dark ice cube frozen in time, alive yet dead. That's when I had my epiphany.

"Walter!" I cried, dragging him close. "We have to shelter!" I could not see him, but sensed the cogs in Merryweather's mind whirring into action.

"No!" he finally screeched back.

"We have to! We must take cover because we'll never walk out of here alive!" I waited a moment but got no response. I thought he'd gone into shock, so dragged him to the floor and started to scrape and scratch at the snow. I sought to dig a bivouac to house us until the maelstrom passed. The storm had reduced me to a cowering fool, but better a live fool than a dead one.

I continued to heap and pile snow to one side supposing Merryweather helped in his way. I was too tired to beg for assistance and too proud to beg. When at last I patted the top of it at a good four feet from the ground, I dug into its side to fashion a cave. The task took longer than I would have hoped, blind as I was, hands numb and uncooperative, but by the time I'd finished, I felt the thing sturdy enough to protect us from the worst of the weather. Crablike, I scuttled in on my hands and knees and reached to my shoulder to pry Merryweather's fingers from me. They weren't there. With flailing arms and swallowed curses, I flapped about my newly erected home, but never once did I touch anything other than the piled boundaries of snow. There was no human form to be found. Merryweather had gone, and despite not wanting to give a damn, I did.

Chapter 27

Albino

It was the strangest sensation, movement, without propelling oneself? Rigid limbs detected the passage of land and air, which was a relief after the numbness of the storm, but disturbed in my assuredness that I wasn't actually doing anything.

"I wish you'd let us hurt him, Ragnar."

"Quiet, Verstra, we don't want to wake him."

"Serstra," came an indignant retort.

However, it was much too late for those who manhandled me; I was wide awake even if still unable to unlock my eyes. This was not such a bad thing. I'd always had the annoying habit of fluttering eyelids whenever pretending to be asleep. I had used the method on the Marquise many times although her lusty nature rendered it pointless. She, like others, always saw through my ploy, as it was almost impossible for me to remain still. Playacting was not in my nature, so I luxuriated in the opportunity to eavesdrop whilst stillness was forced upon me: I listened, and I listened well.

"Whichever of you, the same applies. You know mother's feelings on the matter," Ragnar continued.

"We could lie," one twin replied.

"She would know."

"Don't tell us you're as scared of her as you are of Grella."

There was a slowing of step, a decrease in momentum, as tension rippled through my legs via Ragnar's oversized muscles.

"If you even think to speak like that again I shall cease dragging my burden and do something to the pair of you that only you will regret."

"Sorry, brother," came one twin's voice, a slight tremor tingling down one arm.

"Apologies, Ragnar," came the other, sending a similar jolt of fear down my other arm. "It's just…"

"Just what?" came the booming tones of their more powerful sibling.

"Shush."

I thought the twins pushed their luck then, but Ragnar appeared not to notice.

"I said, just what?" he repeated slower, but no quieter.

"He hurt us."

"Your point being?"

"Our point being," said the two as one, "we have fought wars and whales, and never once had a finger laid upon us."

"True," Ragnar interrupted.

"And the one time we are not only harmed but slandered, we are unable to correct it."

"You know the law," Ragnar grumbled like an aftershock.

"The law is obsolete," Verstra replied.

I felt I began to tell the twins apart more easily than their brother did. Verstra walked to my left, whilst Serstra to my right, a guard of honour to their hated foe, namely, moi.

"If there was no law, there would be no you."

"What!" Serstra blurted.

"I would have polished the pair of you off years ago."

Ragnar chuckled to himself like a landslide mid-fall.

"Oh, ha, ha," the two voiced in sarcastic unity.

"Things will change when there is a new power on the Nordic throne. I hope I can still count on you, brothers?" Ragnar growled the latter in a no-mood-to-argue tone.

"Oh, yes," said one.

"I don't see why not," said the other.

"Good, because sedition is a crime best served cold."

"Well, we're in the right place for it then," Verstra shot back much to his twin's amusement.

"Hm, well, I have no desire for it to remain that way."

"Us too," the twins replied in unison.

"All this running around the countryside after Aurora has given us a taste for freedom," Verstra went on.

"Then you wish to leave as much as I?" Ragnar enquired.

"More so," replied the two.

"Then it is settled. We strike at the first opportunity and pray to Odin it's before this damn planet is as dead as mother."

"Ha! We like that," said the twins.

"Just make sure you're ready to move."

"I don't see why it should be so hard to finish her," said Verstra.

"I agree," replied his twin.

"What makes you say that?" Ragnar asked.

"Grella being gone, of course. Poor Jean-boy here has inadvertently done us the biggest favour of all in sorting him out."

"We cannot be certain he has," Ragnar's booming baritone replied with an air of caution.

"He must have. Grella would not have left him not even if Aurora *had* been with him."

I did not like the emphasis placed on had but resisted the urge to share my lucidity. Accordingly, I carried on eavesdropping.

"That disturbs me," Ragnar puzzled.

"What does?" said the two.

"If Aurora went to all that trouble to run after him, and then follow this vagrant halfway across Europa, why would she leave him?"

"He probably killed her, too," said one twin.

"He's known for it," said the other.

"I suspect us misinformed," Ragnar replied.

"How so?"

How I desired to add by whom, but restrained myself.

"He does not strike me as the mindless killer we were led to believe."

"Look what he did to us," the twins interjected.

"It is because of that."

"What!" A joint show of disbelief.

"Believe me, it was easier to kill than maim you, brothers. He knew you'd heal and did no more than necessary to demonstrate his displeasure."

"How can you say that, Ragnar?" Verstra questioned, and I thought him about to burst into tears.

"It is the truth," Ragnar replied.

Ironically, it was, and I felt a sense of newfound admiration for Ragnar in that he had both recognised and acknowledged it. At the time, I was surprised he had not aided them, foul of temper as he was, but his words explained much.

"I still don't believe he could best Grella," pouted Serstra.

"Don't say you agree with Ragnar and not me, brother," Verstra sounded most put out at the suggestion.

"Frankly," boomed Ragnar, "it's Aurora being the missing one that troubles me most, for I know with indisputable certainty, he could not kill her."

"You always overestimate her," the twins chirruped.

"Better to be over than under, boys," Ragnar replied less forcefully, and I realised he'd tried to crack a joke; he needed further practise.

"Bah!"

The twins' jovial responses were too jovial for a man being dragged against his wishes. So, as my eyelids, at last, became unstuck, I made my move.

"Good morning, boys, if it ever is morning in this godforsaken hellhole," I declared. The shock to the three was apparent by the slack jaws that gawped like broken coffin lids. "Are you taking me for a ride?" I winked.

Ragnar was the first to speak quite unworried by my awakening, unlike the twins, whose contorted faces tried and failed to dispel their fear. I hadn't realised until that moment just how much my humiliating them had affected each. "It would be best for you not to resist, little man. We have been instructed to collect you, but not in any particular bodily state," he grumbled.

"Why would I resist; this is great fun. I do so hate travelling by air and get to see so much more of the place from down here. Hang on, I may have got that the wrong way around?"

"You think you're so funny, don't you," spat one twin.

"Yes, funny," agreed the other.

"Better to think it than look it."

By reflex, Verstra put his free hand to his still half-closed left eye.

"Oh, God, I hope your brother doesn't put his hand where I stuck the other whalebone."

The kick to my ribs was excruciating, but worth it. The twins were mine to harangue, and Ragnar knew it.

"Don't bloody listen to him!" he roared, tightening his lock about my elevated feet.

"Good advice," I quipped. "I never listen to me either if I can possibly help it."

"You sound just like…"

"Hush your mouth!" Ragnar bellowed, cutting Serstra off mid-sentence.

"Sorry, brother, I wasn't thinking."

"Ah, that's your problem, so young and impetuous," I teased.

"We're far more ancient than you," his twin brother snapped.

"Well, boys, in that case, I offer my humble apologies. I'd always had you pegged for infants."

"I know what you're attempting, Jean," Ragnar rumbled.

"Do you? Regale me with your knowledge."

"You seek to antagonise us into doing something we may regret. Perhaps, even into releasing you. We shan't though. The only way you are leaving is over our dead bodies."

"Either way is fine," I chuckled.

Ragnar's fury almost burnt a hole in the back of his head, but he continued his steady march north.

"You have my admiration, Ragnar."

"Do I?" he replied, without turning.

"Indeed, you do," I enthused. "I think you're doing well to even walk straight after the ease with which Grella put you down." Ragnar did not respond, but the cracking of my ankles showed my jibe had hit home. "By the way, as seen as you've already alluded to him, have you seen my good friend Sir Walter Merryweather running around anywhere? I lost him in the snowstorm and am growing worried for his well-being."

"For who?" said Verstra.

"I doubt you've concerns for whoever-he-is or anyone else," said Serstra expanding upon his brother's question.

"Why do you say that?"

"You don't feel for anyone."

"You sound very sure of yourself."

"We know things."

"Do you now," I replied.

"Be quiet, Serstra," Ragnar boomed, stirred once more into action.

"I will not," Serstra bit back.

I listened intently as the two shouted and cursed at each other; it was quite entertaining in its own way. But in between the bravado and the moments of silence, I caught a definite lapping sound. If we were near the border of the ocean and ice, then we had almost reached Hvit. I chanced raising the stakes, unwilling to turn up at their mother's door trussed between the three like a hunter's trophy.

"You're quiet," I said turning to Verstra. "Scared I'll hurt you whilst the other two argue?" The response was instant as the flames of anger stirred him. He required both hands free to retaliate and the instant his grip loosened, I struck.

Catching Verstra by the wrist, I swung the albino as hard as I could towards his twin. The two clattered together in a crunch of bones that even I winced at. Ragnar, caught off guard, felt my fist to his jaw, as I doubled over at the waist to punch him. He let go in obvious pain, but the blow did not floor him, which frustrated as it had been my best shot. Survival being the wiser side of valour, I ran.

As the elder Nordic reeled and the other two writhed about each other entangled in a snowdrift, I ran for all I was worth. The darkness of night was to my left, the lapping ocean to my right illuminated in the dusk of a perpetual ruby glow. The sun winked over the distant horizon and I knew myself to be heading in the right direction. But time was against me. The Nordics were quicker than I even if their orca fuelled might wasn't up to their usual standards. I had only the element of surprise, and I used it to its fullest. I sprinted as though my life depended on it, which it probably did. My legs creaked in protest; I ignored them. My arms pounded the Arctic air aching from my imprisonment; I refused to let them hinder me. I ran like the wind but knew it not fast enough.

The snow and ice shot past in a haze of neutrality. I might almost have been running on the spot so little did the scenery change. All that marked my passing was the sputum topped waves and the occasional berg that drifted in some perpetual dream of finding warmer climes. I'd have enjoyed watching their journeying, but knew without feeling it, there were none.

The world was cold like the hearts of those who dwelled in it. Soon, it would be just as dead.

I caught a glint, a flash of reflected ruby to my left, and saw that one twin, bedecked in owl-like goggles, already flanked me. I could not tell which and frankly did not care. The albino kept a respectable distance between us until his brother sped up along-side him then overtook at a velocity to marvel at. The two ran so light-footed, they barely left imprints in the snow, unlike my own furrowed passage. They endeavoured to outflank me and I dared say allow Ragnar time to sneak up and deliver the blow they thought would finish me. Determined and resolute, I would not allow it and fate came to my aid.

I watched as the twin who'd taken point caught his foot on something, whilst preoccupied with me. He tripped and crashed into the snow causing such a disturbance I had to leap over his sprawled form high into the air. The view from my greater height was an unpleasant one. I spied tinges of brown set against the snow, maybe limbs, but without investigating, I couldn't be sure. I was certainly not about to do so.

I hurtled on across the Arctic wastes, my black form mirrored by a single white blur. With only one brother flanking me, I felt confident I could not be brought down: I was wrong. But it was not Verstra, or Serstra, or even the mighty Ragnar that felled me, but an object of polished mahogany: a discard coffin. I skidded face first into a heap of what had once been Hispan-ics and their portable, wooden homes. By the looks of things, Chantelle had come this way, but her entourage had lessened somewhat. Whatever the Marquis had done to them, Raphael's kinsman had become less than impervious to the cold and had been dumped in unceremonious fashion in the snow, a light-ening of the load, as had I. My face came to rest mere inches from the contorted features of a Hispanic female. She held such a look of terror, of absolute fear, that an Eternal should never have known; the look of someone who realised their own mortality.

I had no time to mourn, nor dwell on detail, as I felt myself pinioned to the ground by each arm. The twins had caught me. The gigantic shadow that was their brother engulfed my own, and I knew I was right out of luck.

"Friends of yours?" boomed Ragnar.

"No friends of mine, you oaf."

The pain from his blow cracked my spine and almost rendered me unconscious, the anguish as the twins turned me to face their brother, even more so.

"I have decided you were right, Jean."

Ragnar's words surprised me, but the blood swilling around my mouth prevented a response.

"Are we to kill him, brother?" the twins voiced together.

"Yes, boys. I have had my fill of the inkblot that is Jean."

"Or soon will be," one of the two returned.

I couldn't even turn my head, the pain of Ragnar's well-judged blow was too complete: I could not speak; I could not resist; I could only die. What was worse, I was going to die within reach of my dear, sweet Linka without gazing upon her beauty one last time. I would die in the weak rays of the sun and felt nothing but regret.

"I am not a man of many words and you seem all out of puns, my ravenesque descendent, so I will end this quick. In your own twisted way, you've earned that, Jean. We shall tell mother you fell and return your shattered body to her. What she does with it, I care not." Ragnar spoke with the solemnity of someone conducting a eulogy, I just never envisioned it my own.

My head hung against my chest as I waited for that final blow. I watched as two feet planted before me, Ragnar poised. His shadow's arm lifted, his mighty body flexed, and I awaited death.

The crack almost split my head asunder, and I wondered if the ringing sensation in my ears was that of the afterlife, then realised an Eternal lived the afterlife, and presumed it something else. Perhaps it was finality that precursor to nothingness? I knew not, nor cared not, as I awaited obsidian night.

Another crack, and I suspected myself already dead. Surely I witnessed Ragnar beating me to a pulp from the beyond: I was wrong, yet again. The twins tensed, then released me. My short fall to the snow at Ragnar's feet caused unparalleled pain. My eyes rolled back as a fissure split the ice and the boots I thought to crush my skull were grasped by two slim, porcelain hands. They locked about his ankles with a power mightier than anything I'd ever witnessed. Ragnar's aghast look was one of sheer terror, as they dragged him through the fissure and into the cold oblivion of the ocean below.

* * *

That was the last thing I saw, felt, or wanted, as darkness took me into a realm beyond realms.

Chapter 28

Cinnamon

I stirred to the sound of a tinkling waterfall, its droplets pitter-pattered against my bare cheek to a magical rhythm. The thought I must have descended into an underworld of cascading water and permanent night was most prevalent in my mind. When all was said and done, there could have been fates far worse for a man with my history.

Something soft brushed against my brow, it tickled, and I twitched involuntarily. The shudder that shot through my body re-established the fact I was still alive; pain does that to a person. At least, I hoped so, for if it was Hell and an eternity of such agony my penance, then it was more hurt than I could endure.

I tried to open my eyes. They refused to respond allowing only the faintest chink of ruby light to filter into my retina. Redoubling my efforts, I tried again, and woke to the glistening purity of a snow-white angel: Aurora. My joy was short-lived as the fog in my mind cleared and the dear girl grew into focus. She wept as though the world had ended. For her, part of it had.

"Je…an," she stammered. "Oh, Jean, what have I done?"

I endeavoured to lift my hand, to wipe away the tears that flowed from those beautiful sapphire eyes, to take hold of the hand that stroked my brow, but could not. "I do not know, dear girl, but I thank you for saving my life," I said, instead.

"But at what cost?"

"I'm sorry, Aura, I know not of what you speak."

Her answer was to remove her hand and hold it out to view. What should have been pale as new-fallen snow dripped in vivid crimson. The girl had killed.

"You see?" she beseeched. "You see what I've done?"

"Ragnar," my one-word response. A nod of her handsome face confirmed it.

"I have murdered my step-brother. The worst shame is, if they had not fled, I should have murdered the twins, too. As it is..." she began, then trailed off.

I gasped in horror as the arm I was cradled in tilted me forward and I regarded the torn off limb of a Nordic prince settled in the snow. The thing twitched in crimson liquid like an eel in a hellish sea.

Aurora, as if sensing my pain, rested me back in the snow, stood and collected the torn off arm, and paced to the waterside. The fingers attached to it were still clenched shut, as though resistance had been desperate, but futile. The pale princess stroked her step-brothers torn off hand, then flung it limb and all into the waiting waters. I did not see it sink beneath the waves, but frankly, I was glad to see it go.

"Grella?" I called softly.

"Gone," a bitter reply.

I felt as though the world had tilted out of orbit, everything sent askew. "He was a good man, Aura," I offered as consolation.

"He was more than that, Jean, he was my brother."

I was about to offer more, some crumb of comfort to her, but my body surged with such pain that I coughed into the half-light, my essence pooling as red spittle in the snow. Aurora saw it and hurried back to my side.

"You look worried," I said in between grimaces.

"I am worried."

"Please, don't be. I will heal, Aura. Being an Eternal has some benefits." I attempted a smile but coughed up so much blood as to spoil Aurora's porcelain robes. If the girl noticed, she did not show it, instead, just looked on more concerned than ever. "Do not fret, my dear, I just need to rest. I promise I shall heal."

"You shall not," a blunt response.

"Don't sugar-coat, will you."

"How else does one state the truth? Ragnar is dead and Serstra soon will be. Grella is lost, and so am I. Soon, I will not only be lost, but I fear, alone."

She cast me such a look of pity, I wished I were dead, so she would not have to do so again.

"What else is there to say?" she persisted. "Hvit will relocate and Mother shall live on. We shall not."

"You can, Aura," I encouraged. "Leave me, I care not, just promise to get Linka away from that accursed city of yours. I ask for nothing more."

It was a good job too because I was seized by another fit of such excruciating coughing, I thought it should end me.

Aurora wiped her hands in the snow, then took some clean and mopped my face with it.

"I cannot leave you, and I cannot go home," she said at length once I'd settled again.

"You must!" I implored.

"I cannot. I do not know how?"

"What!" A jar of protest rippled through my frame.

"What I told you before of never having left Hvit was the truth. I have never strayed more than yards from its door. Only when hunting orca and surrounded by others was I allowed my freedom and even then only in the water."

I must have frowned for Aurora's eyes flickered with concern.

"I don't understand?" I wheezed.

"Only my elder kin were privy to Hvit's secret entrance. The city's citizens and I were not ever trusted with how to find it.

That way they and I should never have dared leave. So, dear Jean, we are indeed stuck here in the middle of a barren wilderness with nothing to do but starve and die."

The poor girl looked so resigned to her fate it almost tore what remained of me apart. She had always seemed so strong, so sure of herself despite her restrictions. It pained me to see her spirit broken, it was so very wrong.

"I can find it," I stated, with as much confidence as a crippled man might.

"You what?"

"I said, I can find it. And I can, Aura, I know I can."

"How?" She looked at me in disbelief, her jaw set, lips poised to argue.

"I can smell it."

"Smell it?"

"Yes, the lavender. If we pass anywhere near the entrance to Hvit, I feel confident I will smell it."

"Of course, how stupid of me. I have grown so used to it over the centuries. All this time, I have used my eyes when it was my nose I should've trusted. I could have strayed further in my cloak, run with Nordvind, lived. Escaped, too," she said as an aside that ran right through my dead heart. "The lavender, the accursed lavender, if only I'd thought."

"You are no more short-sighted than I, Aura. I have lived a lie. That is far worse than being unable to escape one."

"Hm, perhaps, but to be caged by one's family's shame is beyond ridiculous."

"What do you mean?" I tried to lift my head, then regretted it.

"The lavender. You are still unaware why they shower themselves in it?"

"I am," I answered, the time for subtleties departed.

"They decay."

"They what!"

"They are dead."

"We all are."

"No, Jean, we are not. Just because our hearts do not beat does not mean they cannot. Just because we have lived off blood for aeons does not mean it was always so. But for my family things are different. They are albino through inbreeding, not fluke, not Darwinism. If it not for the orca blood that surges through their frames reinvigorating long dead cells with false purpose, they would disseminate within days. Perhaps, sooner, I do not honestly know. But I know this, I am the only child of Hvit to be born to an outsider since records began. I am the only child of Hvit that is and has not been dead for centuries. That is why I am despised. That is why my mother hates me so. I have what she has lost."

"And what is that, dear girl?" I asked, enthralled by her account.

"I have promise, Jean, the ability to reproduce, the thing she lost for good with my birth. I was a miracle, you see, as I suspect were you. That is the one thing I will both love and despise my father for. He has cursed me with a gift I will never live to use."

"I'm sure it's overrated," I said and instantly regretted it, as the tears flowed from her eyes. She put her head in her hands and wept as though she'd never cease.

"I'm so sorry, Aura, please forgive this petty, bitter man I've become." She did not stir, so I tried again. "I see so much in you I am unable to verbalise. You are amazing. I wish you could see it, too. I don't know how else to put it. I wish my friend the old Sunyin was here, he'd know what to say." But the thought of the old monk all confused and on the cusp of death brought great pain to me, far worse than that which wracked my body.

Aurora gave me a strange look then, lifting her water-filled eyes to my own, as though seeing me for the first time in an age. She took my hand in her own although I could barely feel it and spoke with conviction. "You shall see him again, Jean, I promise it. If you say you can find the doorway, I believe you."

"It won't do you any good whilst I'm laid here," I wheezed through the suffering.

"You will not be," she replied. And, with the gentleness of a mother caring for a newborn child, the one thing my darling Alba had always wanted, she slid her arms beneath me and raised me from the snow. That was the last thing I remembered, as the pain hit like the bomb Vladivar had used on The Hierarchy but going off inside of me, instead. I whirled, grimaced, my mind blacking out and fell into the obsidian slumber of the dead.

* * *

"Ah, you are awake." It was the voice of my guardian angel.

"Where am I?" I asked, then felt rather foolish.

"You and I are on our way home," Aurora replied.

"But what if we've missed it whilst I've slept?"

"We have not."

"That's very certain for someone who does not know the way."

"I know the way just not where the door lies."

"And we have not passed it?"

"We still have a long way to go, Jean. You must rest."

But her words already faded away.

* * *

I cannot remember if I argued with her as I slipped in an out of uncomfortable darkness, but whenever my heavy eyelids opened, she was there. Aurora walked without complaint taking the greatest care not to jar my battered body. I might have lain on a bed of goose feathers, so soft was my passage through her lands. How long we travelled that way, I couldn't say, but I knew that every time I woke from my enforced rest her beautiful face appeared more and more concerned. I had an awful feeling that at some point, I would not wake at all. At least twice, I remembered with clarity, Aurora laying me in the snow and leaping into the sea's irritated waters. I presumed it was to hunt. She risked her own life for me as she had for Grella.

There was a time when I would've said she was far too good a sister for that man, but I'd judged him harshly. Grella had not deserved to die, especially not for me. I dwelt on that fact both in and out of consciousness and told myself it was all due to Serena's machinations, and through no fault of my own. However, my fault or not, there was now a princess without a brother and a future without a king.

The thoughts never lasted long, so erratic was my passing through that nightmare, yet like the sudden desisting of an Alpine storm, my torments ended.

* * *

"Drink."

I heard Aurora's cool command as if from a great distance.

"Drink deeply, Jean, I can spare it now."

I didn't need telling twice and suckled at the free-flowing juices as though my life depended on it, which it surely did.

"Now, open your eyes."

I tried, but failed.

"You can do it. Imagine Linka is here looking down on you."

And just like that, I was awake. For a second, I thought Linka did look down on me, but as my eyes refocused to the ruby haze of perpetual twilight, I realised it Aurora.

"What's that godawful stench?" I bemoaned pulling my mouth from Aurora's proffered arm.

"That's not much of a greeting for someone who's just saved your life."

"It was an honest one," I said, laughed, and realised with some relief, I felt as good as new.

"Well, it isn't me," she smirked, indicating I look left.

"Good grief! What on earth is that?" A mountainous cinnamon-coloured beast lay with its back to me. If it had been dressed in silken finery, I might have thought it the Marquis, so rotund was it.

"I believe they were once called walruses."

"Then, I presume that is walrus blood?" I pointed to the stream of crimson which ran down her robes to collect as puddles on the ground.

"That would be correct. Not quite orca blood, but not bad, not bad at all."

The beast lay sprawled on the ice like an overstuffed marshmallow. I marvelled at its obesity and wondered how the thing had survived the dying seas.

"Thank you," I said, whilst Aurora splashed seawater all over herself at the edge of the ice.

"My pleasure," she replied when finished. "I think you'll find my own blood better than that of the beast," she grinned. "I only wish I'd dared gift you it earlier, but I thought myself too weak. This," she gestured to the behemoth, "was an unexpected bonus."

"I'll say. How did you capture it?"

"Stand, Jean," her blunt response.

I was about to argue my wounds too severe when I realised to my joy, they were not, and I fairly leapt to my feet.

"Does it feel good?"

"Unbelievable," I answered, stretching out and cracking my bones with unrestrained glee.

"That is what it feels like to drink orca blood even if it is diluted with a little walrus."

"It didn't feel like this the last time I had it."

"I doubt very much my mother would have fed you our orca liquor. I would guess it that awful synthesised stuff."

"Synthesised?"

"Yes, the blood that disgusting man provides when we are in need of it."

"What man?"

"The man that makes all the inventions. I do not know his name."

"But I was told your people had no interaction with the outside world."

"That is true, apart from him."

"Might I ask something, Aura?"

"Of course," she said raising one quizzical eyebrow.

"Would I be far from the mark in saying he looked rather like the beast you slew?"

Aurora looked between the walrus and me before bursting into laughter. It was joyous to hear, almost elemental.

"I would say very much so."

The irony of having compared the Marquis to such a creature for years, though never having actually seen one, other than in the pages of my father's crumbling books, was lost on me at that moment.

"We must redouble our efforts," I said. I brushed myself down, straightened my cuffs and shook the creaks out of my neck.

"Why?"

"Because, my dear girl, the man I describe is the Marquis, the one I have bemoaned on our travels, and if it is he, he knows the way to Hvit."

"And?" Aurora queried, looking suddenly more concerned.

"And, we are in a lot more trouble than I first reckoned."

We said no more, merely turned and fled in the direction we both recognised as north. I prayed we fled fast enough.

Chapter 29

Limestone

"Run, Jean, run. Feel what it is to be Nordic," called Aurora, her voice in my ears and blood in my veins.

And I did. I ran like the wind, faster than I would have ever thought possible. I felt I might have run forever, outrun the night, the light, my past, everything. Aurora's blood flowed like magical rivers through my Eternal frame and I experienced the bliss of true power. If a slow death was the cost for consuming orca blood, then I considered it a small price to pay. Perhaps, I would have said differently if cooped up in Hvit without friend nor fancy, as Aurora had, but to be Grella and free to roam with feelings such as those that sped through my every fibre... well, it should've been a dream.

A second scenario swept through my mind as we shot across the glacial plain. I couldn't quite place it. There was some nagging thought dragging at my subconscious, something I'd missed. My temples tightened in concentration, Aurora's blood throbbing at my taut skin. I cogitated and deliberated, mulled over my introduction to Hvit and Aurora's dismissive reply of why the Nordics gave me synthesised and not orca blood, when like the Zeppelin crash I'd survived, it exploded over my consciousness.

"Aura, I have been duped." I spat into the snow with contempt.

"How so?" she replied, ignoring my ill-manners.

"Your blood."

"What about it?"

"I have never tasted it before."

"We agreed you had not." Aurora glanced my way, a blur of white motion, feral, a puzzled goddess.

"But why not?"

"As I stated, I would not expect mother to share it with you."

I came to a skidded stop, which Aurora matched, a plume of snow shooting into the sky toward the sun's ruby rays transfusing it into a wall of insipid tears.

"I was an unexpected guest, yes?"

"You were."

"You would think she would try to impress, not hide her might, so there must have been another reason for it. I believe I now know that reason."

"Enlighten me."

"Because a dangerous man is far more so if empowered."

"And you are a dangerous man."

"Aura, my dearest friend, I can assure you, I am becoming more so with every step."

"That does not sound good, Jean."

"It won't be for anyone that gets in my way."

"I am sorry," Aurora said, looking as disheartened as I'd ever seen her.

"For what?"

"I feel so stupid."

"You have no need to."

"I should have known the man you hate and sought was the same as Hvit's benefactor. If only I'd recognised, paid more attention to his bulbous presence in New Washington, but my eyes were fixed on your main tormentor."

"Dearest Aura," I said, taking her by the shoulders and looking her deep in those bluest of eyes. "There is only one person who has and continues to act the fool, and that is me, not you. Others have used me to achieve their goals, not mine, and I have only ever looked to the end of my nose for answers. I have lost my true love to a woman who has tested my professional services as a confirmed killer. A test she confirmed at the expense of her own sons' lives."

"By mother, but how?"

"She did not send her children out for you, I am quite certain of it, despite what she may have told them. She sent out all four of her male heirs with one purpose."

"What purpose, Jean? I am not following."

"To be killed, Aura. To be murdered by me in some faraway land where they would die unknown and unheralded. A land neither of us would've found our way back from. She seeks to rid herself of all who'd usurp her."

"You are certain of this?"

"It is irrefutable. She, like all who sense the end, strive for even a second longer amongst the living. There is no greater enticement than a fraction of a moment extra to those who face the torments of the damned."

"And you suspect the Marquis integral to this?"

"I believe so. The man is a master manipulator. He has twisted her mind and has used me, his blunt and unwitting tool, to carry out her plan. I fear my Europan wanderings have already facilitated the murder of most of those who could have opposed him."

"Do you think he knows of the sunlight?"

"I envisage he suspects, but being the coward he is, he will not risk testing his theory. You Nordics are so different in composition to the rest of us that it could have been a fluke. How could he be sure without testing his theory on others?"

"The Hispanics?"

"Yes. The Marquis would have had to persuade them to the point of absolute certainty as no descendent of our vampire past would risk the light willingly. He has had to change their make-up over time, use subtlety, coerce, because Raphael is nobody's fool. He has used my brother-in-law by enticing him with imagined promises and the hope of walking in the day with his sister. His research, his dabbling with the Sunyins' genetics, as well as Raphael's own people, have shared the single goal of stepping into the light."

"So, why does he need this Chantelle, Linka, the others? I cannot fathom it, Jean."

"Because the Marquis has no heritage. He is not a member of the Hierarchy, nor would they likely ever have accepted him. He requires a face to represent him, and in Chantelle and Raphael he has secured two. Not that either of them will realise it, of that I'm quite certain."

"And Linka?"

"Linka has the gift her mother bequeathed her. She is the only Eternal the Marquis has indisputable proof of having survived the sun. Is she a miracle, or a freak? I am sure he drools over that knowledge, that he has had many a restless night because of it. He has done all this, Aura, for I feel it in my rocklike heart. It is he who's responsible for my parents' death, he who has brought me such misery."

"But why your parents?"

"There were no others with the scientific knowledge required to out-think or outflank him. He had to have them murdered, and I will have his head for it."

"Then, Jean."

"Hmm," I replied as my talons dug deep into ice-cold palms. "Run."

* * *

I seethed with murderous intent. All I envisioned were the bulbous jowls of that most hated man wobbling before me. He bobbed, as if in water, just out of reach, always just beyond my grasp.

The landscape passed in a haze of turmoil, Aurora's anchoring presence the one definite in a world made mad. If she hadn't been there, I thought I should have gone quite mad and wandered enraged into the ocean and the slow death of a watery grave.

"Jean," called my pale angel cutting through the murder in my mind.

Aurora closed the small divide between us pointing ahead and diagonally to our right. At first, I could not see what I was supposed to, there was nothing but snow and ice, curlicues of misting vapour, a freezing fog to disturb the scene. I shook my head to show my ignorance. Aurora's response was to grasp me by the collar and come to an abrupt halt, almost scragging my head off in the process.

"The water," she said.

I followed her guiding finger past the land, through the gathering gloom and out to the waters beyond. "Orca," I proclaimed.

"Yes, Jean, and they feast."

And they did. Twenty or more tar-black faces striped in distinctive white punctured the ocean surface in jaw-gaping joy. They took bites out of something or some things that floated upon the angry waves.

"I would suggest the Marquis has lost more of his prized specimens," Aurora said in her ice-cool way.

"Hispanics, or what's left of them."

"Indeed," she agreed. "If there are that many whales here, we cannot be far from Hvit. The creatures fear straying from us almost as much as we do they."

I watched with dark fascination as the sea wolves rose and fell in time to the undulating waves. With every rising, they would take a mouthful of arm or leg or ragged torso, I even saw a tanned face protrude from between one creature's elongated teeth.

Aurora appeared as entranced as I. She stood there, the greying air lapping against her, cloak flapping in the sea breeze, hair dancing about her shoulders, a sorrowful figure. She pitted those dead upon the water, as she did those that fed on them. The orcas may have been abominations to her kind, but they were abominations with shared ties. The orcas had no freedom, no true liberty, they were as stuck in their domain as she had been, and Aurora felt their frustration.

I would have comforted her then when she looked to need it most, but the faintest, sweet scent caught my nose. I sniffed at the air like one of the Nordics' wolves.

"What is it, Jean?" A prompt acknowledgement of my behaviour.

"I smell it, Aura. The doorway is here somewhere, I'm sure of it."

"This scene does not look familiar," she commented.

"But does Hvit not move periodically?"

"Yes, but that is not due for some time."

"That is not what your mother implied before I left. Serena seeks to guarantee Hvit never being found."

The look she gave told its own story, as Aurora sniffed at the air in female duplicity of my own actions. We paced the area together first in one direction then another, towards the water, then back again to the looming night. Wisps of mist congealed about us like the ghosts of lost lovers stroking at our almost lives. It thickened by the second and I knew it would soon become a grey shawl. It prompted us to greater exertions.

"Jean, the smell is strongest here," asserted my companion.

"Yes, you are right," I said collapsing to my knees. "The snow is permeated with it down here. Dig," I said in earnest.

Aurora dropped to my side and the pair of us scrambled around in the snow. I thought, at first, the Marquis had tricked us, that some false scent had been laid to trap us. But again I worried without due cause as my fingers closed about a horizontal fixture buried beneath thick layers of snow.

"I have it!" I cried. "Help me, Aura."

Drawing back the snow from the solid seam, we soon revealed the faintest outline of the Nordics' most sacred place. Aurora did not dwell on it as she stamped on the thing; the doorway popped up out of the snow catching the faint light in glimmering relief.

"Are you prepared for this?" Aurora asked, her face impassive. "It will be... unpleasant."

"Only for them, my dear, only for them," I growled.

I launched myself onto that dark and brooding staircase. Aurora followed without complaint.

Descending into the black abyss disorientated and confused after becoming so used to the surface's half-light, and it took some seconds for my eyes to readjust from the starburst of retinal change. But an Eternal's natural habitat is the perpetual darkness of night and my eyes soon remembered the same.

"Jean, I would advise caution," Aurora said, catching me by the arm.

"You might advise it, but I will not practise it," I replied.

"So be it."

"Aura," I said looking her in the eyes. She cocked her head to one side in her beguiling way and regarded me with intelligence, a trait I'd found lacking in the world for far too long. "You do not have to do this. If the twins are down there, you may be forced into actions you will regret."

"I will regret nothing. They got, and may still get, only ever what they deserved. My one regret is that Grella does not stand with us; he would have swayed the odds in our favour."

"He was a good man, Aura, and I share your regret. His death is a bitter pill to swallow."

"I just wish I could have caught him, offered solace of sorts, but the orca was too fast. The beast had fled into the open ocean before I even got close, my brother writhing in its jaws."

"Try not to remember him that way it will do you no good."

"On the contrary, Jean, I have every intention of remembering him that way. It is Grella's pain that my mother shall feel, and any other that stand in my way."

"Then, I am doubly glad."

"For what?" she asked, as the tears pooled in her eyes.

"First, that I am on your side, second, that I shall bear witness to what you do to those who aren't."

I offered Aurora my sleeve, which she took and used to dab at sculpted cheekbones. A slight inclination of her elegant head confirmed her readiness for what lay ahead, and we moved off at pace down the stairs.

When fury builds within a container such as mine all else becomes secondary. I lost all sense of time, all sense of Aurora's presence. The staircase became a dark transition between what had and what would be done. The further we descended the angrier I became, and the further the damned thing seemed to stretch. I paid no attention to the glass walls to who, or what, may or may not have been watching. If orca waited beyond that semi-transparent divide, I cared not. The creatures could wait and have their fill of what we left behind because I had no intention of leaving Hvit in anything other than a broken state.

When my feet finally touched the flat of the glass corridor, I seemed to awaken from my trance-like state. My hands balled into fists, my eyes narrowed, and with a mere glance to check on Aurora's proximity I charged through the grand ice doors of Hvit's throne room and into a massacre.

The city's denizens lay strewn across the ice floor lighted in macabre fashion by the neon glow of the blood-spattered walls. It was a carnage that Aurora's shrill cry suggested was unexpected to her, but for some reason, not me.

However, I did not dally for there was only one person for whom I searched within those eerie walls. The raven hair of my dear Linka was my sole objective. But despite my panic and deepest fears, they proved unfounded. Every one of the dead figures was of the albino caste that marked their bearing. Hair of limestone poured from each of the scattered forms that littered the throne room floor. Linka's own raven locks were nowhere to be found, and much to my eternal shame, I breathed a huge sigh of relief.

My scavenging took me to the foot of Serena's throne. The thing stood empty, cold, bereft of the power that normally occupied it in such ominous fashion, a mere trinket to its decadent queen.

It was to that symbol of Nordic power that Aurora made her wide-eyed way. Respectful of her fallen kin, she made every effort to avoid stepping in the pooled blood of her people, ultimately it proving a futile task for there was too much crimson to avoid. By the time she reached my side, she'd left red footprints all over the floor. When she saw them, something cataclysmic occurred.

It was the throne that felt her wrath. That symbol of Nordic austerity crashed to the floor in shattered pieces at her single strike. And for a moment, even I trembled before her rage.

Chapter 30

Gold

"We must check the living quarters," Aurora commanded, a wild madness rippling like ocean waves in her blue eyes.

I didn't require telling twice and shot through the doorway that led to the bedchambers. I left Aurora to do as she wished for there was but one room on my mind. It was to the door at the corridor end that I ran, the ice walls passing in slow motion as though not moving at all. My fear mounted with each slippery step, hopes mingled with apprehension, as the blood of the Nordic people lay strewn around me. Every surface from the ice floor to glasslike ceiling had been desecrated by a new bright crimson coating. The Nordics had not gone down without a fight, and I wondered whom could have caused such mayhem? Blood still dripped from overhead splashing upon my cheek, slapping against my clothes, but I had no time to waste in wiping it. It felt like running down a hole with an awful surprise waiting at the bottom, a murderous finale to a one-way trip.

And then I was there, the doors to our once room torn from their hinges. The things lay smashed to tiny pieces each fragment reflecting my fear. Whoever had struck them was strong. I cared not, for at that moment I longed to face them.

I hastened inside, the broken ice crunching beneath my booted feet to a scene of wreck and ruin. The bed lay overturned, curtains dragged from the walls revealing an empty ocean with no sign of my sweetheart other than the remnants of her resistance. I would have expected no less from my tigress.

My dark eyes scanned every detail of the bedchamber evidence of Linka's punched and clawed defiance in every inch of the place. Each scratch in the ice, each fleck of Nordic blood led me to believe they'd taken her in a whirl of vortex ferocity. I hoped so, for I could not bear the thought of a prolonged execution.

By the time I staggered from the room, Aurora awaited. Her serene features shared my anguish.

"She is not here," I said.

"Thank God," she sighed. "It makes no sense, though. Who would do this, Jean? Who would massacre my people? For all my mother's faults, and those who did her bidding, they did not deserve this. We never hurt anyone, never even interacted with others. There is simply no reason for what has happened, it defies logic."

"Don't take this the wrong way, Aura, but I noticed the royal house were not amongst the dead."

"What do you mean by that?" she bristled, ice in her voice.

"I mean only that they've either been taken by those who perpetrated this atrocity, or were a party to it. I do not know which, but I shall find out."

"And, Linka?"

"She did not go without a fight. My heart tells me she is an unwilling participant in this, at least, I must hope so."

If Aurora had not pulled me close and wrapped her beautiful yet deadly arms about me, I should have wept until I was no more, but she did, and I didn't.

"We must search the rest of the city, Jean." Aurora spoke with a calm determination drawn more from fancy than fact.

"This is the city?"

"No, my friend, the other doorway leading from behind the throne, that is where our real home lies. Hvit is much more than you were permitted to witness. Come, there is nothing left for us here."

Aurora took my hand and led me away at a sprint back whence we'd came, out into the throne and its jigsaw of death and through the second doorway into architectural wonderment. I had seen much majesty in my time: homes created to their master's whim, magnificence beyond imagining, colour and texture as one, but I'd never seen such as I beheld. It was like a master craftsman had combined the dreams of generations, spun them together in a tapestry of unreality. The glasslike austerity of the Hvit I had roamed was as much a facade as the Nordics' lives. I had, in my usual way, judged before thinking, categorised without knowledge: I would not make the same mistake again.

The throne room was cavernous, a giant of creation, but with every doorway that Aurora cast aside, I realised, I'd seen nothing. Walls of gold inset with every imaginable gemstone twinkled in the light of myriad chandeliers. Velvet cushioning adorned mahogany chaise longues, silk drapes hung from ornate ceilings. Paintings of times long since past adorned almost every square inch of wall, tapestries and murals filling what remained. It was a record of sorts of memories passed down through the generations. I could have marvelled at them for years, but I only had seconds to spare. Every precious metal, every glimmering jewel was present in those decadent halls, those throwbacks to gothic beginnings and I understood what the Nordics truly protected. Theirs were not creations, not fabrications of scientific minds, but the real masterpieces of a people unparalleled. Millennia had rolled by in the sculpting of Hvit, and I revelled in its magnificence. If I'd cared to admit it, I would have said the place perfect. If someone, or someones, were to spend eternity anywhere, then the city under the sea was the place to do so. How it must have pained Serena to find out it would all end? Who could have borne such news without a hint of madness? To see the legend of a race as old as time itself erased, forgotten, lost to star stuff, it was almost beyond comprehension.

How many halls we passed through, I could not honestly say, but when Aurora paused before one ebony doorway of an immensity unparalleled, I realised something amiss.

"What is it, dear girl?" I asked, taking her hand in my own. Aurora trembled as though about to shake apart, a flower in a hurricane.

"This is as far as I have ever been. What lies beyond these doors is unknown to me, Jean."

"You have never been allowed free wanderings of your own home!" I said, astonished.

"No. What lies beyond these doors was for the select, I was not one of them."

Aurora's voice welled with shame. A girl, or really woman, of such majesty, such stature as she, deliberately kept at heel like a pet, the thought turned my stomach. To be both a princess and slave, how Aurora had stood it with the grace and resigned dignity she had was beyond me. Only through such a revelation did I appreciate the magnitude of what her following me had entailed. She was a braver person than I'd ever be. She had left everything and nothing for a dream.

"Aura, let me help," I said taking hold of one of the ivory handles. The inlaid coral decoration felt soft in my palm, less abrasive than the rest of the place. "We'll do this together."

"Together," she breathed, and closed her eyes.

We turned the two handles as one and let the mighty doors swing open of their own accord. It was not what I expected to see.

"What is this, Jean?"

"I'm glad it's not just me."

"This is no time for humour."

"Who's being humorous!"

"But, what is it?"

I took a staccato step into the chamber and tried to interpret what I beheld. The area was smaller than the other halls, but still vast. Darkness prevailed in the place, but that was no object to Aurora or I. The perimeter of the chamber was furnished with one almost continuous length of table that stood laden with objects and artefacts the likes of which I had no perception of. The chamber looked like a repository for everything from scrap metal to the most delightful objet d'art. Stuff littered every tabletop to the extent I could not see even one fraction of revealed surface. That paled into insignificance compared to what lay heaped on the floor.

"What could mother have wanted with all this rubbish?" Aurora glided over to the nearest conglomeration of so-called rubbish and prodded it with her toe. "Have you any idea what it's for?" she asked, moving to the next.

I considered an appropriate response but just mustered a, "No." There seemed no pattern, no practical explanation for the piled accumulations. "Are you sure you've never seen this place?" I asked, still unable to accept her confession.

"Do I need to dignify that with a response?" she answered coolly.

"You just did. But I find the whole thing so incredible. This chamber reminds me of my home, though it is centuries since I last saw it. My parents used to have a plethora of half-dismantled devices strewn about the place. I can't remember a time when there wasn't some strange object begging for attention. My father would say they needed to know how the things worked to assist them with their understanding of humanity. Knowledge was power, my mother would add, or some such nonsense. I remember them lecturing some minor lord on what buttons to press to change the colour of his garden. The man looked at them with such disinterest, I thought they would kill him. They both despised those who disliked their precious sciences, which was pretty much everyone."

"I know nothing of such things," Aurora replied. "I prefer magic over science like that of my cloak."

"Do you not think it a thing of science that simply appears magical?"

"Perhaps, but to me, it will always be magic. I hate to think what kind of woman I would be, or where I would have been, without it."

"Yes, I imagine it should have been a most helpful gift. Did nobody else know of it?" I asked, as I trailed after her. Aurora sashayed between the towers of junk taking in the scene without, like I, actually understanding it.

"Oh, no, if they had, they would not have allowed me to keep it. They all knew what it meant to me, of course. Once, Narina even pretended to take it. She cast the cloak over her shoulders and pulled it closed whilst I held my breath, but it did not work for her as it always worked for me. I think it was only ever meant to be mine, Jean. I have clung to that fantasy."

"A fine fantasy to have, Aura, but I don't think it, or we, are best served perusing this place. We should move on."

"I agree," she said and made for the opposite side of the chamber.

Another double doorway stood parallel to the others but of a less grand design than any we had thus far passed through. These opened out into a chamber of similar proportions and wreckage to the last. However, I recognised one portion of scrap amongst the many others. There surrounded by a melee of metal sat a partial cockpit almost identical to the one within Captain Scott's Zeppelin.

"Jean, there is something strange here I have only just recognised for what it is." Aurora stopped dead in her tracks and tilted her head one way then the other.

"What is it?"

My enquiry was met with a finger brandished to red lips. "Do you hear it?"

"I hear nothing," I answered truthfully.

"Exactly, for the first time in my life, Hvit is silent."

"That cannot be right."

"I assure you it is." Aurora's eyes narrowed. A revelation abounded.

"What is it, dear girl?"

"Do you not think it strange that Hvit is deserted, all dead, and the music has stopped?"

"Perhaps, they murdered the orchestra, too," I offered. Her look of disgust made me wish I'd kept quiet.

"Or there was no need for sound if there was no one left to hear it."

"I thought it was to drown out the orca calls."

"So did I, but what if, instead, it was to drown out the sounds of people working? What if it was to quell any inkling of lives unlike our own?"

No sooner had the words left Aurora's lips than another piece of the puzzle that was my life slipped silently into place. Someone *had* been hard at work and not one of the Nordic peoples had known of it.

"But why, Aura? Why all the subterfuge, the secrecy? There has to be a reason. There has to be!"

"Secrecy has been the key, Jean. Have you noticed the walls are neither curtained, nor ice, but solid? Nobody was meant to see what transpired within these chambers from within, or without. Having hunted, swam the ocean in battle with our mammalian foodstuffs, I can attest to the fact these walls are as disguised on the outside as the entrance to them was on the inside."

"Then onwards, whilst there is still a chance of finding…" But my words were cut short by a crashing and banging of such magnitude, I thought Hvit's walls had shattered. I expected tonnes of saline ocean to come roaring in, to envelop me, consume me, crush me in a watery grave. I feared the embrace of the sea.

But I had no time to dwell on such thoughts as Aurora shot forward through the piles of scrap and out of the adjacent doors. She disappeared into a corridor of physique cramping narrowness. It was so small in proportions that Aurora ran through the thing stooped over, her head almost to the floor. Yet even in so awkward a position, the girl moved at an incredible pace; I was less fortunate. There was no way one such as I, a specimen of a more formidable frame, could do the same. I wiggled and shoved my way along in her wake, more worm than man. By the time I caught up, she'd burst out from her warren-like confines into the vastness of the main burrow, its gigantic roof shattered into revealing an obsidian night high above.

An Arctic breeze swept across me like a slap to the cheek, a sobering draught free from lavender residue, it was the draught of a hall open to the elements, roofless, contents disgorged.

I would have marvelled at it, stood in awe of the great chunks of ice that littered the floor, but we were not alone. I sensed his presence; heard his tears; saw the wreckage of his rampage, long before I saw him. The forgotten Merryweather had beaten us to the scene, and the chamber trembled at his torments.

"Walter," Aurora cried, speeding over to him and grasping the wretched man by both shoulders. "Walter!" she bawled, as his arms flailed about him striking at her repeatedly. He raged like a madman kicking, screaming, biting at the air. His eyes, blood-red and manic, displayed, at last, the true essence of a vampiric past. Merryweather the man had departed. Merryweather the beast had replaced him.

"She said she'd wait!" he howled like a tortured wolf. "She said she'd wait for me!" he implored, as Aurora wrapped him in a spectral embrace.

If Merryweather found comfort in her touch, he did not show it, instead, venting his fury upon her. Aurora did not waver, did not move an inch, never once batted an eye. She stood resilient, took the pummelling, as he tore at her hair, spat in her face and wailed to the sky until he could swing and wail no more. She held him constricted until he collapsed utterly spent into her arms like a flower destroyed by the cold.

I wanted to say something, to call out to him, comfort him, but was struck mute, for eyes bred for the night, bred to hunt, bore witness to the craft that rose into a distant, dark sky. Only when the first tinge of ruby light kissed its Zeppelin skin, a last glinting farewell, did I turn and scream.

Chapter 31

Epilogue

Sir Walter Merryweather found the small, white envelope amidst the aftermath of his rampage. He passed it over with a sneer of utter contempt, Aurora by his side.

I sliced the thing open with a razored fingernail to an overpowering stench of lavender and tipped its contents into my hand: a single sheet of folded paper and a necklace with a silver cross, my cross.

My eyes closed, world stalled, stomach fell away. Fumbling fingers tugged free what I wished them to not as dark eyes re-opened to four little words.

Merryweather reacted first, his face raised to the sky in scarlet, snarling fury, as I roared to the ground. But it was Aurora who put a voice to the message written in bold, italic script. It was Aurora who put sound to my torment as she read those words written in blood.

Dear Jean.

Too late.

To be continued in book three
The Eternals: Into Eternity

<<<<>>>>

About the Author

Richard M. Ankers was born a dreamer. From an early age, if Richard was not out in the fresh air playing sports, he was lost inside a good book or secretly writing his own. A lover of everything from Marvel comics to classic Fantasy and Science Fiction, he allowed his mind to wander to these fantastical places and never quite came back. Heavily influenced by authors ranging from Michael Moorcock and Gene Wolfe to such wonders as Haruki Murakami and Margaret Atwood, Richard enjoyed being entertained, whisked away to places unknown. Every book had something to offer, snippets of the unimaginable, twists of fate and spectacular universes and Richard soaked them up like a sponge. These were the makings of his mind.

Born and bred in rural Yorkshire, England, Richard squirreled his words away in shyness without showing them to anyone until plucking up the courage to place them online to be read and judged. Fortunately, that went better than he could ever have dreamed and hence decisions were made. Richard resigned his position as a Company Director and gave up everything he was to become the writer and person he wished to be. People have said it a brave decision but, in truth, it was the only decision he could ever have made. There would never be enough hours, minutes and seconds remaining in Richard's lifetime to uncover all the words and worlds he had to unleash. Work began in earnest, and The Eternals came to life.

Three years in the making, The Eternals Trilogy was born from a vision of moonlight waltzes and a dying sun. Our distant future was to end and those who thought themselves immortal would be proved less so. This is the time and place that Jean is born to and wishes he wasn't.

When Richard is not tapping out stories on his laptop, or adding poetry and writing to his own website, richardankers.com, which he nearly always is, you'll find him running and taking in the scenery. Running has offered a sense of peace and relaxation only ever matched by writing. A lover of the great outdoors, he is lucky enough to have visited many of the world's most beautiful countries such as Norway and Switzerland both of which he could happily have never left. If he could sit with a view of the mountains with a river flowing by and birdsong, a quite corner set aside in which to write with a view of the former, you'd probably never see Richard again.

Words and the stories formed from them have brought Richard much joy over his lifetime. Now, it is his turn to hopefully return the favour to others. Modern life is a hectic place and time is precious. Richard hopes those stolen moments with his words can bring some relief from the tedium as the authors he has read have done for him. There are few things that could make him happier.

Richard is a passionate believer in the natural world. Our Earth is a delicate place and everybody should do their bit to look after it. There is so much beauty to be seen if only people opened their eyes. He hopes that more and more are doing so these days, and prays that it's not too late for those to come. He is also a strong advocate of never letting anyone tell you, you're not good enough. If you want to do something with a passion you cannot explain, you should. Life is too short for regrets and everybody is good at something. As long as that person is happy and content, nothing else really matters. So, good luck with your own futures and Richard thanks you for being a part of his.

Richard.

Lightning Source UK Ltd.
Milton Keynes UK
UKHW021057051020
371040UK00012B/798

9 781715 505196